The Meddlers

June Drummond

ROBERT HALE · LONDON

© June Drummond 2004
First published in Great Britain 2004

ISBN 0 7090 7546 4

Robert Hale Limited
Clerkenwell House
Clerkenwell Green
London EC1R 0HT

2 4 6 8 10 9 7 5 3 1

Typeset in 11/14½pt Sabon by
Derek Doyle & Associates, Liverpool.
Printed in Great Britain by
St Edmundsbury Press, Bury St Edmunds, Suffolk.
Bound by Woolnough Bookbinding Ltd.

The Meddlers

I

'And there, devil take them, go the last of the carrion crows!'

Dominic Barr turned abruptly from the window where he'd stood to watch a long line of carriages wind through the park to the gates of Melburn Hall. He moved to a table still laden with the remains of a funeral repast, and addressed the other occupant of the room, a portly gentleman ensconced in an armchair near the fire.

'What will you take, sir?'

'Nothing, I thank you.' Mr Amyas Beacher, watching his host toss down a generous measure of brandy, found himself hoping that the new Lord Barr would not fall into the hard-drinking habits of his late father.

Granted, the past week had been enough to test the fortitude of any man. The deaths of Justin Barr and his elder son John had shocked the whole of West Dorset. A flash flood, occasioned by prolonged and tumultuous rain, had destroyed the old bridge on the River Rem at the precise moment that the two men were attempting to cross it in a racing curricle. The torrent swept all away – carriage, horses, driver and passenger, and it was not until fourteen hours later that the bodies were recovered from a point far downstream.

The double tragedy had drawn mourners not only from Twyford Lindum and its surrounds, but also from places as far afield as Bath and London, a crowd greater than the little Church of St Dunstan could accommodate. The funeral cortège had been delayed for over an hour as carriages vied for space in the Market Square.

To cap it all, Dominic's mama had arrived at the church with him, and had remained in the family pew throughout the obsequies, a target for the stares and whispers of those who deplored her desertion of her husband and sons, her scandalous divorce, and her subsequent marriage to her lover Ivor Savernake.

She did not stay for the burial rites, nor join the throng that filled the reception rooms of Melburn, but there could be no doubt that her brief visit caused the local gentry and city fashionables to linger long past the time prescribed by good sense or good manners. Small wonder that by four in the afternoon Dominic had reached the end of his patience.

As the young man came to take the chair on the opposite side of the hearth, Mr Beacher sought to give the conversation a more cheerful direction.

'I thought Mr Pruitt's homily was excellent,' he said. 'Very well phrased.'

Dominic flicked him a sardonic smile. 'I thought it hypocritical cant! To drone on and on about my father's virtues, when everyone knows he had none! He was seldom sober after noon, and on the night he died he was roaring drunk. Beckett warned him he was in no state to drive, and that the roads were unsafe, but he must needs take out a curricle that was hard to handle even in fine weather. John went with him in the hopes of preventing disaster, with the result that John is dead at the age of nine-and-twenty.'

Mr Beacher pursed his lips. 'Bitter as that loss is, I can't agree that your father lacked virtues. I knew him in his heyday. I remember him as a fine sportsman, a man of sound opinions, the best of company. It was only after your mama left him that his character suffered a change.'

'A change indeed! He brought his lightskirts and his gambling cronies to this house, he forbade Mama to have any contact with

John and me.' Dominic set down his empty glass with a bang. 'But that's all in the past. We have more pressing matters to discuss. Let me say I'm very glad my father appointed you as an executor of his will.'

'Thank you. You . . . ah . . . know its terms?'

'Yes. Shipton was here two days ago, and explained in a maze of legal jargon that I inherit everything . . . which means, I take it, all my father's debts.'

'I'm afraid that is the case.'

'How badly was he dipped?' As Mr Beacher hesitated, Dominic said brusquely, 'Don't try to wrap it up pretty, sir. I prefer to know the truth.'

'Very well. This house is heavily mortgaged.'

'Yes, to Horace Pickford. He called on me in London, the morning after the accident. All paint and pomade, smirking and reminding me of his long friendship with Papa.'

'Perhaps that may persuade him to delay foreclosure?'

'Small chance of that. He runs with the Carlton House set and has a misplaced faith in his skill as a gamester. Word is, he's deep in debt. He'll foreclose as soon as the law allows. What else do you have to tell me?'

'The unredeemed loans and bills amount to more than sixty thousand pounds, and we don't yet know the whole. You'll need to consult Shipton on that score.'

'Will the banks help?'

'They are not prepared to sanction further advances.'

'One can't blame them. What about the house in Town?'

'Barr House belongs to your mother. Justin settled it on her when they married, and he would never consent to altering that arrangement. I felt sure you knew of that.'

'No. I've been remiss. Never troubled my head with the business of the estate.'

Mr Beacher sighed. 'A family failing. Justin didn't speak to me of his difficulties until three months ago, when he confessed he was in deep water. He'd been gambling on 'Change, y'see, and when that didn't bring him about, he applied to the Greeks. I lent him enough to get those bloodsuckers off his back, but I fear it was a drop in the ocean.'

'You'll be repaid in full, Mr Beacher, my word on it.'

'Tush, there's no hurry, you have more immediate claims on your purse.' Mr Beacher studied Dominic's face, wondering how to say the unsayable. Nick was very like his wayward mama; the same dark good looks, a shade too aquiline for the general taste, the same blunt honesty and sharp intelligence, the same disastrous tendency to act without thought for the consequences. Mr Beacher took the bull by the horns.

'Your land is unencumbered. You could sell part of it.'

'How much would I have to sell?'

'If you sold half, you could meet your most pressing obligations . . . perhaps stave off foreclosure . . . but there'd be precious little left over for the running of the farms.'

'Robbing Peter to pay Paul. It won't fadge. As it is, we use every inch of pasturage. If I sell land, I must sell the stock it supports. We would be living on capital, ploughing nothing back. The tenant farms would go to rack and ruin, and the cottagers would be driven to seek work in the North. I won't do it, I won't condemn Melburn to a slow death. I'd rather sell up, and be done.'

'Surely that must be your last resort? The Barrs have owned Melburn for centuries. It's unthinkable that you should leave.'

'I know, but what else can I do?'

'You might borrow. You have wealthy friends. Savernake might be prepared, for your mother's sake, to—'

'*No!*' The word was spoken with such force that Mr Beacher raised a temporizing hand.

'I merely suggest that that is an option.'

'Not one I can stomach. I'll not crawl to the man who seduced my mother and destroyed my family.' Dominic paused, and continued more calmly, 'Pray don't think me ungrateful. You've stood friend to my father and me, I shan't forget your kindness.

As to the future . . . I'll speak to Shipton, reach a full assessment of what I owe, but I believe it's clear what my final decision must be. Melburn will have to be sold.'

'There could be an alternative.' As Dominic looked up enquiringly, Mr Beacher coughed delicately. 'You could marry.'

Dominic blinked, then gave a grunt of laughter. 'For money, you mean? Join the ranks of the gazetted fortune-hunters? I'm not sure what price a bankrupt peer might command, but I suppose that might easily be discovered!'

'Naturally, you would do nothing to impair your good name, my lord; but if you were to contract a match that everyone must approve . . . with a young woman of impeccable breeding who also enjoys a handsome jointure . . . that surely could not be repugnant to you?'

'More likely it would be repugnant to the lady! How would you suggest I approach her? "Madam, my pockets are to let and I am like to be hauled off to a debtors' prison, but I beg you will do me the honour to become my wife." '

'You must marry some day to secure the title.'

'Time and enough for that. I'm in no hurry to set up my nursery, especially as I might be unable to house or feed the brats.'

Mr Beacher was silent for a moment, then said, 'May I be frank with you, my lord?'

Dominic smiled faintly. 'I've never found a way to check people who use that phrase. Pray be as frank as you please.'

'Is it your attachment to Lady Cheveley that makes you reject the idea of marriage? Forgive me, but I know Lord Cheveley. He will never consider a divorce.'

'Nor, I assure you, will her ladyship. She's made that abundantly clear to all her suitors. And that is all I propose to say on the subject.'

Mr Beacher bowed his acceptance. 'Then it comes to this. You will marry one day, not for romantic but for dynastic reasons Why not now? Marry to your advantage. Choose a girl of the right age and background, one with charm and wit and a fortune to boot.

Can that be such a dreadful fate?'

Dominic regarded his guest through narrowed lids. 'I'm almost persuaded that you've already found this paragon.'

'I have. I have.'

'May one ask her name?'

'Certainly. She's my niece by marriage, and your nearest neighbour.'

Dominic stared. 'Kate Safford? She's hardly out of the school-room!'

'She's turned eighteen. She was to have made her come-out last year – she did in fact attend some of the earlier events of the Season – but her father fell ill, and she returned to Twyford to nurse him. He died last July. I believe you were abroad at that time.'

'Yes, in France.'

Mr Beacher nodded affably. 'Well now. How does the notion strike you?'

'Of marrying Kate? It's out of the question.'

'Why so? She meets all the requirements I've mentioned. Her lineage is as long as yours. She's personable, accomplished, and the sole owner of Safford Manor, its lands, a house in Curzon Street and a villa in Lombardy. Her income is handsome, and when she marries she'll have the capital as well.' As Dominic started to protest, Mr Beacher raised a hand. 'May I also remind you that it was the earnest hope of your father and hers that she would marry your brother John. Now that he's gone . . .'

'I can't be John's surrogate, Mr Beacher. I lack his sterling qualities.'

'I think you underrate yourself.'

Dominic made an impatient gesture. 'When I marry, it will be to please myself.'

'Would it displease you to marry Kate? You've known her since she was in leading-strings. Surely you don't hold her in dislike?'

'I neither like nor dislike her; I remember her only as a four-teen-year-old, all eyes and freckles . . . .'

10

'Changed, now,' Mr Beacher said.

'But I knew Clive Safford; I had the greatest respect for him, and I respect his daughter too much to make her an offer she must see as an affront. The thing's impossible. I wonder you even suggest it!'

'Let's say I take the long view, which is that you're a man of sufficient character and resolution to redeem your father's mistakes. The marriage would cement a friendship enjoyed by your two families for generations. Your lands march with the Saffords', and to unite them must benefit everyone in this valley.' Aware of Dominic's growing annoyance, Mr Beacher leaned forward in his chair. 'Be advised, my lord, a man in your situation cannot afford to indulge in false pride.'

Dominic bit back a stinging retort. Mr Beacher was a meddler who stuck his nose in where it wasn't wanted, but he was also a friend of long standing. He'd lent his money and his moral support when they were needed, and even this last idiotic proposal was made with the best of intentions.

'I'll bear what you say in mind,' Dominic said.

'I ask no more.' Mr Beacher heaved himself to his feet. 'Now I daresay you'll be wishing me at Jericho, so I'll take myself off. Emily and I will remain with Kate for a few days, then we return to Bath. Our Anna expects her fifth next month, and Emily wants to be at hand for the event. Perhaps we'll see you in Bath, one of these days?'

'Yes, I must talk to Shipton.'

Mr Beacher nodded. 'A sound man, of course, but I wonder if you might not be better advised to employ a London firm? Bath is a long way from the major banks and financial institutions.'

And from the rich Cits with marriageable daughters, thought Dominic, but all he said was, 'Shipton suits me very well. If I sell Melburn, it will very likely be to a West Country buyer, and I'll need a man on the spot to guide me.'

Mr Beacher perceived that he'd said enough, and took his leave. Lord Barr accompanied him to the front door, and watched his carriage roll away towards the river road, and Safford Manor.

It was now past five o'clock, and the westering sun was dipping towards Twyford Tor. Its rays cast a copper burnish on formal gardens, pastures and crops, cottages and barns. It was a prospect to warm any heart, one that Dominic had accepted all his life as his birthright.

Every inch of these woods and fields recalled some boyhood memory. Beacher had spoken the truth. His father had been admirable once, John a close companion, and Melburn home to a close-knit family; but that time was past, and vain regret would serve no useful purpose.

He walked to the stable yard and spent an hour going from one loosebox to the next. The horses must be sold at once; they couldn't stay here, eating their handsome heads off. He would speak to Keeler, the head groom, tomorrow.

As he turned towards the house, his brother's cocker spaniel ran whining to meet him. He was a country dog, who would be miserable in the confines of the city. Dominic bent to pat him.

'Don't fret, Brag, you shan't go to strangers. I'll find a good home for you, I promise.'

II

Safford Manor was cited in the guidebooks as being of great antiquity and historical interest.

It could in no way match the Palladian grandeur of Melburn Hall, for successive owners had added rooms at whim, and linked them by such a profusion of passages, antechambers and stairways that visitors frequently lost their way entirely. Despite this, it was a comfortable house. The chimneys never smoked, the roofs never leaked, and the whole property was kept in apple-pie order by servants who knew precisely how to go about their duties.

The drawing-room, which enjoyed a maximum of light and sun, was hung with wheatstraw silk that admirably set off the amber brocade of chairs and sofas. Sage-green velvet curtains were drawn back from three tall windows with leaded panes, and fine Chinese carpets covered the floor. In the wide fireplace massive logs burned, casting a rosy glow on the two ladies seated nearby.

The older of them, Mrs Emily Beacher, was a plump matron of forty-seven. She was very much at home in these surroundings, for as the youngest sister of the late Sir Clive Safford, she had lived in the house until her marriage. She was still attired in the black gown she had worn to the morning's funeral, but she had kicked off her shoes and thrust her feet into a plaid-lined footwarmer. Her right hand clutched a phial of smelling-salts, and in her lap lay a novel newly delivered from London. She was making no attempt to read, her brooding gaze being fixed on her niece-by-marriage.

Elinor Crane was twenty-eight years old, but looked younger, for she was blessed with a fresh complexion and a trim figure. Her light brown hair was drawn back in a chignon. Her gown was of blue cashmere, her slippers of matching Morocco leather. An intaglio brooch was pinned to her breast, and from her belt dangled a châtelaine of household keys. She was engaged in unravelling a switch of hair, the strands of which she laid carefully on the table at her side.

Mrs Beacher found this absorption provoking. Elinor was competent, kind and good, but she was not companionable. She had no conversation. She did not know how to chat. In Bath, one had only to visit the Pump Room or the Assembly Rooms or the Library to find a dozen bosom friends, eager to share the latest on-dits, enjoy a coze, settle the affairs of the world. Why, when Letitia Savernake entered the church today there was a positive buzz of dismay, but all Elinor found to say was that the poor soul must be devastated by the death of her son, and Dominic did quite right to bring her to the service.

Mrs Beacher gave voice to her annoyance.

'Say what you will, my dear, I think Letitia Savernake must have a heart of stone! Not one tear did she shed, not one! While I, who claim no kinship with the Barrs, was in floods! A funeral quite oversets me.'

Elinor forbore to point out that her aunt was also overset by marriages, christenings, sentimental ballads and the singing of *Rule Britannia*. She said placatingly, 'Indeed, dear ma'am, you are all heart.'

Mollified, Mrs Beacher set down her smelling-salts and leaned forward in her chair.

'Pray tell me, is that human hair you're busy with?'

Elinor smiled. 'Yes. My own, in fact, though from many years ago. I found the plait in my old trunk in the attic, and thought it the very thing for poor Lady Jane.'

'Lady Jane? Lady Jane who? Is the poor creature bald?'

'As a coot.'

'Merciful Heavens! But surely she should apply to a qualified wigmaker? There are excellent men in Bath.'

'Alas,' sighed Elinor, 'that wouldn't serve. She cannot stir from home, and can neither read nor write. I am her sole hope.' As Mrs Beacher shook her head in concern, Elinor laughed and, reaching into the workbag on the arm of her chair, drew out the china head of a doll.

'You see how desperate is milady's case. Selina Pruitt left her unattended, and the puppy found her and left her as you see, clean-shorn. I undertook to try to mend the damage.'

Fascinated, Mrs Beacher stared at the porcelain head. 'How will you contrive to attach the hair?'

'There are holes already drilled for it, you see? If I thread it through from inside, and knot it, and secure all with a dab or two of glue, I fancy the result will be respectable.'

'How kind you are, to go to so much trouble.'

'It's no trouble. I'm fond of Selina.'

'Of all children, I think. It's a pity you have none of your own.' As Elinor made no answer, Mrs Beacher continued, 'How long is it since Hugh was killed?'

'Six years.'

'And have you never thought of marrying again? I'm persuaded you must have received eligible offers.'

'Some.' Elinor met her aunt's inquisitive gaze. 'We were so very happy, Hugh and I, that everyone else seems . . . well . . . second best.'

'That I can understand. Hugh was a model husband, as well as a gallant soldier. Still, my dear, as one grows older one learns to settle for less. Aside from the joy of having children, companionship and security must count for a great deal.'

'I am already secure, Aunt. Hugh left me well provided for. As to companionship, I have you and Uncle Amyas, and Kate, and my circle of good friends.'

'Lord knows we've no wish to be rid of you. When my brother lost his Laura, he was at his wits' end to think what to do about

Kate . . . only thirteen years old, and missing her dear mama so dreadfully. You've filled a void in her life, as well as seeing that this house is properly run. For that we all stand in your debt; but the fact remains that Kate will marry some day, and you will find yourself alone again.'

'I'll worry about that when the time comes.'

'That might be sooner than you think. I believe it won't be long before we see our Kate happily betrothed.'

A certain smugness in her aunt's voice made Elinor look up sharply.

'Has Uncle Amyas received an offer for Kate's hand?'

'Why, no,' replied Mrs Beacher, turning a little pink, 'but you should know that your uncle and I plan to invite both of you to join us in London for the latter part of the Season. We will make it our business to see that Kate meets suitable partis, and I venture to say that she must receive a number of creditable offers.'

'That I don't doubt,' agreed Elinor. 'Whether she will accept any of them is another matter.'

'You are thinking of her recent loss, I suppose. Indeed, we all hoped she would wed John Barr, but since that hope is destroyed, we must turn our thoughts elsewhere.'

Elinor frowned. 'I don't believe she considered herself betrothed to John. They were friends, no more.'

'Fond friendship often leads to marriage.'

As Elinor shook her head, Mrs Beacher gave her an arch smile. 'You suspect her affections are already engaged? An attachment exists, perhaps, to some other gentleman, someone she's known for a considerable time?'

'She's said nothing to me on that count. In any event, it's something you should discuss with Kate herself, not with me.'

Elinor made a show of searching in her workbag for needle and thread, and Mrs Beacher did not press her further; but her expression as she picked up her novel and began to read was one of deep complacency.

*

On Mr Beacher's return to the Manor, he did not alight at the front door, but directed the coachman to drive round to the stable yard. Entering the house through the kitchen quarters, he came upon Elinor Crane in consultation with Mrs Puddifin, the cook. He greeted them with enthusiasm.

'Concocting a fine dinner, are you? I don't mind telling you, I'm hollow as a kettledrum. There was such a crush at the Hall, one couldn't come near the buffet. One would have thought those London smarts hadn't seen food for a sennight.' He sidled round the table to eye a smoked gammon on a silver platter. 'A slice or two of that ham, Mrs P., wouldn't come amiss, with a crusty loaf and butter, and a bumper of ale to wash all down.'

Mrs Puddifin beamed. 'I'll make you up a tray this instant, sir. I've a nice Stilton, too, that's beggin' to be ate.'

'Excellent woman! Bring the tray to the morning-room, if you please.' He directed a meaning look at Elinor. 'Bear me company, won't you, m'dear?'

A short while later, uncle and niece were settled in the little parlour, the tray at Mr Beacher's left elbow and the flagon of ale at his right. Between mouthfuls, he described the gathering at the Hall. Only when he'd filled and lit his pipe did he come to the nub of his report.

'I stayed at Melburn till the rag, tag and bobtail left,' he said. 'Wanted a private word with young Barr.' He puffed smoke ceiling-wards. 'I needn't remind you that it was my brother-in-law's hope that Kate would marry John Barr.'

Elinor was tiring of this theme. She said tartly, 'The hopes of match-making relations often come to naught!'

'And more's the pity, I say. In my young day, parents felt it their duty to arrange good marriages for their children, based on mutual respect and material security. Today, romance rules the roast, and a fine old mess that makes of things!'

'Kate looked on John as a friend, not a potential husband.'

'Because,' said Mr Beacher slyly, 'she had eyes only for Dominic, ain't that what you mean?'

17

'Good God, no! What put that in your head?'

'Got a good memory, that's what. Recall how she used to trail after him and hang on his lightest word.'

'That was puppy-love, Uncle, the admiration of a fourteen-year-old for a dashing nonesuch!'

'And is she cured of it now?' Mr Beacher stabbed the air with the stem of his pipe. 'Answer me that.'

'Of course she is. If you must know, she thinks poorly of Dominic because he's neglected Melburn and left all its problems on John's shoulders.'

'Criticisms to mask her true feelings.'

Elinor regarded her uncle with deepening suspicion. 'What are you trying to say?' she demanded.

'That Kate would jump at the chance to marry Nick Barr.'

'That is a most indelicate remark.'

'It's the truth, none the less.'

'Has Lord Barr offered for Kate?'

'Not yet.' Mr Beacher's voice held a note of defiance. 'He will, though, if he takes my advice.'

'Advice?' Elinor was thunderstruck. 'Do you mean to tell me you've advised Nick to make such an offer, when the whole world knows he's heir to a bankrupt estate?'

'Not quite bankrupt. Severely encumbered, I grant you. Crippled, if you like, but not yet dead and buried. No need to talk of selling, yet.'

Elinor paled. 'Does Dominic talk of selling?'

'Yes, and I told him Melburn's prime land, and can be restored to prime production. All that's needed is money.'

'Kate's money, I presume? I find that an infamous idea.'

'Damme Elinor, spare me these niminy-piminy airs. Kate is already wealthy, and when she marries will be excessively rich. Take my word for it, if she comes to London with us this year, you'll see every fortune-hunter in Town paying court to her. Like it or not, it's the way of the world.'

'I know little of the world, but I do know Kate. She will find it repugnant if Dominic courts her only for her money.'

'Who's to say that would be his only reason?'

'Oh, come, Uncle! They've scarcely set eyes on each other, these past five years.'

'That's easily mended. We'll arrange a few parties, see they become better acquainted.'

'You're all about in your head,' cried Elinor in exasperation. 'The man's a rake, his interest is already fixed . . .'

'On Madeline Cheveley? That's common knowledge, but I assure you, the woman's a mercenary. She'll soon rid herself of a lover whose pockets are to let.'

'There you mistake. I've seen how she behaves towards Nick. She's jealous as a cat. She regards him as her personal property. She may drop others of her *cicisbei*, but she'll never let him off the hook.'

'Well, we shall see.' Mr Beacher brushed a crumb from his sleeve. 'Does Kate know about La Cheveley?'

'How could she not? In London last year, the affair was food for gossip wherever one went.'

'Hasn't put Kate in dislike of him, has it? She was perfectly civil to him at the funeral this morning.'

'What else would you expect?' Elinor's gentle face was pink with annoyance. 'Your intentions may be good, Uncle, but I tell you to your head, you shouldn't meddle so. You go beyond what is acceptable.' Gathering up her skirts, she started for the door, but turned back to say, 'Depend upon it, Dominic will never propose marriage to Kate. Whatever his faults, he's too much the gentleman to serve her such a backhander.'

On this note of reproof, she quit the room. Mr Beacher, not in the least abashed, broke into a wheezing chuckle. Then, noticing that his pipe had gone out, he set about rekindling it with a taper drawn from the hearth.

Elinor found her cousin in the still-room, sorting jars of preserves.

Kate Safford's detractors were prone to lament that she had not inherited her late mama's beauty. Though conceding that her figure was excellent, they argued that her height of five feet and four inches lent her no distinction. While her eyes were certainly fine, her complexion lacked a fashionable pallor, her cheeks being far too rosy, and her nose lamentably inclined to freckle.

Her manners, they further maintained, were altogether too free, no doubt because her papa had encouraged her to express her opinion on every subject, and had allowed her to join him in his rambles round the country, when she should have been at home minding her books, or learning how to comport herself with propriety.

Her style of dress was apostrophized as unsuitable, for she disdained insipid muslins, and favoured garments of decided colour and dashing cut.

Kate paid little heed to her critics, who tended to be the mothers of plain females who failed to take with the ton. She enjoyed life, whether it was in rural Twyford, provincial Bath, or the great metropolis of London, and she was generally thought to be an agreeable girl, with no false airs about her.

At the moment she was contemplating a row of glass jars with marked disapproval.

'Tomato jam,' she said in disgust. 'Can you believe that Cook has put up thirty bottles of the horrid stuff? I shall donate them all to the Church Fair.'

'Most unchristian of you,' said Elinor, and Kate chuckled.

'I suppose you're right. Very well, they shall have ten of the tomato, ten of strawberry, and ten of sweet pickle.' She began to pack the jars into a basket. 'Is Uncle home?'

'Yes, I've been talking to him. He complains there was a sad squeeze at the Hall, and he got nothing to eat. The guests outstayed their welcome. Dominic was quite out of temper with them.'

'And with himself, I imagine.'

'Why do you say so?'

Kate paused in her task. 'It must gall him that John and his father died in that silly, wasteful way. I felt just the same about Papa's death. If only he hadn't ridden up the Tor in a rainstorm, if only he'd changed his wet clothes when he came in, if only I'd been here to make him do so, instead of which I was gallivanting round London. He died at fifty-three, his life's work unfinished, all that knowledge lost to the world. I feel I'm so much to blame.'

'I doubt if Dominic's conscience is so nice,' said Elinor drily. 'According to Uncle, he's in a rage with his father, his creditors, and the world at large. He talks of selling Melburn.'

Kate's eyes widened in dismay. 'Oh, he cannot! There must be some other solution. Surely he can borrow?'

'It seems the Barr credit has run out.'

As Elinor spoke, she was debating whether to mention their uncle's latest blunder. Her thoughts went to that uncomfortable occasion of the Prestons' ball, last year in London.

She and Kate had been conversing with a Mr and Mrs Montford when Dominic appeared in the entrance to the ballroom. On his arm was Madeline Cheveley, dressed in a gown as immodest as it was modish, spectacularly jewelled and coiffed, and proclaiming by her whole demeanour that Dominic was her property.

Mr Montford, made foolish by red wine, enquired with a hiccuping laugh why that precious pair wasted time in a ballroom, when a bedroom was clearly more to their taste. His wife affected indignation.

'They are shameless,' she said. 'They make no attempt at discretion, and Cheveley turns a blind eye. If he had any proper feeling, he would call Barr out.'

Her husband shook his head. 'T'wouldn't fadge, m'dear. For one thing, the law don't allow duelling these days. For another, Barr's a deuced fine shot, and Cheveley couldn't hit a haystack at five paces.'

Catching sight of Kate's white face and blazing eyes, Elinor laid a warning hand on her arm, but Kate remained silent. She took care to avoid any encounter with Dominic, and an hour later said she had the headache, and asked to be taken home. Elinor could not tell if her anger was sparked by the Montfords' ill-bred comments, or by the discovery that Dominic had a mistress in keeping.

Nowadays Kate laughed off her childhood hero-worship, and the few times she met Dominic, treated him with the same easy friendliness she showed to her other Twyford neighbours. But what if Uncle Amyas was right? What if she still nursed a tendre for Dominic, and he offered her marriage simply to settle his debts? Might not her feelings be deeply hurt?

Kate interrupted Elinor's musings. 'What's amiss, Nell? You look as sick as a parrot.'

'It's nothing,' said Elinor hastily. 'I was wool-gathering.' Kate regarded her shrewdly. 'Is it Uncle Amyas? Has he committed another *bêtise*?'

Cornered, Elinor took refuge in a half-truth. 'He's taken it into his head that Dominic must marry you, to save Melburn.'

Kate burst out laughing. 'Good God, did he say so straight out? Poor Nick, I wish I might have been a fly on the wall, to see his face!'

'It's not such a wild notion, Kate. According to Uncle, Dominic holds you in high respect.'

'Maybe so, but he certainly doesn't wish to marry me.'

'You must remember that his situation is . . . is very difficult at present.'

Kate's hazel eyes glinted. 'You mean he may be hard-pressed enough to offer for me?'

'No, no! At least, he may feel that a marriage of . . . of convenience is his duty. You know how Gothic the Barrs are about Melburn.'

'Gothic or not, Dominic won't ask me to marry him, for the very good reason that he knows I'd refuse him out of hand.'

'You would?'

'Certainly. To marry in such circumstances must make us both miserable. He knows that as well as I do.'

Elinor heaved a sigh of relief. 'I'm glad you take it so calmly. I thought you might be angry with Uncle.'

'Lord, no. I know his quirks too well – and so, I hope, does Dominic.'

Kate spread a clean white cloth over the contents of the basket.

'There!' she said. 'That's done. Gemmel shall take it to the vicarage, and I hope they will receive the tomato jam with Christian forbearance.'

III

After dinner that night, Kate found an excuse to draw Mr Beacher into the library for a private discussion.

'Elinor tells me that Dominic talks of selling Melburn,' she said. 'Is that true?'

'Alas, yes.' Mr Beacher heaved a dolorous sigh. 'How sad it is to think that but for malign Fate, you might have been mistress of that beautiful house, and all its acres.'

Kate gazed sombrely at the fire. 'I admit I love Melburn. I was sometimes tempted to marry John for the sake of the estate, which would have done him a great injustice; but that's all past. We must think what's to be done now.' She faced the old man. 'I would like to lend Dominic whatever he needs.'

'Impossible, puss. Your capital can't be touched till you turn twenty-five, or marry, whichever comes first.'

'I have a large income.'

'Indeed you do, but it couldn't provide a tenth of what Barr needs to clear his debts. However, there's no cause to despair. He'll come about, not a doubt of that.'

'How?' demanded Kate.

Mr Beacher assumed a look of such cherubic innocence that she longed to slap him. 'Perhaps an advantageous marriage,' he said. 'There are those to whom a peerage is a powerful inducement. More than one City nabob would come down handsome to make his daughter Lady Barr.'

Since this was undeniably the case, Kate didn't bother to argue the point. She spent the rest of the evening deep in thought, and when the family retired to bed did not follow them, but went instead to the large room which her father had set aside for his work.

During his lifetime it had been wonderfully untidy, its cabinets stuffed to overflowing with his notes, its shelves laden with his reference books, its vast central table buried under his folios of maps and sketches. These papers, collected over a period of more than twenty years, were the raw material of his planned *History of the County of Dorsetshire*. No one had been permitted to lay a finger on them.

After his death, Kate had tried to reduce them to some order, but she quickly found that a single page in his crabbed handwriting might include references to a dozen different subjects, and how to determine its proper place in the files was a puzzle.

At last she wrote to Mr Theophilus Lombard, whose publishing house had from time to time printed learned articles by her papa, and to whom Sir Clive had intended to submit his final manuscript. Mr Lombard, invited to stay at the Manor, spent several days burrowing mole-like through the mass of records, and emerged flushed with excitement.

'You have a treasure here, Miss Safford, a veritable crock of gold! I have long been an admirer of your father's research, but I had no idea that he'd unearthed so much new information. Translations from Old English, Latin, even Welsh! A new vision of old events. I promise you, it will shake the realm of academia to its foundations, and elevate Sir Clive to the highest rank of historians. The collection will be a triumph! A veritable triumph!'

'Collection?' said Kate, bemused.

'Why, yes, dear lady, there is far more here than can be contained in a single volume. Five at least are needed.' Mr Lombard's eyes became misty. 'Suitably bound in levant morocco, with gilt embellishment. A respectful dedication to His Majesty may be within our reach.'

'It all sounds very splendid,' said Kate doubtfully, 'but who is to write the book?'

Mr Lombard returned to earth.

'That, Miss Safford, is the nub of the matter. Had Sir Clive lived to finish his *magnum opus*, it must have been hailed not only for its factual revelations, but also its literary excellence. I don't scruple to say that many historians are dead bores, but your papa was as witty as he was well informed . . . a master of the felicitous phrase, the precise word. To find his match will be no easy task. I can find *a* writer, but can I find *the* writer, the man who will bring the facts into proper sequence, then set them out in sparkling prose?

'I confess I can't immediately think of the genius who combines these skills, but that can wait. First, the material must be codified, and an index compiled that will include every item of information, with a proper system of cross-reference. I dare swear I know the very man for *that* job.'

So it was that Mr Sidney Trumble arrived to take up residence at Safford Manor. He was a small man, like a pig in spectacles, who spent his days and sometimes his nights locked in the workroom, and treated the other inhabitants of the house with profound indifference. Such was his proficiency, that by Christmas-tide Sir Clive's records were in apple-pie order.

Towards the end of January, Mr Lombard wrote to Kate from London, saying he had thought of just the man to write her father's *History* – a Mr Henry Godbold of Winchester, who was not only an acknowledged authority on manuscripts of the Middle English period, but also the author of several books whose lively style had won them wide popular appeal. Unfortunately he was not at present in England, having gone on a lecture tour to Rome and Sienna. He had, however, answered Mr Lombard's initial letter with courtesy, and had promised to call at the publisher's office when he returned home in a few weeks' time.

'I am sure,' concluded Mr Lombard, 'that once he has seen Sir Clive's papers, we shall have him firmly on the hook.'

27

Kate began to hope that her father's labours might at last bear fruit.

Tonight, though, her mind was not on the projected *History* of Dorset, but on the contents of the large desk that stood in the bay of the workroom. In it were stored Sir Clive's personal treasures – the letters he had received from his wife over the fifteen years of their marriage, miniatures of her and Kate, a collection of old coins, a snuffbox given him by Charles James Fox, and other small articles of purely sentimental value.

Seated in her father's chair, Kate unlocked the central drawer of the desk, and lifted out a large, flat box with a japanned lid. From this she took a sheet of paper, which she spread before her. It was the last letter her father had written to her before his death.

My dearest daughter,

You have always held that your nature is not romantical – a claim that would win you the praise of my fellow antiquaries, who say it's facts that count, and that myth and legend are beneath the notice of a serious historian.

My own view is that in these tales, handed down by word of mouth, told and retold round the winter's hearth, embroidered by bards and distorted by bigots, lie the seeds of historic truth. Dorset has many such tales, not the least intriguing of them being that of the Twyford Gold.

According to standard histories, in the year 1015, when the Army of Cnut the Dane ravaged this land, a great store of treasure was brought from Sherborne to Twyford, for safekeeping in the stronghold of Cynric of Melburn; but the pursuing Danes laid siege to the place and at length overran it, killed all the defenders, and carried off the gold as tribute to their leader.

All very fine. However, history in this case depends upon a sixteenth-century text by Simon of Sherborne, who based his account on reported sermons (now lost) by Wulfstan of York and Aelfric of Cerne. The facts, you see, are no better than second or third-hand, and cannot be verified by reference to the original eleventh-century writings.

If we turn to the heroic poem, 'The Song of Edina', we find a rather different outcome to the siege of Melburn. The poet relates that though the Danes vanquished Cynric 'by foul witchcraft', he had hidden the gold so well that the rievers never found it. The treasure remains somewhere in the Rem Valley, to be recovered in the course of time by a 'brave and virtuous champion'.

I think there is more than a grain of truth in this bushel of make-believe, and I have said as much to Mr Humphrey Dymoke, whose History of the Second Danish Invasion you will find on my shelves. Dymoke pooh-poohed my belief, and is convinced that the gold was found, and that the Song is mere fiction.

Alas, I don't have time to wander down this charming byway, but you may find it amusing to do so. You've enough of me in you to enjoy poring over the old fables. You are both brave and virtuous, and who's to say that a champion must always be a man?

I suggest you begin by reading Dymoke's book, and the texts I attach to this letter. Then go on to consult living authorities, in particular Dymoke himself, Dame Celia of Midsomer Norton, and Father Francis Tuckitt of the Cathedral of Wells.

Good hunting, my Kate, and may you find the crock of gold at the end of the rainbow.

Your loving

Papa

Kate had never been able to discuss the letter with her father, for by the time she arrived home from London, he was already dying. Sunk in delirium, he called for people long gone, and mistook Kate for her dead mother. Sometimes he lay silent, his congested lungs fighting for breath. Once, apparently fancying himself back in the days of Cnut and Cynric, he rambled about the Danish Gold and Dunstan's Cross. The night before he died, he caught Kate's wrist in a burning grip, whispering, 'Remember, child, the blackthorn is anathema! You must find the dry river. Find the dry river!'

Trying to soothe him, she said, 'I will, Papa, I promise, but now you must rest.' Soon after, he lapsed into the coma from which he never woke.

In the months after his death, Kate studied the other papers in the japanned box, and read Dymoke's book, a boring tome full of prosy footnotes, but she was far too busy to act on her father's suggestion. Safford Manor was a large estate, and it took her all her time to learn its workings, and to convince her factor, her bailiff, and the other farm workers, that her orders were to be taken seriously.

Still, she could not forget Sir Clive's last words to her, nor convince herself that they were no more than the ravings of a fevered mind. He had meant what he said, he had urged her to search for the treasure, and she had promised to do so.

Now that her affairs were running smoothly, and the *History* of Dorset had been placed in competent hands, she felt in duty bound to keep her promise.

There was the added incentive that if by some miracle the gold was found, Melburn would be saved. She was not sure of the laws governing treasure-trove – she thought that whatever was found became the property of the Crown, but that a substantial reward was paid to the finder.

Her solicitor could advise her on that point. In the mean time, she would write to Dame Celia of Midsomer Norton, Father Tuckitt of Wells, and the tedious Mr Dymoke.

She carried the japanned box up to her bedroom, and settled down to study the documents it contained. The first of these was a slim pamphlet printed and issued by the historical Society of Bath.

THE DESTRUCTION OF OLD MELBURN HALL BY THE ARMY OF KING CNUT THE DANE

At the close of the tenth century, the Viking Sweyn Forkbeard, son of Harald Bluetooth of Denmark, led his army of raiders against Britain. By the year 998 they were pillaging Wessex, and four years later they exacted from the embattled populace a tribute of 14,000 pounds of silver and gold.

From 1005 to 1007, Sweyn harried the eastern coasts and the West Country. His pirates marched from Reading, past Wantage, and down to Avebury, laying waste the country. They defeated the thanes of Wiltshire, then turned eastward with their loot, bypassed Winchester and reached the coast. That same year they were bought off by a toll of 26,000 pounds of coin.

The Danish assaults continued over the next decade. Oxford was sacked, and Ipswich, and London itself was threatened. King Ethelred fled to Normandy.

After Sweyn's death in 1014, his second son Cnut took up the attack. In 1015 he assailed Poole Harbour and rampaged through Dorset, destroying many villages and holy shrines. Thinking to save something from the invaders, the nobles of the King's court loaded wagons with treasures of the Crown and Church, and sent them northward towards Glastonbury. However, rumours came that the Danish fleet had already sailed round Cornwall and taken command of the whole of the Severn Estuary. The treasure train was therefore diverted to the stonghold of Cynric Cerdinga of Melburn. He was a staunch Christian, kinsman to that same Dunstan who built the first church in Twyford Lindum, and who later became Archbishop of Canterbury.

The Hall of Melburn was fortified by earthworks and a ditch, and for eleven days it withstood the besieging Danes. At last, by a subterfuge, the Danes succeeded in overrunning the place. The defenders, man, woman and child, were put to the sword. The gold and holy artefacts, which included a pectoral cross said to have belonged to St Dunstan, were seized, and Melburn Hall was destroyed, so that not a stone was left standing.

Pinned to the back of the pamphlet was a document in her father's hand.

'From cold fact,' he wrote, 'I turn to legend. It's to be found in a poem, "The Song of Edina", attributed to the bard Nairn, who lived in Sherborne at the start of the twelfth century. Several versions exist, the earliest and most authentic is in archaic English. I give you my own prose translation.

' "When the fair Edina became the wife of Cynric of Melburn, the marriage was solemnized by her kinsman, Dunstan of Glastonbury, a priest who came to stand high in the favour of Edgar, King of Britain. Edina besought Dunstan to cause a church to be built at Twyford Lindum, so that people might there worship God. Dunstan granted her request, and the church was built that*

31

bears his name.

' "Heaven blessed Edina and her thane. Three sons and three daughters she bore, and she was known throughout the shire for her piety and good works.

' "When the ravening wolf, Cnut of Denmark, began to tear the flesh of this land, the keepers of the King's treasure sent much store of gold and holy vessels, including the Cross of Dunstan, to Glastonbury for safekeeping.

' "But ere the wagons had travelled many miles, word came that the sea-wolves had seized the Severn coast. The King's men turned north to Melburn, the abode of Cynric and Edina, knowing them to be loyal to the King's cause.

' "The Danish army followed, and as they approached, Cynric sent his daughters to a place of safety, and begged his wife to go with them, but she refused. Cynric caused the treasure to be hidden.'

'At this point,' continued Sir Clive, 'there's a break in the text, presumably the part that described the hiding of the treasure, and the eleven-day siege of Melburn. The story resumes where the defenders realize that defeat is inevitable:

' "Now the Danes made such terrible assault on the Hall that the ditch was filled with the dead, and the ravens feasted on their bodies. Cynric's sons fell, and many others, until there remained less than twenty of his fighters. Then Cynric said, 'When night falls we will make a sortie, and draw the wolves to us, while my lady Edina, with Muir and Kennet to protect her, rides out through the postern gate, and God willing makes her escape.

' "This plan they followed. Under cover of darkness, Cynric and his small band sallied forth, and fought mightily until weight of numbers overcame them.

' "Edina and her two protectors stole out, wrapped in dark cloaks and with the harness of their horses muffled. They could not cross the bridge, for it was held by the Danes; but Edina prayed to the saints for aid, and was granted a miracle. The party passed safely over the dry river-bed, and rode to find sanctuary in the Abbey at Glastonbury.

' "There they were received with honour, but Edina's heart was broken by the death of her husband and sons. She spoke no word to anyone, and a few

days later she died, and was buried in the sacred precincts of the Abbey.

' *"From that day to this, many have sought to know where the Twyford Gold lies hid, but those who knew its hiding-place are dead, and Cynric's Hall is utterly destroyed. Neither the wolves of Cnut, nor the good folk of Twyford, have found trace of the treasure. It is said that Dunstan has set a seal upon it, which will be broken by a brave and virtuous champion, who is yet to come.'*

Kate laid the pages down.

The poem left so much unanswered. What had happened to the two men who accompanied Edina on her last ride? Had one or other of them survived to relate the saga of Melburn? How else had Nairn found the material for his poem?

It was most unsatisfactory. Yet her father had believed that somewhere in those lines of verse lay a seed of truth. He had urged her to find the dry river, the one Edina and her companions crossed the night Melburn fell.

Try as she might, she could recall no dry river-bed in the Twyford valley. The present village, like Safford Manor and Melburn Hall, stood close to the banks of the Rem, and it was a matter of local pride that its waters never failed, even in the driest season.

It was accepted fact that after the razing of Cynric's Hall, Melburn had been rebuilt on a new site. How could one possibly locate the old one, after a gap of eight centuries?

Sighing, Kate took a third document from the box and spread it open on her lap. It was a map Sir Clive had drawn a year ago, of Twyford and its surrounds. It showed the winding course of the Rem, the principal farms and houses of the valley, the roads and cattle-paths, and the village itself with its Roman bridge, its market square, and at its centre St Dunstan's Church.

Somewhere in this wide territory, Cynric Cerdinga had hidden the contents of the treasure wagons. There had not been time to move them far. The gold, if it existed, must lie buried close to Old Melburn.

The week before his death, her father had revisited Twyford Tor. He'd been caught in a rainstorm, and he'd contracted the inflammation of the lungs that killed him. What had driven him to those exposed heights in foul weather? Had he hoped to test some half-formed theory, something that related to the legend of Edina?

The blackthorn. Anathema. The dry river.

It made no sense at all.

Kate folded the documents away. Tomorrow she would ride to the crest of the Tor, and from that vantage point make her own survey of the landmarks on the map.

She rose early next day, donned her riding-habit, and ate a hasty meal in the breakfast parlour. The other members of the family were still abed, a fact for which she was grateful, as she had no wish to be quizzed about her plans.

The morning was cold, the encircling hills blue with frost, and she put on a warm cloak with a hood. Her favourite hack, Waldo, was waiting for her in the stable yard, and before mounting she placed Sir Clive's map and a small spyglass in the saddlebag.

Quitting the yard by its northern gate, she set out along the road that led to the village. At its outskirts she turned left, and followed the causeway on the eastern edge of the marsh that gave Twyford Lindum its name. It was a solitary place, the home of wildfowl and small beasts, and the local people shunned it, claiming it was haunted by bog-bogles.

From the far end of the causeway, the path climbed steeply to the summit of the Tor. The soil here was clay and sand, very different from the dry chalk reaches of south-east Dorset, and from the spongy turf rose the many springs that ran down to the mere, there to combine as the headwaters of the Rem.

Her father had told her the Tor was a place of refuge since time immemorial. 'The Celts built a fort here six centuries before the birth of Christ,' he'd said. 'One can still see the ramparts they threw up. The Romans added a watch-tower to give them early warning of barbarian raiders. Had to protect their fine villas, down in the vale.'

'I never saw any villas,' Kate said.

'They're there, none the less, buried under our pastures. The ploughs turn up traces . . . coins, pieces of broken pottery. The Romans were here for four hundred years, y'know. Built roads, and a canal to drain the marsh, brought in yew and cherry trees, roses and violets, all the things we think of as typically English. Then the legions had to go back to defend Rome against the Goths, which left our coasts open to a fresh wave of invaders.'

'Who?' Kate demanded.

'Saxons from north-west Germany and Friesland. Cerdic led them, fellow who founded the Cerdinga line of kings. Cynric's ancestor, and ours, most likely.'

His passion was the history of Dorset. His days and years were spent poring over old manuscripts, visiting the houses of the great and the graveyards of the forgotten, gathering every scrap of information that might put a stitch in the threadbare fabric of the past.

Kate was roused from her reverie by the honking of a skein of geese that winged down towards the marsh. She dismounted and tethered Waldo, took the map and spyglass from the saddlebag, and walked to a rocky ledge that overhung the valley. Behind her was the line of rough-hewn stones that marked the foundations of the Roman tower, and before her stretched the Vale of the Rem, which wound away to join the distant Frome.

The air was clear enough for her to pick out every detail of the village, from Fishway on the east, to the Corn Store and the New Mill on the west – though why the mill should be called 'new' when the date above its door was 1662, was a mystery.

Three miles from the foot of the Tor, on the west bank of the Rem, lay her own Manor, and closer in, on the opposite bank, stood Melburn Hall, its three wings ringed by gardens and parkland, a home wood and an artificial lake.

The spring that fed the lake was vigorous enough to supply the

Hall's needs, and various other streams criss-crossed the Barr lands, but none of them was large enough to be termed a river.

According to the legend, Edina had escaped from her besieged home through the postern gate, and a miracle had allowed her and her bodyguards to cross the dry river-bed. Had the Melburn of those days been closer to the Rem than its successor?

People built close to water. Certainly the Romans, with their passion for bathing, would have done so.

In the Old English tongue, Melburn meant 'mill stream'. It took a strong flow of water to turn a mill-wheel, and the flow must remain constant throughout the year. Was Cynric's Melburn situated near an ancient mill? Did watermills even exist in the eleventh century, or was the grinding done by hand?

Kate's spirits sagged. With such vast gaps in her knowledge, how was she ever to solve this puzzle?

She turned back to the map. South of Melburn stretched arable and pasture land, dotted with tenant farms. Her father had marked these with crosses. Some of the families who worked the farms had lived here as long as the Barrs and Saffords, perhaps longer.

Three roads met at the village – the one from the Manor, the one from Melburn, and the one that connected with the pike road to Sturminster Newton.

Her father had marked two other features on the map; the Tump, and Pony's Field. The Tump was a rounded hillock which the villagers called the Devil's Footfall. From the heights where she stood, it did resemble the print of a cloven hoof stamped deep in the turf, its central mound dark with thickets of blackthorn and holly.

Pony's Field was a stretch of common which the Barrs let the villagers use as pasture for their livestock.

Kate folded the map and put it away. She was no closer to knowing where in all these rolling miles she should begin her search, but it would not do to lose heart. Her father had told her to begin with the living rather than the dead, and since the treasure, if it existed, lay on the Barrs' land, the first person to consult must be the new owner of Melburn, Dominic Barr.

She would visit him as soon as may be.

IV

Two days after the funeral of Justin and John Barr, a racing curricle turned through the gates of Melburn Hall and swept up the driveway to the shelter of the main portico.

Its driver, whose smooth round face and ingenuous expression belied his thirty-three years, was dressed in the height of fashion. His greatcoat, frogged in the Cossack style, hung open to reveal a jacket of Bath weave and a glimpse of a lemon-yellow waistcoat. His buckskins admirably set off a fine pair of legs, and the tops of his boots were trimmed with tan leather that matched his gloves. On his head was a hat with a curling brim, such as was favoured by the sporting set. It was apparent to the meanest eye that Mr George Walcott was not only a notable whip, but also a pink of the ton.

Handing the reins to his groom, and directing him to 'see the tits safe-housed', Mr Walcott climbed the steps of the mansion, flicked the nose of one of the stone lions guarding the portal, and rang a summary peal on the bell. The door swung open to reveal not the butler, but Lord Barr himself.

'Come in, George,' his lordship said. 'Don't hang about in the cold.'

Stepping inside, Mr Walcott divested himself of his outdoor garments and handed them to the young footman who hurried forward.

'Where's Beckett?' he demanded. 'Don't tell me he's jumped ship.'

'No. He's ill abed.' Dominic was steering his guest towards the library. 'He was with my father for thirty years, and takes his death hard. Parry's quit, though. Got an offer of a post with Hetherington, and in the circumstances I couldn't stand in his way. I'm afraid you'll find the house at sixes and sevens. You'd be a dashed sight more comfortable at The Grey Goose.'

'No, I shouldn't. Come to bear you company. Would've been here for the funeral, if it hadn't been for Lizzie's weddin'. M'mother was in a blind panic, convinced Liz was goin' to do a bolt, but she didn't. Flew all her fences like a thoroughbred. Asked particularly to be remembered to you. Everyone did.' Mr Walcott dropped into an armchair and regarded his lordship with a keen eye.

'Bad, has it been?'

'Devilish.' Dominic turned his head to stare out of the window. 'The place feels so empty.'

'Friends been callin', I daresay?'

'To tell truth, I'm no longer sure who are my friends. Some folk toad-eat me for my new title, and others seem to regard me as a kind of Panthéon Bazaar, bargains to be had for the asking. On the day of the service, Foster Flint offered to buy John's greys for a thousand guineas.'

'Don't consider it. He's not called Skin Flint for nothing.'

'Beggars can't be choosers,' said Dominic harshly. 'Fact is, I'm at ames ace, and everyone knows it.'

George rubbed his nose. 'Tell you what, Nick, when you come to sell the hosses, make me your broker. I'll take 'em north, arrange things so folk won't know who's sellin'. That way, you'll avoid the nipcheeses.'

'Thank you.' Dominic spoke with real gratitude, for Mr Walcott was one of the best judges of horseflesh in the country, and to have him handle the sales would save not only money, but a deal of embarrassment.

George cleared his throat delicately. 'I hope . . . I trust . . . it won't come to sellin' this place?'

'I may have no alternative, but I mean to put up a fight. I'll go up to Town soon, to try if I can raise fresh loans. If I fail, I'll consult the property dealers. One can't in a moment dispose of a place this size, and if I sell I must do so to best advantage.'

'Quite so.' Mr Walcott studied his fingernails. 'I take it you'll be havin' a word with Savernake?'

'No, I will not.'

'Pity. He's rich as Croesus, and don't mind stakin' his blunt in a good cause.'

'I don't choose to be the object of his charity.'

'Not even to save Melburn?'

'Not even to save Melburn.'

Mr Walcott knew better than to argue against a man's pride. He shifted to safer ground. 'Your mama's well?'

'Yes. She came down for the service.'

Mr Walcott nodded. Bath had been a-buzz with that titbit of gossip. He held Lady Letitia in high regard, and wished that for her sake the breach between Dominic and her second husband could be healed, but there seemed no hope of it.

He suggested to Dominic that they go and take a look at the horses. They made a leisurely tour of the loose-boxes, and discussed what price should be set on each animal.

'Prime stock, in prime condition,' Mr Walcott said at last. 'You should do nicely out of 'em.' He scanned the well-equipped yard, and the coach-house with its row of shining carriages. 'At least your father went down with all guns blazin'.'

'Oh, Yes,' said Dominic bleakly. 'We Barrs are bankrupts of the very first water.'

Mr Walcott remained at Melburn for several days. He accompanied Dominic on his rounds of the estate, and as the son of a country squire, was able to offer sound advice on many points. In the evenings, sitting late over a bottle of port, or playing a few hands of piquet, he chatted or was silent as his host's mood directed.

He knew that beneath Dominic's surface anger lay a very

genuine grief. Whatever had been the tensions between the members of the Barr family, the ties that bound them were strong. Now, bereft at a stroke of father and brother, Dominic had to accept that his comfortable world was shattered. His generous income, his position as a man of fashion, his friendships and his home seemed lost for ever.

He appeared to be dealing with his situation in a practical manner. His secretary, housekeeper and librarian were already engaged in drawing up inventories of the contents of the Hall, and his stockmen were making account of his flocks and herds.

What obviously weighed heavily on him was his inability to help those who had looked to Melburn for their livelihood. Some of his employees had already left, others were on the lookout for new positions, but many clearly hoped against hope to remain in Dominic's service, and he found the anxiety in their eyes very hard to bear.

'I can make provision for pigs and cows,' he said, 'but not for the people who've served us faithfully all these years. I tell you, George, if I survive this shambles, I will never again allow myself to fall into debt.'

George sighed. 'You might consider goin' abroad for a spell,' he suggested. 'Very cheap livin' to be had in Italy, I'm told.'

'I won't quit,' said his lordship flatly. 'I won't leave England, not if I have to earn my bread as a dance-master, or peddle pies in the street like Colly-Molly Puff!'

At Safford Manor, Kate stood before the pier-glass in her bedroom and scowled at her reflection.

'Do you consider I look dependable and resolute?' she asked.

'You look delightful,' Elinor replied uncertainly. Indeed, the morning gown of saffron challis displayed Kate's pretty figure to advantage, and the bonnet lined with matching satin lent sparkle to her eyes.

Kate's scowl deepened. 'It's provoking to own nothing sufficiently dowdy.'

'Why in the world should you wish to be dowdy? Where are you going, may I ask?'

'To Melburn.' Kate's tone was abstracted. 'I suppose I could wear black, but that seems altogether too dismal. One should aim for a note of optimism, I believe.'

Elinor shook her head in bewilderment. 'Dominic will hardly expect callers to wear mourning. He never stands on ceremony.'

'Lord, I wasn't thinking of that. It's that I have a proposition to put to him, and I wish him to take it seriously.'

'Proposition?' Elinor turned pale with misgiving. 'What kind of proposition?'

Kate's only answer was a glinting smile. She tied the strings of her bonnet under her chin.

'It will have to do,' she said. 'I doubt Nick will notice, one way or another.' She picked up the pelisse and reticule that lay on a chair, and started for the door. Elinor darted after her.

'I'll go with you,' she said.

Kate batted demure lashes. 'But that would quite defeat my purpose, Nell. What I have to say must be said in private.'

'Kate,' said Elinor desperately, 'if you have the least thought of acting on Uncle's lunatic suggestion . . . .'

'I don't, you goose.'

'Then tell me why you're going to Melburn!'

'Very well. I wish to ask Dominic's leave to search for the Twyford Gold.'

'The Twyford . . . ?' Elinor made a snatch as Kate whisked past her. 'Kate, come back here! Come back this instant!'

But Kate was already running down the stairs and across the hall, to the carriage waiting at the door.

'The Twyford Gold?' said Mrs Beacher blankly. 'My love, whatever can you mean? The gold is just an old wives' tale.'

'No, it ain't,' said her husband. 'It's in all the history books. Must be true.'

Elinor sank down on a sofa. 'True or false, Uncle, it's been lost for centuries; it's ludicrous to think of searching for it now. What's more, to plague poor Dominic when he's knee-deep in trouble is unforgivable. I can't imagine what's got into Kate. I offered to go to Melburn with her, but she said she must speak to Dominic alone.' Elinor saw the flash of satisfaction in her uncle's eye, and said tartly, 'I devoutly hope she won't say anything indiscreet.'

He had the grace to look guilty, but Mrs Beacher was beaming happily. 'I think Dominic will be grateful for Kate's kind offer. What's more, if he agrees to her plan, I daresay Kate will need to visit Melburn quite frequently. All things considered, I believe she has acted just as she ought, and nothing but good will come of it.'

When Lord Barr perceived from his study window that the Safford carriage had halted at his door, and that Miss Safford herself was mounting the front steps, he was tempted to direct Beckett to deny he was home.

To be pursued by hopeful ingenues and their ambitious mamas was nothing new to him. It was a natural hazard of London life. One flirted casually with the prettiest of the girls, treated their mothers with courtesy, and at the end of the Season allowed the ebb tide to carry them all beyond the far horizon.

Kate Safford, though, was in a different category. She was a close neighbour, and might have married his brother. She must not be offended in any way. One could only send up a prayer that that numskull Beacher hadn't told her of their conversation.

Dominic's annoyance with Mr Beacher increased daily, and his expression as he strode to meet his guest was far from welcoming. Kate, for her part, was fighting the urge to turn tail and run. It had taken all her courage to come this far, and though she was outwardly calm, her heart was thumping and her hands icy.

What might have been an awkward encounter was eased by the arrival of the cocker spaniel, Brag, who came scurrying from the kitchen quarters and greeted Miss Safford with cries and caperings of delight.

Kate bent to pat him, saying, 'Poor old Brag! Are you missing your master, poor old boy?'

Dominic, entering the hall at that moment, saw there were tears in her eyes, and forgot his ill temper.

'Kate, how good to see you. I hope this animal hasn't muddied your skirts.'

'No, not at all.'

She held out her hand and he shook it, exclaiming, 'Lord, you're frozen! Come into the library and warm yourself!'

He settled her in a chair and gave her a glass of sherry wine. For a while they exchanged formalities, but once it was established that Dominic was well, that he was entertaining his friend George Walcott for a few days, and that next week he planned to go to London on business, Kate drew a deep breath and broached the purpose of her visit.

'Uncle Amyas tells me you may have to sell Melburn.'

He nodded stiffly. 'In the last resort, yes.'

She met his eyes. 'We've known each other a long time, and needn't mince words. I am a wealthy woman, and nothing would please me more than to help you with a loan.' She saw his expression grow wary, and continued quickly, 'In fact, I suggested it to Uncle Amyas. He explained that it's not possible. My capital is tied up, and can't be touched for some years yet.'

'You're very good. I appreciate your concern.'

She ignored the coldness in his voice, and plodded on. 'My father used to say that when reasonable measures fail, one must try the unreasonable.'

'Chance one's arm, you mean?' Dominic's smile was ironic. 'My father would have applauded that sentiment.'

She lifted her chin. 'I think he would have risked a great deal to save Melburn.'

'If he'd risked less, Melburn would be safe today!' Dominic saw the colour flood into Kate's face, and said in a quieter tone, 'I beg your pardon. I shouldn't rip out at you. It's not your problem.'

'But it *is*! Don't you see? It's the problem of everyone in this valley. The Barrs belong here, their blood and sweat is soaked into the very soil of Twyford. I know it's an impertinence to speak of things you must consider private, but surely if there's a chance of keeping this estate in your hands, you must seize it?'

'I mean to try if I can raise money in London.'

'And if you fail?'

'I'll cross that bridge when I come to it.'

Kate leaned forward. 'What if there is something we can do here and now?' she demanded. As he gazed at her frowningly, she reached into her reticule and brought out a small, shining object which she held out to him.

'Do you know what this is?'

He took it from her, and examined it briefly. 'An old coin. We have one or two in a cabinet, I fancy.'

'It's an *Agnus Dei*,' she said, 'minted in the time of King Ethelred the Second, who reigned from 976 to 1016. You see it has the Lamb of God on one side, and the Dove of Peace on the other. Papa thought it the most beautiful coin ever made.'

'Very likely.' He gave her a wry smile. 'I fear it won't suffice to clear my obligations.'

'Not of itself, of course; but what if it were part of the Twyford Gold?'

'My dear Kate, that's a legend, nothing more.'

'My father believed it existed. When he was dying, he urged me with the last of his strength to search for it.'

'Indeed? Did he say where?'

'Yes. He said I must find the dry river.'

Dominic's brows rose. 'Dry river? Was that not perhaps the fever speaking?'

Her face set. 'Do I have your permission to begin the search?'

He stared at her, half-irritated and half-amused. 'Not if you mean to pull down this house about my ears. Cynric's Melburn is probably buried beneath mine, you know.'

'No. Old Melburn lay on another site.'

He smiled. 'Near a dry river?' He saw her flush, and relented. 'There, I don't mean to tease. Start your search when you choose.

Consult with my factor. He'll see you don't upset my cattle, or dig up my crops.'

'I don't intend to dig,' Kate said. 'At least, not yet. I plan to talk to people Papa recommended, people who are experts on ancient history.' She rose from her chair. 'If I learn anything of value, I'll tell you at once. I think that if the gold is found, it will belong to the Crown, but you'll be entitled to claim a substantial reward.'

'Thank you,' he said politely.

He escorted her to her carriage and handed her up into it. As it drove away, Mr Walcott appeared from the direction of the stables.

'Nice turn-out,' he said. 'Who owns it?'

'Miss Safford, from the Manor.' Dominic directed a bland look at his friend. 'She believes there is treasure buried on my land, and seeks leave to search for it.'

'Treasure?' Mr Walcott blinked. 'Dicked in the nob, is she? Only nineteen shillin's in the pound?'

'No, she's sane enough, but her papa had a bee in his bonnet about finding the Twyford Gold, and she feels obliged to comply with his dying request.'

Mr Walcott nodded sagely. 'Inbred, the folk in these valleys. Present company excepted, of course. Pity one can't weed out the poor stock, as one can with horses. Speakin' of which, I have a buyer for John's team.'

'Really? Who?'

'Me. Happy to give you three thousand for 'em.'

'I'm not looking for charity, George.'

'No question of that, my dear fellow. Sweet goers, mouths like silk; they're worth every penny of three thousand, so you may tell old Skin Flint to act the cheapskate elsewhere.'

At luncheon that day, Kate found herself the focus of all eyes. Mrs Beacher plied her with questions. How were things at the Hall? Was it true that the household staff had deserted poor Dominic? What were his plans for the future?

47

Kate replied that she had not noticed any mass exodus of the Barr employees, and that Dominic was to leave for London in a day or so, to try to recruit funds.

'That hare won't run,' said her uncle, with a lugubrious shake of the head. 'He'll end by marrying some frumpish commoner, you mark my words.'

He stole a sly glance at Kate, but she ignored the lure.

Elinor said hastily, 'Did you speak to him about the treasure?'

'Yes, and he gave me leave to set up a search for it.'

Mr Beacher snorted. 'It'd take an army of engineers a dozen years to probe the whole of this valley!'

'I agree,' said Kate.

'So what's your plan, may I ask?'

'I'll seek an interview with Mr Humphrey Dymoke.'

'Dymoke the historian? No harm in that. I'll drive you to Weymouth; we'll pick the fellow's brains and enjoy a breath of sea air into the bargain.'

'You're very kind,' said Kate firmly, 'but you know you must be back in Bath for Anna's confinement. Elinor will go with me, and Ben Coachman will drive us, with Harry on the box. We will deal very comfortably, I assure you.'

Mr Beacher agreed to the arrangement, and began to reminisce about past sojourns in the little coastal town, in the days when it was in high favour with the Prince Regent and other of the royal dukes; and no further mention was made of Melburn, or the plight of Dominic Barr.

V

George Walcott left Twyford on Thursday, to return to his father's house at Solsbury Hill, near Bath, and on Friday Lord Barr set out for London. He travelled at an easy pace, broke his journey at Reading, and at noon on Saturday arrived at Barr House in Grosvenor Square.

He had always thought of the handsome building as a family property, and it had come as a shock to learn from Mr Beacher that it belonged to his mother. It seemed that every day brought fresh proof of how little he knew about the estate.

The knocker of Number 17 was tied up with black crape, indicating a house of mourning, and the table in the entrance hall was laden with letters, which he guessed were expressions of sympathy. He was turning them over when he heard a step behind him, and the housekeeper hurried towards him, dropped a curtsy and said in a trembling voice,

'Oh, Mr Dominic . . . your lordship, I should say . . . I'm right glad to see you. Lady Letitia is here, and looking so pale as a ghost, but lie down and rest she will not, say what I may.'

'Is his lordship with her?' asked Dominic, hastily peeling off his gloves and greatcoat, and tossing them on to a chair.

'No, my lord, she came alone, wishing to hear all the news of Melburn, I daresay. Oh, sir, it's past all bearing, so it is. It breaks my old heart to think on it.'

Dominic put a hand on her shaking shoulder. 'Don't cry, Mrs Rudge. We must all try to keep our courage up. We'll talk later, shall we? But now I must go to my mother. Where is she? In the red room?'

Mrs Rudge nodded dumbly, and Dominic ran up the stairs to the small parlour that the family reserved for their private use.

Letitia Savernake was standing at the window, but she turned at the sound of Dominic's step, and came towards him. She wore deep mourning, which emphasized the waxy pallor of her skin, and the shadows under her eyes. Her countenance, so like her younger son's, bore the marks of past as well as present suffering. Her divorce from Justin Barr had created a great scandal, and though her charm and wit, allied to her new husband's vast wealth, had broken down many barriers, the high sticklers of society still refused to receive her.

Dominic embraced her warmly and led her to a sofa. 'I meant to come sooner,' he said, 'but George came for a few days. How are you, mama?'

'I'm well enough. People have been very kind.' Tears sprang to her eyes. 'I feel so guilty, Nick. So much to blame for what happened.'

'No, that's nonsense.' He took her hand and held it firmly. 'My father was responsible for his own disasters.'

'No,' she insisted. 'I was wrong to marry him. At sixteen I was dazzled by his title, and his social consequence. Justin was a man who needed love, and loyalty, and I gave him neither. I deserted him, and my children, to satisfy my own selfish desires; I can never absolve myself of that. But I'll say no more. No more of that. You have enough cares of your own. Ivor tells me Justin was deep in debt. Is that true?'

'I'm afraid it is.'

'How bad is it?'

'As bad as it can be.'

She gazed at him in distress. 'Surely Melburn is safe?'

'No. I might be forced to sell.'

'Dominic, no! It doesn't bear thinking of.'

'It has to be faced.'

'I'll speak to Ivor. He can so easily—'

'No, Mama. I forbid it.'

'My dear, this is no time to be on your high horse! At least let him help you to raise fresh loans. He knows a great many wealthy people.'

Dominic was about to make a repressive reply, when he saw the anxiety in her eyes. To refuse her help would cause her needless distress so he said abruptly, 'There is something he can do. I propose to sell off the valuables in the house – furniture, pictures, china. If he can provide me with a list of reputable dealers, I shall be grateful.'

'I'll ask him at once,' she said. 'How long do you mean to be in Town?'

'Not above ten days. There's so much to be done at Twyford, and I must visit the property agents in Bath and Dorchester.' He hesitated. 'If you'll permit me to stay here in this house . . .'

'Of course.' She kissed him and rose to her feet. 'I shall call again when you've had time to gather your wits, and Ivor shall send you the list of dealers tomorrow, without fail.'

When his mother's carriage had driven away, Dominic went to the study to deal with the accumulation of mail.

There was a depressingly large number of bills, which he set aside for Mr Shipton's attention. The letters he opened and read. Some were carefully formal, some fulsomely sympathetic. A few of his close friends, evidently aware of his financial straits, offered to lend him money. On reflection, he added these letters to Shipton's pile. Humiliating as it was to hold out the begging-bowl, it was less shameful than bilking the tradesmen of Twyford.

Near the bottom of the stack, he found a note addressed to him in a flourishing hand, and sealed with purple wax. He opened it, frowning.

'My dearest,' it ran, 'all my thoughts are with you at this sad time. I saw the notice in *The Times* and was so much shocked! To lose father and brother in that tragic way! No more of that now. I shall provide what solace I can when next we meet. C has gone

51

off to Bath on some matter of business, so I am quite alone. I long to see you. Come to me soon, I beg.'

The note was unsigned, but no member of the ton, or for that matter of the household staff, could have any difficulty in identifying the writer as Lady Madeline Cheveley. Truly, thought Dominic, her indiscretion amounted at times to lunacy. He carried the sheet of paper to the fireplace and dropped it on to the flames, where it curled and fell to blackened ashes.

The following afternoon, coming in from a solitary ride in the Park, Dominic was informed by a flustered Mrs Rudge that the Marquis of Savernake was waiting to see him.

'I told him you was from home, my lord, but he said it was a matter of great importance, and he'd bide till you came. I put out the best sherry, my lord; I hope I did right.'

'Quite right.'

Dominic dropped his hat and gloves on the hall table, and crossed to the library. He found his uninvited guest comfortably ensconced in an armchair, a glass of sherry in one hand and a copy of Byron's *Don Juan* in the other. He rose at Dominic's approach, and laid book and glass aside.

He was a man of no more than medium height, and slender build, with a swordsman's powerful wrists and thighs. In youth he had fought a number of duels, one of which had left him with a thin scar above his right eye. His colouring was fair, his eyes of a light, cold blue. Looking at him, Dominic felt the accustomed surge of dislike, and with difficulty extended his hand in greeting.

'Forgive the intrusion.' Savernake's voice was lazy rather than apologetic. 'Letitia insisted I must brook no delay.' He took up a scroll of papers from the table at his side, and handed it to Dominic. 'The first two pages list those collectors and dealers who reside in England. The rest live abroad, but are known to employ agents to bid for articles of special interest. I believe Melburn contains such items?'

'My grandfather was knowledgeable about art,' said Dominic

coldly. 'We have Titians, Corregios, a Rubens, as well as a number of more modern works. The Sèvres porcelain is generally admired, and there are pieces by Cellini and Clodion which are thought to be valuable.'

'My felicitations. Obviously, merchandise of such high quality must be marketed with care. I think you'd do well to speak first to Angerstein. He's a gentleman as well as a connoisseur, and won't allow you to be gulled.'

'Thank you. I appreciate your advice.' Dominic knew he sounded ungracious, and made himself meet Savernake's gaze. 'I am truly grateful for your help.'

'In accepting it, you've made your mother happy. That, I think, is what concerns us both.'

'Yes . . . It is some consolation to know that her future at least is secure.'

'Of that you may rest assured.' Savernake touched a finger to an eyebrow. 'Lord Barr, if at any stage you can bring yourself to accept my financial assistance . . .' Savernake saw the quick darkening of Dominic's expression, and left the sentence unfinished. 'There's something else that must be said. It relates to your presence here, in this house.'

'I've told Mama I'll be out within two weeks. However, if that's inconvenient . . .'

'Not in the least, but should you wish to remain longer, perhaps you'll be good enough to let her know? She's decided to sell, you see, and if a buyer is found at once, some agreement must be reached about the date of occupancy.'

'Sell? What do you mean? She must not, I won't allow it!'

'I'm afraid, my lord, that you have no say in the matter. Barr House is hers, to do with as she pleases.'

'She's only selling to help me. Please tell her that under no circumstances will I accept money from her.'

'Your creditors may feel differently, don't you think?'

'This is intolerable. Don't tell me you approve of her plan?'

'I've no right to approve or disapprove. Your father gave the house to Letitia, and I've always respected his decision. If she chooses to sell the place and use the money to settle some of your debts, so be it.' Savernake flicked invisible dust from his sleeve. 'It may ease your conscience to know that if I die tomorrow, Letitia will be able to live out her life in the utmost comfort.'

Dominic made an impatient gesture. 'I shall call on her, and persuade her that I would find such a sacrifice abhorrent.'

Savernake sighed. 'If you think it a sacrifice, you're more of a fool than I took you for. You are very dear to your mother. She wishes to help you. To refuse that help would be both short-sighted and churlish.' He strolled towards the door. 'I bid you good-day, Barr. Accept my best wishes for the success of your dealings. If I can be of any further service to you, you know where to find me.'

The interview with Savernake was the start of an unpleasant week. Dominic went doggedly from one banking-house to the next, and though he was received with courtesy, it was made plain to him that no one in the realms of high finance was ready to throw good money after bad.

Worse, he became aware of a falling-off in the attentions of people he had counted his friends. Few invitations decorated his chimney-piece. He told himself that hostesses knew him to be in mourning and unable to attend balls or routs, but the suspicion remained that he was no longer welcome in their drawing-rooms.

On visiting White's Club in St James's, he was greeted with a forced cheerfulness that made him vow not to repeat the experience. Poverty, he realized, made a man a leper. In losing his fortune, he'd committed the one gaffe the polite world couldn't forgive.

Late one evening he visited the house of Lady Cheveley. He found her just returned from an assembly at Carlton House, very grandly attired in a gown of champagne lace cut low across the bosom. She was a voluptuous creature, with tawny hair and eyes, and the emeralds that sparkled at her neck and wrists somehow emphasized her predatory grace, like jewels on a tigress. She held out her arms and Dominic caught her to him, kissing her lips and bare shoulders.

Freeing herself at last, she said with a pretended pout, 'I've waited all week for sight of you. Did you not have my letter?'

'I did.' He dropped down on a sofa, stretching his arms along its back. 'I've been deuced busy. Tonight is hail and farewell, I'm afraid; I go to Twyford tomorrow, and to Bath the following week, to parley with Shipton.'

She moved to pour him a glass of brandy, and came to sit beside him.

'Drink up! You look in need of some Dutch courage.'

He smiled wryly. 'If I don't have a care, I'll end as great a drunkard as my fine papa.'

She shook her head. 'Say what you like, Nick, you'll miss him.'

'Not I.'

'You'll miss him. Now he's gone, who else will you blame for your mistakes?'

He grinned ruefully over the rim of the glass. 'You've a cursed sharp tongue, my love.'

She shrugged her smooth shoulders. 'I've no turn for pretty speeches. I never knew your father or your brother. Would you have me pretend a grief I don't feel?'

'It's customary. You should begin by mumbling a few words of sympathy; express concern for my health and enquire how my poor mother does. After that, you may withdraw to find more convivial company, or if you are peculiarly thick-skinned, you may offer to relieve me of various of my possessions, at rock-bottom prices.'

She seemed unmoved by the bitterness in his voice. 'I heard you were in Queer Street,' she said.

'Oh, yes, it's all over Town. Barr's troubles are bandied about in every club and tavern.'

She reached casual hands to the magnificent necklace she wore, unclasped it and dropped it in his lap.

'Sell it,' she said.

He looked at her blankly, then gave a crack of laughter. 'Sell the Cheveley emeralds? My dear, have you lost your mind?'

'Not at all. I dislike them. The settings are so old-fashioned.'

'And how, may I ask, will you explain the sudden disappearance of a family heirloom to your husband?'

'Oh, I shall say it was stolen.'

'While I, meantime, attempt to peddle it to some felon in Seven Dials? I think it wouldn't be long before the Bow Street Runners took me in charge!'

'You needn't risk arrest. Jewels can be sold in Holland, no questions asked.'

He looked at her curiously. 'Do you speak from experience?'

'No,' she said coolly, 'but it's often done. Not all my friends are as stiff-necked as you.'

He picked up the necklace and placed it in her hand.

'I've not yet reached the level of dealing in stolen goods, my pet. Don't think me ungrateful, it was a handsome offer. At least the past few days have shown me who are my true friends. Here's Savernake willing to vouch for me to every art expert in Europe, and I've been made a present of the Cheveley emeralds, not to mention the Twyford Gold.'

'The Twyford Gold? What is that?'

'A legendary treasure, supposed to be buried at Melburn. Kate Safford has undertaken to find it for me.'

Madeline frowned. 'Safford? Is that the chit who was the Beachers' protégée, last summer?'

'The same.'

'Evidently she's developed a tendre for you.'

'On the contrary; I suspect she thinks me a poor fish.'

'She's rich, is she not?'

'Extremely rich.'

'You have your solution, then. Borrow from her.'

'That's not possible.'

'Why not?'

'Kate can't touch her capital till she reaches the age of twenty-five – or marries.'

Madeline eyed him narrowly. 'You're well informed on the subject. I wonder who was your informant? An ambitious relation, perhaps? Or does the lady cast out her own lures?'

A coldness in Dominic's glance warned her not to persist, but she ignored it. Smiling brilliantly, she said, 'If she inherits on her wedding-day, why, there's your chance! Marry her out of hand. It need make no difference to us; you may have your cake and eat it.'

'I fear it would choke me!'

'You're very nice in your feelings, all of a sudden.'

He shrugged impatiently. 'Cannot you understand? The Saffords have been our neighbours and friends for as long as I remember. I won't make an offer for Kate merely to meet my debts. I've lost everything but my self-respect – at least leave me that.'

'*Respect?*' Madeline sprang to her feet. 'How dare you speak to me of respect? How much respect do you show me? You leave my letter unanswered for days, then appear in my house without so much as an apology! You treat me as if I were some doxy from a whorehouse!'

He stood up to face her. 'I'm sorry. I've had other things on my mind, if you recall.'

'Why, so you have, Miss Safford among them! You refuse my gift, but you don't mind accepting help from a lovesick milkmaid who promises you fairy-gold: And what payment will she expect in return, may I ask? I'll warrant she wants more than a brotherly kiss or two!'

'Kate asks nothing for herself,' he said furiously. 'She's honest and she's kind, qualities you'd do well to emulate.'

He tried to step past her, and suddenly afraid she caught hold of the lapels of his coat and pressed herself against him, trying to wind her arms round his neck. He thrust her aside.

'Leave me be, Madeline. I'm in no mood for your tricks.'

She backed away from him, white with rage. 'Get out of my house!' she screamed. 'Get out, go, and don't come back! Get out!'

He stared at her for a moment, and then without a word turned on his heel and strode from the room. She listened to his footsteps fade on the back stairway. A distant door banged and silence filled the house.

Swinging round, she ran to the great gilded mirror that hung above the fireplace. Her reflection glared back at her, contorted and streaked with tears. She ran trembling fingers over her cheeks and throat.

Were there fresh lines about her eyes? A slight sagging of the flesh beneath her chin? She was thirty-three years old and in the prime of her beauty, but it couldn't last for ever. She'd never lacked for lovers, never failed to draw and hold any man she chose. None of them had ever broken with her; it was always she who decided when an affaire should end, but there was a coldness in her now that said Dominic was different. He would not come back to her.

She banged a fist on the marble mantel. Nick must marry some day, but somehow she'd always imagined he'd choose some dowdy country female who'd be content to remain in Dorset, raise a brood of brats, and turn a blind eye to what her husband did in London.

Kate Safford wasn't dowdy. She had a pretty face and figure, she was vivacious, and had a decided sense of fashion. The high-nosed patronesses of Almack's approved of her; they said she had charm and character.

And she was rich, very rich.

If Kate Safford set her mind on marrying Dominic, she might well succeed.

Staring into the looking-glass, Madeline faced the bleak truth. Her liaison with Dominic was over, and all London would know of it within hours. Looking down the years she saw herself in the ranks of those ageing women who covered their blemishes with paint, and were forced to pay young popinjays for their favours . . . . A target at best for pity, and at worst for salacious jokes.

The anger in her boiled over, and she snatched up a porcelain vase and sent it crashing on to the hearth. She was reaching for a crystal travelling-clock when a voice spoke behind her.

'No, Madeline, not the clock, I pray. It's pretty, and keeps good time.'

She spun round, her mouth drooping. The man in the doorway sauntered towards her. He was not tall, but his build was powerful, his heavy shoulders and thick neck giving him the look of a prize-fighter. His black hair was cropped short in the Brutus style. His skin was white and smooth, his hands surprisingly small, and ringless. His only jewel was the ruby pin in his cravat.

Madeline stretched a hand towards the bell-rope, and he shook his head.

'Don't waste your time, my dear. I sent the servants to bed. We can be quite private.'

Reaching her side, he took a handkerchief from his pocket and held it out to her. She dabbed at her tear-stained face, glaring at him.

'What are you doing here?'

'I live here.'

'You went to Bath for a week.'

'I returned this afternoon.' He strolled across to the sofa where Dominic had sat, and bent to pluck her necklace from its cushions. He held it up to the light so that it flashed green fire.

'Did you offer it to Barr, my love?'

Madeline clenched her fists. He always knew. He was a devil, those black eyes pierced through flesh and bone to the very core of one's mind. She'd feared him once, but not any more. Now she could match his cunning and cruelty with her own. She smiled at him.

'Yes,' she said. 'I told him to sell it. He refused.'

Lord Cheveley gave a grunt of laughter. 'A pity. Had he taken the bait, I'd have had him on the hook, and you would have had the satisfaction of seeing him hauled off to Newgate. Now we must be content with consigning him to a debtors' prison.'

'That will never happen,' said Madeline bitterly. 'His dear friend Miss Safford has undertaken to find the Twyford Gold for him.'

'Foh! A fool's mission, if ever there was one.'

'And if she fails, why then they may marry, and live happy ever after on her wealth.'

Cheveley's eyes narrowed. 'Did Barr speak of that?' As Madeline made no answer, he came to stand close to her, and ran a finger over her bare shoulder. 'My poor dear. A new experience for you, to be discarded.'

She thrust his hand away. 'He did not discard me! I told him to go. I never wish to set eyes on him again.'

'I think your wish will be granted. He strode from the house like a man whose mind is made up.'

'You've been spying on me, haven't you?'

'There was no need, people gossip so.' He took her hand and placed the necklace in it. 'The stones are fine, but the setting is clumsy; I'll have it remodelled for you.' He stretched out a foot to nudge aside a shard of porcelain. 'Don't you wish to know how I spent my time in Bath?'

'Making mischief, I'll be bound.'

'For some, yes.' He leaned back his head, watching her under his lids. 'I discovered who holds the mortgage on Melburn Hall.'

'Who?'

'Mr Horace Pickford.'

Madeline grimaced. 'He was friend to Justin Barr, he won't foreclose on Justin's son.'

'He'll have no choice.'

Fascinated, despite herself, she said, 'And Kate Safford? What of her?'

Cheveley smiled benignly. 'There I shall need your help.' He slid an arm about her waist. 'We both have scores to settle with

Barr, my love. Come to bed, and I'll tell you what I plan.'

Before leaving London, Dominic called on his mother. It was the first time he'd set foot in the Savernake mansion, and he was unprepared for its splendours. The exquisite delicacy of the panelling, the magnificence of the painted ceilings, the fine pictures and *objets d'art* that met the eye at every turn, were proof that Ivor Savernake was a connoisseur of the highest order.

Lady Letitia received him in her private salon, a small room furnished in the French style. Dressed in a lilac silk peignoir, and a lace cap, she looked less drawn than she had in her mourning black, and her manner was less strained.

'Nick!' she exclaimed, lifting her face for his kiss. 'What a happy surprise.'

'I'm off to Twyford today,' he told her, 'and wished to talk to you about Barr House.'

A trace of anxiety showed in her eyes. 'I hope you don't mean to bandy words with me,' she said. 'My mind is quite made up. In fact, I've already engaged an agent to arrange the sale.'

He smiled at her. 'I haven't come to quibble, but to thank you. I admit that when Savernake told me you planned to sell, I was totally opposed to the idea, but as he pointed out, the place is yours to do with as you please. If you agree, I'll use the money to put Melburn in better order, which will increase the asking price. So, thank you with all my heart, my dear.'

Lady Letitia breathed a sigh of relief. 'Then that's settled. It's a joy to me to be able to help you. It makes me feel that I'm truly part of your life.'

'You've always been that.'

She nodded and patted his hand. She was wondering if she dared beg him again to borrow from her husband, but decided that that would be tempting fate.

Instead she began to question him about Melburn, and in particular the plight of the staff and tenant farmers. She displayed less interest in the Twyford gentry, for most of them had taken

Justin's part when she deserted him. Of the Beachers and Kate Safford she spoke warmly, saying that from the Manor at least Dominic need expect nothing but kindness.

'I cherished the hope that John would marry Kate,' she said. 'He wrote to me last year, hinting that he'd formed an attachment to her. Did he never speak of it to you?'

'No. We weren't in the habit of exchanging confidences.' Dominic's tone was abrupt, and Lady Letitia at once dropped the subject and spoke of mundane matters until it was time for him to leave.

VI

Kate had written to Mr Humphrey Dymoke of Weymouth, requesting the privilege of an interview with him, and he had replied at once that he would be charmed to meet Sir Clive's daughter and niece, at any time before the end of the month – 'after which,' he explained, 'I repair to Bath, to take the waters and deliver one or two public lectures.'

He could not, he regretted, offer her and her party the hospitality of his own home, since he was a bachelor; but he suggested that very comfortable accommodation was to be had at the Royal York Hotel, which was close to the sea and extremely well appointed.

Kate accordingly reserved rooms in the hotel for herself, Elinor, and their maid Mary Hobson, and in the staff quarters for Coachman Sedley, the groom Tompkins, and the postillion Jarvis. Early one morning in the third week of March, this cavalcade rolled through the gates of the Manor, and headed south for the coast.

A spell of warm weather had caused an early burgeoning of leaf and blossom, which put all the members of the party in a cheerful mood. Though Elinor was a little perturbed at the thought of females staying in a hotel without male protection, Kate assured her that the Royal York was a family establishment with a most respectable reputation.

'Papa and I stayed there nine years ago, after I had the scarlet fever,' she said. 'Dr Trayle recommended sea-bathing, and I must say that once I'd grown accustomed to the motion of the water, I enjoyed it immensely.'

Elinor murmured that she could not feel it modest to bathe on a public beach, where one must run the risk of becoming the target of vulgar ogling. Kate laughed.

'I assure you, a bathing-dress is far more modest than any ball-gown, for it extends from neck to ankle, and is as voluminous as a tent! One changes in a bathing-machine which carries one down into the shallows, and the steps lead directly into the sea, so there's precious little opportunity for any rudesby to ogle. Even the driver and his horse retreat to a discreet distance along the shore! It was King George III who first made sea-bathing popular, you know, and no one can accuse *him* of impropriety. He visited Weymouth regularly, year after year, and had his own bathing-machine with the royal arms emblazoned on the sides. A second machine always accompanied him, carrying musicians who played *God Save the King* as he stepped down into the water, which I must say I consider excessively grandiose.'

'I suppose,' conceded Elinor, 'that if the Royal Family adopts sea-bathing, there can be no objection to it.'

'None at all,' agreed Kate. She forbore to describe the antics of some of the younger members of the royal brood when visiting the resort. The Duke of Kent, for instance, had often lodged in Gloucester Row, close to the house His Majesty had built, but because of his spendthrift ways he was constantly harrassed by duns, and on one occasion escaped from them by hiding in a coffin, and having himself conveyed by hearse to the top of neighbouring Ridgeway Hill.

'The Royals don't favour Weymouth, these days,' she said. 'It's been all Brighton, since Prinny built his Pavilion.'

They reached the town soon after five that afternoon. Kate bespoke a light meal, which she and her cousin enjoyed in their private parlour, whose windows commanded an excellent view of the half-moon bay.

As Kate's appointment with Mr Dymoke was for the following

morning, they were able to spend an hour walking along the beach. Though it was far too early in the year for even the boldest spirits to think of swimming, the soft and silvery sands were well populated by the owners of the fine houses that fronted the shore.

Rows of bathing-machines, their octagonal turrets painted in bright colours, were drawn up above the high-water mark. There were riders a-plenty, some on horseback and others on donkeys with side-saddles. Children raced along the edge of the surf, flew their kites and built sand-castles, while elderly citizens averse to strenuous exercise took the air in donkey-carts or Bath chairs. It was altogether a delightful scene, and Kate and Elinor returned to the hotel in high spirits.

'This is a lucky venture,' declared Kate. 'I feel in my bones that Mr Dymoke will set us on our way to finding the Danish gold.'

It was a prediction that was to prove woefully wide of the mark.

Mr Dymoke's residence was not on the sea-front, but one street removed from it, and within sight of the New Assembly Rooms. The house was small, but of elegant design, with balconies in the Spanish style and graceful fluted fanlights.

A liveried servant admitted Kate and Elinor, and conducted them to a parlour overlooking a neat garden. Mr Dymoke swirled to greet them with cries of delight, led them to chairs in the bow-window, and asked whether they would prefer ratafia or a dish of tay. His guests opting for tea, he made a great show of preparing it, lifting a copper kettle from the hearth-ring and pouring the boiling water on to the leaves, which he said were his own blend, sent to him by his merchant in the City of London.

Studying him, Kate found his manners affected and his appearance decidedly odd. Though over sixty years old, he affected the fashions of a far younger man, wearing light fawn pantaloons, a striped waistcoat, and a tight-waisted, full-skirted coat. His hair, which was of an unlikely chestnut shade, was arranged in elaborate waves and puffs, and his complexion owed much to the rouge-pot. His long nose snuggled between plump and pouchy cheeks, his eyes were small and greenish, and his mouth was never still, curling, pouting and grimacing even when he was silent. It was not thought Kate, at all a comfortable face.

After an exchange of polite commonplaces, he began to speak of his association with Sir Clive. 'We were at Oxford together,' he said, 'though he was somewhat my junior. A brilliant intellect, Miss Safford, and one brimming over with ingenious notions. It was a veritable tonic to hear him discourse – one never knew what he would say next! Even in later life, he never lost that youthful enthusiasm, that astonishing energy. One could not always concur with his theories, of course, but one always found them entertaining.'

Mr Dymoke selected a macaroon from a dish and nibbled on it daintily. 'His views on the Danish Gold, for instance – you referred to them in your letter, as I recall – were highly diverting. *Highly* diverting! He was convinced it lay buried in what was virtually his own backyard, and spoke of setting up an archaeological task-force to find it. I venture to think I succeeded in dissuading him from that piece of folly.'

'You don't believe the treasure exists, Mr Dymoke?'

'I believe it *did* exist, dear lady. If you had read my book on the Second Danish Invasion of Great Britain . . . .'

'I have read it.'

Mr Dymoke's eyebrows soared. 'Indeed? I am flattered! You will be aware, then, that in my opinion the gold was discovered by the Danes, and carried off as the spoils of battle. I follow the line taken by Simon of Sherborne and Wulfstan of York – champions of the Church, Miss Safford, who did not confuse fact with colourful fiction.'

'And "The Song of Edina"? Do you give that no credence?'

'Certainly, as a work of immense *literary* value. No man of cultivated mind will deny its importance in that sense, but its historical accuracy is quite another matter. An historian, even such a distinguished one as your papa, may go badly astray if he takes such old tales for gospel truth.'

'Cynric Cerdinga really existed, did he not?'

'Oh yes, and one accepts that he lived at the time of King Cnut, in a fortified house named Melburn. What one does not accept is that the house was in *West* Dorset.'

'But the legend specifically mentions Twyford, and the Church of St Dunstan.'

Mr Dymoke smirked. 'I think you cannot have read the poem in the Old English version.'

'No, only in Papa's translation,' admitted Kate.

'Then let me enlighten you. The bard wrote of Twyford, not of Twyford *Lindum*. Twyford means 'two fords', and there are a dozen such hamlets scattered across southern England. 'Melburn' may be translated as 'mill stream', and you'll admit those exist everywhere. As for the church – St Dunstan was a Wessex man, and many places of worship in this part of the country bear his name.'

Mr Dymoke took a lace-edged kerchief from his sleeve and brushed crumbs from his lapel. He beamed at Kate. 'Study the Song again, and you will see that Cynric's stronghold must have been in *South* Dorset. The reference to the dry river-bed confirms that.'

As Kate opened her mouth to speak, Mr Dymoke waved a minatory hand. 'Think, think, dear lady. Where is it that we find dry rivers? Why, in the south, to be sure, in the chalk country, the Winterborne country, where certain streams run only at the season of winter rains. In summer the water table does not rise, and the river-beds are dry. You must have heard of the phenomenon?'

'I have, of course, but . . .'

'There can be no buts, my dear. You have only to consider the place names of South Dorset . . . Winterborne Abbas, Winterborne Strickland, Winterborne Tomson, Winterborne Whitechurch. It is in that territory that Cynric dwelt, and fought

67

the Danish sea-wolves. Long, long after, the bard Nairn heard the tale and made a song of it, and over the centuries other bards have written their own versions, altering the details to please different audiences. Legends are not carved in stone, you know, they are not immutable. They are not, in short, history.'

'If the gold was buried in the Winterborne area,' asked Kate, 'why have so many searches been conducted in our part of Dorset?'

'Because,' said Mr Dymoke, kindly, 'those good folk fell into the same error as did your revered father. They mistook legend for fact. The great weight of informed opinion discards your Twyford as the site of the siege, and supports my own Winterborne theory.'

His smug expression put Kate quite out of humour. 'I think,' she said tartly, 'that informed opinion may alter when Papa's five books of fact are published.'

'Books?' The smile faded from Mr Dymoke's face. 'He has published books recently? I knew nothing of . . .'

'He gathered the material,' Kate said. 'Mr Lombard is to publish . . .'

The smile reappeared. 'At some distant date, I surmise? It takes time to put material into workable order.'

'That has already been done.'

'Ah! And who is to be the author of the great work? Will you undertake the task yourself?'

'No. We have engaged Mr Henry Godbold.'

For a moment Mr Dymoke's mobile features were perfectly still. His eyes grew sharp with malice. 'Godbold?' he said. 'Another of the romantic school, and something of a *flâneur*, I must warn you. I cannot myself admire the type, but no doubt his efforts will be acclaimed by the uninitiated.'

'I very much hope so.'

Mr Dymoke seemed to sense that he had overstepped the bounds of courtesy, and said more mildly, 'Pray don't think me harsh, Miss Safford. It is merely that in my eyes, the demands of history are sacrosanct. I am apt to condemn those who fall short of my own exacting standards.' He touched his fingers to his lips, watching Kate. 'Tell me, did your father have fresh evidence of the hiding place of the gold?'

'I think perhaps he had,' said Kate.

'You *think*? You don't *know*?'

'In his last illness, he spoke of the treasure. I gained the impression that he had developed a theory . . . an idea that had come to him very recently.'

'But he was not able to tell you precisely what it was?'

'No.' Kate turned her face away. 'He was dying.'

'Ah, yes. A tragic death, a loss to us all.' Relief stood plain on Mr Dymoke's face. 'Well, well, I wish you luck in your quest.' A thought struck him. 'Do you . . . ah . . . intend to seek other advice in this matter?'

'Yes. I hope to meet with Dame Celia Sickert.'

Mr Dymoke permitted himself a falsetto giggle. 'Lud, child, why waste your time?'

'Papa spoke of Dame Celia as an authority on Ancient Britain.'

'There was a time when she might have been so described. Now she is a recluse; she will admit no strangers to her ruined domain and answer no letters, no matter who the sender. I take it you have already written to her?'

'Yes.'

'And has she replied?'

'Not yet.'

'Nor will she. She's quite mad, you see. The people of Midsomer speak of her as a witch, and though I deplore such archaic superstition, I do advise you to avoid annoying her in any way.

'I met her but once. She attended a lecture I gave in Wells, on the early Christians of Britain. Her behaviour on that occasion was obnoxious. She announced to the audience that she was a descendant of the family of St Patrick, and thereafter interrupted my address with a series of quite irrelevant observations. It was only her great age that prevented me from having her forcibly removed from the hall.'

Looking at his incensed face, Kate began to think she might like Dame Celia very well. She had had more than enough of Mr Dymoke, and soon afterward signed to Elinor that it was time to leave.

Their host accompanied them to the garden gate, and expressed the hope that when Sir Clive's *History* of Dorset was published, Kate would send him a copy.

'I may be able to puff it off a little among my friends,' he said. 'I shall be happy to lend my name to his support.'

As they strolled back to the hotel, Kate gave vent to her pent-up feelings.

'What a vain, posturing, pompous creature!' she exclaimed. 'No wonder his writings are so dull!'

'He's certainly fond of his own voice,' agreed Elinor, 'but I suppose as an acknowledged expert he has a right to be a trifle opinionated.'

'Acknowledged by the *old* school, not by the moderns. Papa used to say that some historians become embalmed in their own theories, like flies in amber, and cannot bear to have their views challenged. Dymoke doesn't wish us to search for the gold at Twyford Lindum, because if we find it, his precious book will be discredited, and his reputation tarnished.'

Elinor sighed. 'I must say I could not like him, but his argument about the Winterborne streams was very convincing.'

'Papa wasn't convinced,' said Kate stubbornly, 'and I'll back Papa against that odious little fribble, any day of the week. It will give me the greatest satisfaction to prove him wrong.'

'How?' asked Elinor doubtfully.

'My first step must be to talk to Dame Celia.'

'But how may that be achieved, if she never replies to letters, and won't let visitors cross her threshold?'

'A way must be found,' Kate said. 'We'll go to Bath, stay with Aunt and Uncle Beacher, and draw up a plan of campaign.' Seeing

70

Elinor's nervous expression, she smiled. 'Don't worry, Nell, I shan't try anything rash. I'm no more eager than the next person to find myself turned into a toad.'

VII

Removing to Bath, even for so short a period as a month, required a good deal of organization. Though the housekeeper, Mrs Horning, and the butler, Broome, could be relied upon to keep things running smoothly in her absence, Kate had to consult with her bailiff and factor, and her head stockmen and gamekeepers, while Elinor had to ensure that adequate supplies were laid in to feed a large staff.

Mrs Beacher, to whom Kate had written the moment she returned from Weymouth, replied expressing delight at the proposed visit, and listed the varied entertainments that awaited her nieces:

> Nothing ostentatious, of course, since we are all still in half-mourning for our dear Clive, but I'm sure no one will cavil at small private parties, confined to our own close circle of friends. Balls and assemblies must remain taboo, but there can be no objection to concerts and lectures. You mentioned Mr Dymoke in your letter. He is to deliver a discourse – I cannot for the moment recall its title – but I don't doubt that we will find it most enlightening.
>
> The town is full to bursting-point. Colonel Tucker is among the visitors, also the Crichtons and the Montagu-Crofts, as well as others known to you. We have Anna's two youngest staying with us – she has been somewhat below par of late, and as it is now her eighth month, Dr Duby recommends complete

rest. They are pretty-behaved children, and I know will not be any nuisance to you.

We look forward keenly to seeing you on Thursday.

Your affectionate

Aunt Emily

PS Your uncle joins me in sending fond love, and bids me tell you that according to Mr Shipton, Lord Barr will arrive here shortly, on matters of business. He is to be the guest of the Walcotts of Solsbury Hill, but will no doubt condescend to take his pot luck with us some evening.

This footnote drew different reactions from the cousins. Kate said anxiously that she hoped Nick wasn't in a rush to put Melburn on the market, while Elinor sent up a silent but fervent prayer that Uncle Amyas would not persist in his self-appointed role as latter-day Cupid.

In the period when Beau Nash ruled as uncrowned King of Bath, the hub of fashion lay in the oldest part of the town, at the Pump Room built above the ancient Roman temple and baths, the Lower Assembly Rooms, and the great Abbey of St Peter.

More recently, interest had shifted to the northerly areas, to the New Assembly Rooms built by John Wood the Younger, and the light and graceful crescents of Palmer and Eveleigh.

The Beachers enjoyed the best of both worlds, their home being situated between the two, in Queen's Square. In wealth and standing they equalled the Pierrepoints and Pulteneys, being received with deference by the Masters of Ceremonies of the Upper and Lower Rooms, and with eagerness by the tradespeople who served this city of over thirty thousand souls.

Kate and Elinor had always looked on the Beacher house as their second home, and they found a warm welcome awaiting them when they arrived there late on Thursday afternoon.

Their host and hostess came hurrying out to the flagway as the carriage turned into the square. The butler Simmons himself supervised the transferring of their baggage from the fourgon to their bedchambers, and Mrs Peabody the cook appeared in the hallway to say she had prepared all their favourite dishes for dinner. Anna Durrant's two sons, five-year-old James and four-year-old Charlie, descended from the nursery and refused point-blank to return there until they had described in detail their recent visit to Bristol, where they had ridden on a steam-carousel, and watched a schooner unloading a cargo of Jamaican rum.

It was only after the servants had removed the last dishes from the dinner-table that the family found any chance of private conversation. Mrs Beacher began by giving news of Anna, whose state of health still gave cause for concern.

'We drove to Corsham yesterday,' she said, 'and found the poor darling far from well. Her feet and hands are much swollen, which is not a good sign. Her previous confinements have been so free of complications that I never saw reason to worry, but now I cannot be easy in my mind. I mean to go to her at the end of this month, and to remain with her for as long as she needs me after the birth. She's not equal to the strain of running a large establishment, with five young children in it.'

'Dr Duby's a sound man,' said Mr Beacher consolingly. 'If he's satisfied with the way things are going, there's no call for you to be in a panic.'

'A mother's eyes see what a doctor's do not,' retorted his wife. 'Anna is nervous. She spoke more than once of poor Princess Charlotte, dead in childbirth and the baby with her.'

'That was years ago, and why Anna should brood over it now I can't imagine! There's bad blood in those Hanovers. Anna comes of good English stock. She'll be right as rain when her time comes, you'll see.' Mr Beacher turned to Kate, seeking to give the conversation a more cheerful direction. 'I hear you met with Humphrey Dymoke. What did he have to say for himself? Did he tell you where to find the gold?'

'On the contrary, he says the Danes found it centuries ago, and in any case it was never buried at Twyford Lindum, but at some other Twyford in the Winterborne country.'

Mr Beacher scratched his jaw. 'That's South Dorset,' he said, 'and the history books hold that the treasure was sent *north* from Sherborne to Glastonbury.'

A little surprised at this show of erudition in one who seldom read anything but the newspapers, Kate said, 'You're quite right! I wish I'd thought to remind him of that.'

'It was diverted,' Elinor said. 'When the King's men heard that the Danes held the Severn Estuary, they turned aside from their planned route, and made for Cynric's stronghold. That could have lain to the south.'

Mr Beacher sniffed. 'That's mere supposing, Nell. We know there's a Melburn at our Twyford. We know Cynric and Edina lived at our Melburn.'

'How do we know?'

'It's common knowledge. Ask any farmer's boy.'

'Folklore,' Kate said. 'Mr Dymoke doesn't believe in folklore; he puts his faith in facts.'

'What about Dunstan's Church, eh? That's a fact, ain't it? Sits in the square at our Twyford, plain for any fool to see.'

'Dymoke says Dunstan built a great many churches.'

'Dymoke says, Dymoke says! Seems to me you're giving up before the fight's begun!'

'Nothing of the sort,' said Kate flatly. 'One of the reasons I've cast myself on your hospitality is that I want a second opinion. According to Papa, Dame Celia of Midsomer Norton is an authority on the antiquities of Wessex.' Kate saw her uncle puff out his cheeks, and said quickly, 'Are you acquainted with her, Uncle?'

'We've met,' he said grimly, 'but I doubt you'll ever have that dubious pleasure.'

'Why? Is she such an ogress?'

'She's mad as a March hare! Claims kinship with St Patrick of Ireland, and believes that as a Sickert of Midsomer she may say and do as she pleases. Lives in a broken-down ruin of an abbey, and will allow no one to set foot in it, save on payment of what she terms 'due tribute'. Highway robbery, more like. Any reputation she may once have enjoyed as a historian has been shattered by her bizarre behaviour. Why, when the sheriff warned her that her precious bell-tower was unsafe and must be dismantled, she laid a curse on him.'

'Did it work?' asked Kate, fascinated.

'Can't say. The fellow was craven. Dropped the suit and took ship for America within the month.'

Kate chuckled, but Mrs Beacher shot her a reproving look. 'It's no laughing matter,' she said. 'Not only are her manners Gothic, but she's capable of physical violence. Last year when the hunt rode across her fields, she fired a crossbow at the Master. The bolt shaved his head and pinned his hat to a tree. When he remonstrated with her, she said her only regret was that advancing age had ruined her marksmanship.'

'You make me long to meet her.'

'That will never happen, my dear. She detests strangers, and will not receive you.'

'Not even if I offer her due tribute?'

'Don't even consider it, I beg. The woman's a dangerous lunatic, and what is more important, she's not considered at all good ton.'

Kate thought it best not to mention that she had twice written to Dame Celia, requesting a meeting. Her aunt had enough worries in her dish without being plagued by a fresh one.

Her nieces did what they could to lighten her burden, taking it upon themselves to look after Anna's boys. The nursemaid who had accompanied them from Corsham was a fifteen-year-old country girl, and quite unable to find her way about the city streets, so Kate and Elinor formed the habit of taking James and Charlie for daily jaunts.

The Sydney Gardens were within easy reach, across the delightful Pulteney Bridge, with its rows of small shops on either side, where one might purchase all manner of useful and pretty things. The Beachers owned one of the prestigious solid silver tickets that

77

admitted the holder to all the pleasures of the Gardens – superior refreshments, swings, and even a labyrinth. Maps were sold at the entrance to the maze, which emboldened more timid souls to try its mysteries.

The Sydney Hotel, which stood near the main gates, was of handsome design, and provided a ballroom, tea-rooms, card-rooms, and at the rear a bandstand where horns and clarinets played every Wednesday evening. In the basement of the building was a public house known as The Sydney Tap.

Sometimes, when the weather was fine, the nursery party drove to one of the beauty-spots in the hills above the city, and shared a picnic lunch; and one wet morning the boys made the glorious discovery of a toy shop in Bacon Street, and emerged the proud owners of hoops, hobby-horses, and a set of lead soldiers.

Once or twice a week the cousins accompanied their aunt to the Pump Room, where elderly and well-to-do citizens gathered to drink the sultry waters and exchange the latest on-dits. Though the Assembly Halls were excluded from the Beacher programme, their evenings were enlivened by select parties given by Mrs Beacher or one of her intimate circle. Kate found these entertainments delightful, for they were conducted with easy informality, and offered just the right mix of new and familiar faces.

In the first week she acquired two suitors; Mr Corbishley, a sidesman of the neighbouring St Mary's Chapel, and young Mr Montagu-Gore, whose infatuation led him to haunt Queen's Square at all hours of the day and night, in the hopes of catching a glimpse of his goddess.

To the sophisticates of London, Bath might seem very flat and provincial, but to one who had spent the past year cooped up in a remote village, it was a hive of activity. Kate found her spirits lifting. The sense of loss that had weighed her down since her father's death, could not survive the combination of sunny weather and congenial company. She realizied that the time had come to put away mourning and look to the future.

One afternoon, as she was returning from a visit to Millard's

Lending Library in Milsom Street, she happened to see in the window of Madame Elise, the town's leading modiste, a ravishing gown of celadon organdie, the hem and sleeves decorated with ruching of matching silk. Kate knew that she must own it, or die. She advanced into the shop.

Madame Elise, a born opportunist, summoned her chief assistant with a snap of the fingers, and bade her bring out not only the green gown, but also the burnt-orange walking-dress, the *café au lait* half-cape, and the afternoon gown of Berlin damask. In a very short time, Kate had bought all four. Madame, aware that Miss Safford was the protégée of the so-amiable Madam Beacher, threw caution to the wind and included in the packages a pair of Morocco slippers and a reticule trimmed with silver bugle beads.

When the bandboxes containing these trophies were delivered to Queen's Square next morning, Kate was seized with guilt, but Mrs Beacher dismissed these pangs out of hand.

'Nonsense, my love! If your heart tells you it's time to put off your blacks, there's no more to be said. Wear the green to the Ingrams' tonight, Elinor shall wear the rose grosgrain that becomes her so well, and I will wear my violet lace. Your dear Papa always held that to be moping about like a set of wet crows was against nature.'

Later, Kate was to suspect her aunt of harbouring an ulterior motive, for the first person she saw when she entered the Ingrams' drawing-room was Dominic Barr. He was standing talking to Lady Ingram, but glanced round as the butler announced the arrival of the Beachers' party, and for a moment stared at Kate as if he had never seen her before. He made a quick recovery, and as he made his bow said, 'You look charming, Miss Safford. I think you mean to take Bath by storm.'

'No, not at all,,' she said roundly. 'I'm here because I wish to obtain an interview with Dame Celia Sickert of Midsomer. My father believed she could advise me how to begin my search for the gold.'

Dominic blinked. 'I thought the old woman was mad,' he said.

'Papa didn't think so. The problem is, she'll admit no one to her presence unless they pay her due tribute.'

'Tribute? You mean money? Kate, I can't allow you to spend your money on a wild goose chase!'

'It's not money she wants,' Kate said.

'What, then?'

'I'm not sure. I have the feeling that she lives in the past . . . that she follows ancient rules of chivalry. Those who seek her favour must pass some test, like a knight.'

Dominic regarded her in silence, then said slowly, 'And you mean to attempt this test?'

'Yes,' she said simply, but then honesty made her add, 'though I can't for the life of me decide where to start.'

Lady Ingram put a halt to their discussion and swept Kate away to meet the Walcott family. Colonel Walcott was a small, wiry man with fierce amber eyes and a hooked nose. His wife was taller than he by half a head, plump, and vague in manner – a hen married to a kestrel, Kate thought.

Turning to shake George Walcott's hand, she said, 'Mr Walcott and I have already met, in London.'

'Yes,' he agreed, 'at the Asbells' soirée, where La Peronne sang, and sang, and sang.'

She laughed. 'You dislike singers, sir?'

'I've a poor ear,' he confessed, and his father snorted.

'No ear at all, you mean. George is as good as tone-deaf, Miss Safford, an affront to his Welsh blood.'

'You may set your mind at rest, Mr Walcott,' said Lady Ingram. 'We have no musical entertainment planned for tonight; just a good dinner, and pleasant converse among friends.'

Her words were over-sanguine. Though the dinner was indeed excellent, the conversation during the first course languished sadly, and Kate thought she had seldom met a more ill-assorted set of people.

At the head of the table, Lord Ingram engaged his right-hand neighbour on the only subject that interested him, namely hunting, a passion Mrs Walcott did not share, and as his anecdotes of points, checks and kills multiplied, her polite comments faded to a glazed silence.

At the other end of the table, Lady Ingram recalled in her booming voice the past glories of the Barr family, describing the splendid parties she had enjoyed at Melburn during dear Justin's youth, and citing such extravagant touches as a ballroom lined from floor to ceiling with red roses, and musicians dispensing Handel's *Water Music* from a gilded barge on the lake. Dominic received these sallies with poker-faced courtesy, but it was plain that her ladyship's lack of tact grated sorely on his nerves.

Mr Beacher, being unable to break in on his hostess's discourse, devoted himself to his meal, his face growing redder and redder as he sampled dish after dish, and quaffed glass after glass of wine. From time to time he caught Kate's eye, and beamed and nodded in a way that made her feel ready to sink, clearly indicating that he had contrived tonight's encounter for her sole benefit.

Colonel Walcott, chatting to Elinor, quickly discovered that her late husband had served for a time in his own regiment. He was full of praise for Captain Crane, and spoke with regret of his death in action.

'If he'd stayed with us, he'd be alive today,' said the Colonel, 'but he was transferred to Slender Billy's lot, and a worse general than S.B. I never knew. Sacrificed the flower of our army through his incompetence!'

Gratifying as it was to Elinor to hear her husband praised, it was little comfort to know that he'd lost his life through the idiocy of his commander. She was forced to blink away tears, and fumble for her kerchief.

George Walcott alone succeeded in bringing some lightness to the occasion, amusing Kate and Mrs Beacher by telling them the tale of the baptism of the Duke of Kent's daughter, the previous year.

'Prinny was still Regent,' he said, 'and on poor terms with his

81

brother Kent. Jealous, too, of the Kent infant, because she might become heir to the throne. Refused to allow her to be christened Alexandrina Georgiana, said Georgiana could come second to no other name in the land.

'So there stood the Archbishop of Canterbury, with the baby in his arms, waitin' for the Regent to pronounce the chosen name. After a long silence, "Alexandrina," says Prinny. Another pause. Then the Duke tries, "Charlotte?" Prinny responds with a furious shake of the head. "Augusta?" falters Kent. Prinny glares, and roars, "Let her be called after her mother!" So, while mama and the infant sob in unison, the christening is done. *Alexandrina Victoria*. One can only pity the child! What sort of future may she expect, burdened with such a name?'

The first course was removed, and Lord Ingram switched his narrative from the drooping Mrs Walcott to Mrs Beacher. Lady Ingram released Dominic from her reminiscences. Relieved, he turned to Kate, and found her regarding him thoughtfully.

'Did you ever meet Mr Humphrey Dymoke?' she asked.

He shook his head. 'No. I fancy we have his *History* on our shelves, but I confess I never read it.'

'Spare yourself the effort,' she advised. 'Nell and I drove all the way to Weymouth to consult with him, and he proved a dead bore. He refuses to accept that the Danes attacked our Twyford, or your Melburn; according to him it all happened elsewhere, the Danes found the gold and carried it off, so there's nothing left for us to search for.'

'He sounds a regular mar-sport!'

'What we need,' said Kate, 'is proof that the treasure was hidden in our part of Dorset, and not in the Winterborne country. You told me the other day that your grandfather had found *Agnus Dei* coins on your lands. It would be helpful to know just where he found them.'

'I'm afraid I don't know. He was forever going on long rambles, and he put whatever took his fancy into his pockets.' Dominic frowned. 'Last week, when I was going through the contents of his cabinets, I found a collection of old coins, all jumbled together. I showed them to Angerstein's agent, who's come to Melburn to advise me on what's worth selling to the antiquaries, and he identified several of the coins as Roman, of about the year AD 420. There were also a number of *Agnus Dei* gold pieces, which he said are in surprisingly good condition, considering their age.'

Kate brightened. 'Perhaps because they've lain underground, and have not been in common use! Oh, Dominic, do you think your grandfather found part of the treasure, without knowing it?'

'There's nothing to say he did. All that the coins prove is that someone brought Roman and old English money to the Rem Valley.'

'Did your grandpapa never label his finds, or . . . or tell anyone where he came by them?'

'No. He was sadly lacking in method, and collected things for quite the wrong reasons. He had no interest in archaeology for its own sake. I remember he said once that he wished he could discover the site of Roman Melburn, because then we might own a proper bath-house, with a dependable supply of hot water.'

'Was there a Roman Melburn?'

'So he believed.'

Kate paused to help herself from a dish of glazed duckling. 'Have you considered the Tump?' she asked.

'The Tump? In what connection?'

'As the possible site of Cynric's Melburn.'

'No chance of that. It was examined thoroughly some twenty years ago, and identified as an ancient burial mound. It dates back to before the birth of Christ. The villagers say the Old People sacrificed human victims there. They won't go near the place at night.'

'Old People? You mean Druids?'

'I've no idea. At any event, when the Tump was explored, nothing was found to show it was ever inhabited by living beings.'

'Might not local superstition have made it the ideal place to hide the treasure?'

'It might have deterred the local worthies, but the Danish cut-throats wouldn't have been scared off by ghost stories. They worshipped other gods, and looted and burned Christian churches and pagan temples with equal ardour.'

At this point Lady Ingram, realizing that desperate measures were needed to salvage her dinner-party, abandoned formality and made the conversation general. Leaning forward, she bestowed a gracious smile on Kate and said, 'Miss Safford, I heard you mention Dymoke's name. He's to address our Historical Society on Friday morning; shall you attend?'

'Yes, ma'am, with my aunt and cousin.'

'Good, good! And how about you, Mrs Walcott? Should you and your husband wish to attend, I have a number of tickets to dispose of. I find it is always the ladies who must support cultural undertakings. The gentlemen seem to lack the desire to absorb the history of Roman Bath.'

'If you're talkin' about me,' said her lord roundly, 'I don't mind admittin' I've no time for history. Got enough to worry about here and now, without fillin' my noddle with what's over an' done with.'

Mrs Beacher looked pained. 'You must surely agree though, dear Lord Ingram, that it is humbling to reflect that a civilization so ancient could produce art and architecture of such high merit?'

'Doesn't humble me,' said his lordship cheerfully. 'Don't know much about art, to be honest, but I'll say this. That plaque they dug up in '90 . . . forget the name of the thing . . .'

'The Medusa Mask?'

'That's the one. Hijeous, I call it. Somethin' to frighten naughty children. I'm a decent Christian, I hope, and I carry no brief for heathens like the Romans.'

'Good soldiers, though,' submitted Colonel Walcott. 'Built their camps like professionals. Good artillerymen, too; used a ballista machine that fired iron bolts. Made a sorry mess of the early Brits, I can tell you. Must give credit where credit is due.'

Lord Barr then had the happy thought of inviting the Colonel to describe his campaigns in Spain with Harry Smith; and as his account was both accurate and lively, it held the company spellbound until the dessert dishes had been removed, and the ladies left the gentlemen to their port and brandy.

On the short journey back to Queen's Square, Mr Beacher revealed that many of the art treasures of Melburn had already been sent to London for sale.

'Barr told me tonight, that fellow Angerstein has found a lot of good stuff in the house. The money will gain him breathing-space, at least.'

'Can he save Melburn?' asked Kate.

'I doubt it, but miracles do happen. We'll hear more next week. I've invited Walcott to bring his family, and Barr of course, to dine with us.'

Kate made no answer. It seemed to her that the last thing Dominic must want at this time, was to endure the petty rituals and trite conversations of polite society. Tonight he must have wished them all at Jericho, but he had somehow kept his temper. The image she had formed of him as a libertine who shirked all responsibility was patently false, and she found herself wishing with all her heart that she could help him out of his difficulties.

The Walcotts' estate lay a little to the north of Solsbury Hill, towards Charmy Down, and they reached home shortly after midnight. The Colonel and his wife retired at once to bed, but Mr Walcott and Lord Barr, accustomed to keeping London hours, repaired to the library for a dram of brandy.

'I swear I don't know when I've passed a more embarrassin' evenin',' grumbled George, handing his guest a glass and throwing himself into a comfortable chair. 'What with Papa as good as tellin' poor little Mrs Crane that her husband was killed by bad generalship, and Mama dozin' off in the middle of Ingram's exploits with the Quorn, I was ready to cut line and run! Old Beacher, too, quizzin' you about Melburn – I'm surprised you didn't tell him to mind his own business.'

'Melburn *is* his business. He's my father's executor.'

'Doesn't give him the right to stick his nose in where it's not wanted.'

'He's a busybody, I grant you, but he has my interests at heart.'

'If you ask me,' said George shrewdly, 'he's out to marry you to Miss Safford. Not a bad idea, at that! Pleasant girl, wears her clothes well, and doesn't put on false airs.'

'Rich, too, George. Don't forget, rich!'

Mr Walcott ignored the bitterness in his friend's voice.

'Liked her cousin, too,' he offered. 'Fetchin' little thing, with a great deal of sensibility.'

'Oh, absolutely.'

'Engaged to take her and Miss Safford out drivin',' continued George nonchalantly. 'Agreed we'd fix on a date when we meet at Dymoke's lecture.'

This brought Dominic out of his gloom. 'You're going to hear Dymoke?'

'Said so, didn't I?'

'My dear George, have you any conception what a historical lecture is like?'

'Goin' because my mother wishes it, that's all.'

'This filial duty touches me to the quick.'

Meeting Dominic's sardonic eye, Mr Walcott had the grace to grin. 'Got to proceed with caution,' he said. 'Throw Mama off the scent. She don't approve of widows. Feels that any woman who's been careless enough to lose a husband, can't be trusted to cherish me as I deserve.' He glanced at Lord Barr's empty glass. 'Another of the same?'

Dominic shook his head. 'No, or I shall have the devil of a head tomorrow.' He was quiet for a moment, then said abruptly, 'Madeline's in Bath. I found a letter waiting for me at Shipton's office this morning.'

Mr Walcott, who disliked Lady Cheveley, tried to think of a suitable comment, and failed.

Dominic hunched his shoulders. 'The last time we met, she told me to get out and stay out. And to tell the truth, while my affairs are in this tangle, I'd as lief leave it at that.'

'Easier said than done,' murmured Mr Walcott.

'Yes. The problem is, Madeline doesn't abide by the normal rules. She's quite capable of enacting me a Cheltenham tragedy. I don't want her coming to your parents' home and putting them to the blush.'

'No fear of that. I'll tell Keeney that if she tries to intrude, he's to deny her the door. She'll hardly stoop to ambushing you in a public place.'

Dominic had his doubts on that score, but he held his peace.

VIII

Mr Dymoke was to present his lecture in the Pump Room, and Mrs Beacher insisted that they must take up their seats early. 'I fear it will be a sad squeeze,' she said, 'but we will know ourselves to be in the presence of history. We will thrill to the sense that Roman Bath lies directly beneath our feet.'

'The only sense I'm aware of in the Pump Room,' retorted her husband, 'is my sense of smell. That stench of sulphur comes direct from Hell, and as for the water, nothing would persuade me to drink such a witches' brew! With your leave, m'dear, I shall cross the road to The White Hart, and sample something a little more palatable!'

Mrs Beacher and her nieces arrived in Stall Street well before the appointed time, found their places and settled themselves comfortably. Lady Ingram, wreathed in smiles, tacked from side to side of the room, calling greetings to all and sundry – 'like a gunboat firing salutes,' observed Kate. George Walcott ushered his mama into the row behind theirs, and quickly engaged them in conversation, inviting Kate and Elinor to drive out with him on Sunday afternoon.

'Thought of toolin' up to Priory Park,' he said. 'Built for Ralph Allen, y'know, in the grand style. Present owner's a Quaker and constructs canals for a livin'. He's given me leave to drive about his grounds. The view from the heights is very fine.'

Lady Ingram introduced Mr Dymoke to the audience, and he took his place at the lectern and began his address. Kate soon realized that she had underestimated his powers. The plummy phrases and affected posturing that had made him ridiculous at the tea-table were well suited to the lofty spaces of the Pump Room. Moreover, he displayed a shrewd understanding of his hearers, balancing the sober facts of archaeology against gossipy anecdotes of the city's past. Against her will, she fell under the spell of his discourse.

'Just under a hundred years ago,' he said, 'when a sewer was being dug along Stall Street, there was unearthed the magnificent bronze head of Minerva that graces your museum today. In 1755, when excavations were started for a suite of modern baths near the Abbot's House, the diggers struck a Saxon graveyard, and beneath that, part of the original Roman baths. A short fifty years ago, during the reconstruction of this very Pump Room in which we are met, the architect Thomas Baldwin uncovered a Roman pavement, and what we confidently believe to be the collapsed remains of a splendid Corinthian temple. Our history lies all about us, dear people. We are the product of not one, but many civilizations.'

'It's true,' thought Kate. 'True for Twyford as well as Bath, and there's a message in it for me, if only I'd the wit to grasp it.'

When the meeting closed and the company began to disperse, Mr Dymoke minced across to make Mrs Beacher a flourishing bow. 'My dear ma'am,' he cried, 'how staunch you are in your support of the humanities! Mrs Crane, Miss Safford, what a pleasure to find you at my humble lecture! Do you make a prolonged stay in Bath?'

'We'll be here till the end of the month,' Kate said.

'Indeed?' His green eyes glinted. 'And shall you include Midsomer Abbey in your itinerary of visits?'

'I doubt it. I've had no word from Dame Celia.'

Mr Dymoke smirked. 'As I predicted, dear lady, as I predicted. Not that you will lose by the omission. The poor creature is in her second childhood and contributes nothing to our store of human knowledge.'

At that moment Lady Ingram beckoned to him from the far side of the room, and with another simper and bow, he left them.

Sunday's outing with Mr Walcott proved an unqualified success. He arrived at the Beachers' front door promptly at two o' clock, in an open landaulet with a coachman on the box. Mr Walcott, an old hand at dalliance, knew better than to handle the ribbons himself. A man in charge of a team of mettlesome horses had little time for conversation.

There was some delay in setting out, as James and Charlie clamoured to join the party. Mr Walcott firmly rejected the plea, but offered to take them to Astley's farm the following week.

'Jem Astley breeds the finest hounds in the country,' he said, 'and I mean to choose a puppy. You're welcome to come, provided you have your grandmama's permission.'

Lulled by this sop, the boys allowed themselves to be herded indoors by their nurse. Mr Walcott handed the ladies up into the carriage, and it rolled away southwards to Horse Street, crossed the river, and climbed the steeps past Beechen Cliff.

As they went, Mr Walcott regaled his companions with stories of the notables who'd visited the Priory in its heyday – Pope and Fielding, Walpole and Gainsborough, Garrick and Pitt. His talk proved so diverting that Elinor quite forgot her shyness, and was soon chuckling at each fresh sally. Mr Walcott then played a master stroke.

'I knew Hugh Crane at school,' he said. 'He was a prime gun. Finest horseman I ever saw, showed us all the way. Not a cowardly bone in his body.'

Elinor turned pink with pleasure at this tribute, and presently enquired if Mr Walcott's older sister were not the Emma Farqueson who lived near Market Harborough, as did her own sister.

This link established, others were quickly found, and by the time the carriage reached the hills above the city, Elinor and her host were conversing like old friends.

91

Kate was happy to sit quietly in her corner and listen with half an ear to their talk. She needed to think. To make a plan. One part of her was enjoying her stay in Bath, the other grew increasingly restive. She had failed to achieve her purpose. As the days wore on, she became more and more certain that Dame Celia would not answer her letters. Her chances of finding the Danish Gold were as remote as ever, and time was not on her side. In a few short weeks, Melburn would be on the market.

Try as she might, she could think of no way to win the old woman's favour. What in Heaven's name would a madwoman consider suitable tribute?

She was roused from her reverie by Mr Walcott's voice saying, '. . . book of sermons. I ask you, what would a ten-year-old boy want with a book of sermons?'

Elinor answered, laughing, 'People always give you what they would like to receive themselves. Yesterday, Charlie presented me with a bottle full of tadpoles.'

Kate sat up with a jerk. In her mind's eye she was seeing the library at Safford Manor, the long shelves loaded with leather-bound volumes, and her father's hand caressing them lovingly.

There sprang into focus a narrow case of stiffened calfskin, its corners silver-capped, and she knew that this was a gift that Dame Celia would find acceptable.

She could hardly wait for the afternoon to pass and the drive to be over. The return to Bath seemed interminable, and as soon as she was home she hurried to her aunt's writing-desk and dashed off a letter to her housekeeper, Mrs Horning. Early next morning, she took it to the post and obtained an assurance from the postmaster himself that it would reach Twyford Lindum within twenty-four hours.

Mr Dymoke had a double motive for visiting Bath. The city's idle rich provided him with a loyal audience for his lectures,, and the city's hot springs helped his rheumatism.

He had for many years suffered from the disease, and at times the agony of his muscles and joints was so acute that he could not stir from his bed; but the sultry waters of Bath possessed a magic that eased the pain, and made life bearable.

In centuries past, sufferers had been able to bathe in the King's Bath and other public places, but as the city grew, its facilities expanded. John Wood had built a new Hot Bath, and Baldwin added a suite of private baths behind the colonnades of Stall Street.

It was to these last that Mr Dymoke repaired on the Monday after his Pump Room lecture. He arrived at eight in the morning, to avoid the crowds, greeted the attendant Joseph who always looked after him, and was soon luxuriating in the warm water. It induced mental as well as physical relaxation, and he was drifting into a near-trance when Joseph reappeared, to inform him that a gentleman was wishful to speak to him, 'most urgent'.

Mr Dymoke was incensed. 'Impossible,' he declared. 'Tell him I will be pleased to see him at my lodgings at eleven o' clock.'

But Joseph demurred. 'Beggin' your pardon, sir, but the gennel-man did say as it would be to your advantage if you was to speak with 'im. He said I mun give you 'is card.'

He held out the pasteboard, which was already curling in the steam of the bathhouse. Mr Dymoke scanned it, scowled, and heaved himself dripping from the water. Fifteen minutes later, he stepped into the lobby of the building and made his bow to the visitor awaiting him.

'My lord Cheveley,' he said.

'Mr Dymoke.' The man's voice was deep and soft, with an undertone of mockery that made Mr Dymoke wonder if his wig was askew. 'I apologize for this intrusion. I return to London next week, and there is a matter of some urgency I wish to discuss with you before I leave.' His gaze roved round the confines of the lobby, and he sighed. 'This is not the most congenial of venues. My carriage is outside. Do you care to drive with me a little?'

It was on the tip of Mr Dymoke's tongue to refuse the invitation, but he recalled Joseph's hint that it would be to his advantage to accept, and curiosity got the better of him.

The carriage drawn up to the kerbside was black, with the Cheveley arms emblazoned on its door, and the horses drawing it were also black. A groom in black and gold livery lowered the steps and helped Mr Dymoke to mount them. His lordship followed suit and the horses started forward. So smooth and swift was their pace, and the carriage so well sprung, that Mr Dymoke had the feeling they had left the cobbled street and were flying through the air.

Clinging to normality, he said sharply, 'What is it you wish to say to me, my lord?'

Lord Cheveley answered at a tangent. 'I enjoyed your history of Dorset. Most erudite.

'Thank you. However, I fail to see—'

'Why I'm here?' Lord Cheveley smiled. 'Put simply, sir, I'm here to enlist your help. Your erudition and expertise.'

'I don't understand.'

'Let me explain.' His lordship leaned back in his corner of the carriage, as if to marshall his arguments. 'Like you,' he said at last, 'I live by knowledge. I acquire knowledge and turn it into power, and wealth. I employ people who supply me with facts and figures that often prove more valuable than nuggets of gold. I know, for instance, that a short time ago you were visited at your home in Weymouth by Miss Kate Safford, of Twyford Lindum. She sought your advice on the location of the legendary Danish gold.'

Mr Dymoke bridled. He disliked this man, his soft cold voice and his flat black eyes, his insolent knowing smile. There was only one way he could have come by the information he boasted of. He must have bribed the servants. It was ungentlemanly. Intolerable.

He opened his mouth to protest, but before he could speak, Lord Cheveley held up a hand.

'You find my words distasteful, but let me continue. It is a fact that Miss Safford plans to search for the treasure. It is reasonable to suppose that before doing so she will consult with those who are experts in the history of the Danish invasions. You are a leader in that field. I have read your books. Your theory is that the gold was hidden in the Winterborne area, and was long ago discovered and removed. I take it you told Miss Safford as much?'

Mr Dymoke nodded stiffly. 'I did, yes.'

'That must have caused her great disappointment.'

'It may save her the far greater disappointment of searching for something that doesn't exist.'

'Hmm.' Lord Cheveley was silent for a space, studying Mr Dymoke's flushed countenance. At length he said, 'You hold the treasure was hidden in South Dorset, the land of the dry rivers. But what if there was such a river in Twyford Lindum?'

'There was not. It is not chalk country.'

'I understand that in the period when the Romans occupied Britain, a canal was cut to drain the marsh – the lindum that gives the village its name.'

'It was cut, and when the Romans left to go back to defend Rome, the canal was neglected and allowed to fill.'

'Thus becoming dry?'

'Tush, my lord, that happened centuries before the Danish invasion. The canal can in no way be taken for the "dry river" of Cynric's time.'

Lord Cheveley shrugged. 'Rivers come and rivers go, over the centuries. Do you have proof that the canal cut was dry in Cynric's time?'

'Proof, no, but reason supports that belief.'

Lord Cheveley frowned, steepling his fingers. 'Perhaps, sir, we have both of us reached that stage in life when reason should give way to self-interest. No, hear me out, I beg. I have said I make it my business to acquire knowledge. I know a certain amount about you. I have read your books. You have not published any major works for some years now. You have been forced to practise economies. Your lectures are still popular, but for how long will that continue? And the travel that lecturing involves is becoming more burdensome each year, because you suffer from painful rheumatism. That must, in the cold weather, be little short of torture. Having considered all these circumstances, I have a proposal to lay before you. It is this.

'It has long been my intention to sponsor a history of my family. The Cheveley name has been prominent in Wessex for a very long time. I have in my muniments room a mass of documents that must be brought into order. The history must then be written and steered through the process of publication. All this requires an expert's hand. The task will be long, but well rewarded. I wish you to undertake it. I can and will assure you of a comfortable income for the rest of your days. You will have the leisure and the means to travel to warmer climes in the winter months. Egypt, the Holy Land, Italy and Madeira will be within your compass. All I ask in return is that you write to Miss Safford and suggest that she begin her search for the treasure in the old Roman canal cut. By that simple act you will provide a charming young lady with a glimmer of hope, and secure for yourself a comfortable future.'

So saying, Lord Cheveley reached into the pocket of his coat and drew out a folded document, which he laid on the cushioned seat between them.

Mr Dymoke was not a fool, nor was he ignorant of the town gossip. He had heard the scandalous tales about Lady Madeline Cheveley. She took lovers, many lovers. One of the most recent had been – perhaps still was – Lord Dominic Barr, owner of Melburn Hall at Twyford Lindum, and neighbour to the Miss Kate Safford who was so hell-bent on finding the Danish Gold.

Staring at Lord Cheveley's dark countenance, Mr Dymoke saw there something that frightened him, a malign and implacable purpose. Instinct warned him to have nothing to do with this man or his proposal.

But there floated before Mr Dymoke's inward eye pictures of the sunny south, of luxurious travel, ease in his declining years, all to be his at the stroke of a pen.

He reached out a trembling hand and picked up the document. 'I cannot decide at once,' he said huskily. 'I need more time.'

Lord Cheveley smiled. 'Of course. Take a day or two. Come and see me – my Bath address is on my card – and we'll talk. You understand that this is our secret? An agreement between gentlemen?'

'Yes. Yes indeed.'

'Good. And now, do you wish to return to your lodgings, or may I set you down somewhere in the Town?'

Mr Dymoke chose to go home, and within minutes was deposited at his door. Lord Cheveley leaned from the carriage window, his hand raised in salute. The coachman twirled his whip, the great black horses sprang forward, and the carriage rocked away round the crescent.

Mr Dymoke hastened within doors. He was still trembling, and his flesh felt cold, as if he had just concluded a pact with the Devil.

IX

On Wednesday morning, as Kate was making her breakfast, a letter was brought in to her. On breaking the seal, she found to her astonishment that it was from Mr Dymoke. After a number of preliminary flourishes, he came to the purpose.

> It occurs to me, that on the occasion of your visit to me at Weymouth, when we discussed the matter of the Danish gold, I was overhasty in insisting that it could only have been hidden in the Winterborne country.
>
> Though that remains my view, as an historian I feel obliged to consider every possibility, however remote. In this spirit I beg to remind you of the old canal cut. During the Roman occupation of Britain, engineers cut a passage to drain the Twyford Marsh. It is possible than it endured, in shallow form, until Cynric's time, and formed a defence for his fortress.
>
> The Danes may have dammed the canal, thus giving rise to the legend of the 'dry river'. Perhaps you should begin by searching along the bed of the old cut. I do not think you have much chance of finding what you seek, but I offer the small pointer, which you may follow or ignore as you feel best.
>
> I extend my best wishes to your endeavours, and applaud your effort to extend the bounds of our historical knowledge.
>
> I remain, my dear Miss Safford, your obedient servant,
>
> Humphrey Dymoke.

Kate was pleased with the letter, but Elinor, when shown it, was less sanguine.

'Dymoke says himself it's a remote possibility,' she said.

'Any chance is better than none,' Kate answered. 'It was good of him to write to me.'

'Why did he not have the courtesy to call, and discuss the matter more fully?'

'He may have had other more important business on hand.'

Elinor sniffed. 'The tone of his letter is pompous and patronizing. And why the sudden change of mind? I confess I find the man slippery and self-seeking. I do not like him. I cannot trust him.'

Such vehemence in the peace-loving Elinor was unusual, and Kate said soothingly:

'No more can I, but that's no reason to reject his advice. I shall tell Dominic of it when next we meet. The muniments at Melburn may mention the canal cut. It's the nearest thing to a dry river we've discovered yet.'

That evening, the weekly concert was staged in the Sydney Gardens. The warm weather attracted an unusually large crowd, and as the dusk deepened lamps were lit on the bandstand and in the surrounding trees, so that patrons could easily find their way to the chairs set out on the lawns.

The Beachers' carriage delivered them to the grounds behind the hotel, and on alighting they saw the Walcotts' party a little ahead, the Colonel and his wife hurrying to take their places, George Walcott and Lord Barr trailing in their wake. The two young men were deep in conversation, but at Mr Beacher's jovial hail they turned and exchanged greetings.

George offered Elinor his arm, and Dominic fell into step with Kate. He looked weary and out of sorts, and she decided it was not the moment to tell him of Mr Dymoke's letter.

The horns and clarinets were already practising their runs and riffles, and catching a strain from The Marriage of Figaro, Kate gave a sigh of pleasure.

'Mozart tonight,' she said. 'Just the right touch, in this weather, don't you think?'

Dominic nodded. 'You're fond of music, are you, Kate?'

'Oh, yes! I had hoped to attend concerts in London, last year, but I had to leave before the summer season began.'

'Next time you're in Town, I'll take you to the Opera,' he said. He remembered his altered circumstances, and added wryly, 'You'd best make it soon, before the lease on my box expires.'

She gave him a glance of warm sympathy. 'You'll come about, Nick. It's not in a Barr's nature to accept defeat.'

He was touched by her words. The rest of the world had taken it for granted that his plight was past praying for; and though it was ridiculous to value the faith of an eighteen-year-old girl above the opinions of hardened men of business, he was none the less comforted, and smiled warmly at her.

The concert soon began, the transparent melodies floating like gossamer on the balmy air, so that even the rooks fell silent in the boughs of oak and elm. After a time an interval was announced, and Dominic and George Walcott went off to procure lemonade for the ladies and ale for the gentlemen.

Elinor and the older members of the party were content to remain seated, but Kate decided to stretch her legs, and strolled the short distance to the ornamental pond where fish hung motionless among the lily pads. She was about to retrace her steps when she heard a hurried footfall on the path, and saw Lady Madeline Cheveley approaching.

Having no wish to speak to her ladyship, Kate made as if to pass her by, but she found her skirts caught in a grip that almost jerked her off balance.

'Don't try to elude me, Miss Safford. What I have to say to you is in your best interest, and will take only a moment.'

Lady Cheveley moved round to bar Kate's way. She looked distraught, her eyes unnaturally brilliant, and wisps of tawny hair hanging loose about her face.

Kate said bluntly, 'Madam, I think you are unwell. Let me help you to your carriage.'

'I am perfectly well,' Lady Cheveley replied. 'I am here only to warn you against a man who is like to break your heart, as he has broken mine.'

'I fear I don't understand you,' said Kate coldly, and Lady Cheveley laughed.

'Oh, don't play the innocent with me! I saw you promenading with Lord Barr; I saw how he cast sheep's eyes at you. Believe me, he's an old hand at that game! I don't doubt he's made you extravagant promises of undying devotion; he has made them to me, many's the time. It is all lies, nothing but lies!'

'Lady Cheveley, pray release me at once, you should not be speaking to me so.'

'Ah, do you despise me as a fallen woman? Indeed, so I am. I have been everything to Dominic Barr – I have been his paramour, his light o' love; I have put myself beyond the pale for his sake, and my reward is to be discarded without compunction. He has no further use for me. I stand rejected, and you are the reason for it. Yes, that is the truth. He means to lay siege to your heart. He means to marry you.'

'Rubbish!' Kate snapped. 'Kindly stand aside. I wish to return to my friends.'

'No. You must listen to me, before it's too late. It's your fortune Barr desires, not you. You are to pay his debts and hand over everything you own to him. He has told me his intentions. You may imagine what anguish that has caused me. Not only am I to be cast aside, but I am to watch while he entraps his next victim.

'I know you seek to help him. I've heard from his own lips that you will search for lost treasure at Melburn. He thinks that a fine joke, I can tell you! He says that there is no such treasure, but your gold will suit him very well. Easy meat, he called you. He will take advantage of your youth, he will marry you, and once you are married there'll be an end to any pretence of love. He will show himself in his true colours, as a shameless libertine.'

Lady Cheveley leaned closer, and her mouth twisted in a travesty of a smile. 'Why, he has even boasted to me that marriage

102

with you need make no difference to our relationship. I have only to be patient, he says, and in a few months we will be lovers again. You may stare, Miss Safford, but those were his very words. I entreat you to spare yourself the pain and humiliation I have endured because of Dominic Barr. I urge you to be rid of him, once for all.'

With these words, Lady Cheveley relinquished her grip on Kate and hurried away towards the gates of the park. Kate stood for a moment, gazing after her. Was the woman quite mad, to invent such a Banbury tale? Did she really expect to be believed? Clearly Dominic had grown tired of the creature, and she sought to be even with him by spreading these slanders.

She will learn her mistake, thought Kate grimly.

The musicians were resuming their places on the bandstand, and she moved quickly to rejoin her party. Dominic, in the chair next to hers, looked at her in some concern.

'Are you all right, Kate?'

'Perfectly. Why do you ask?'

'Your face is a little flushed.'

'The heat, nothing more.' She smiled at him. 'I have news to impart. I had a letter this morning, from Humphrey Dymoke. He suggests that the only dry river in Twyford is the old Roman canal cut. Do you think there might be reference to it in your records?'

He frowned, shaking his head. 'There could be. It's an interesting idea. I'll send word to my people to initiate a search at once.'

He spoke with such enthusiasm, and looked so much more cheerful, that Kate was able to believe his token consent to her plans had grown to be a genuine wish to share in them.

The following day, her uncle and aunt having gone out to make a round of morning calls, and Elinor having taken Charlie and James to inspect a new steam pump at the Scientific Society, Kate retired to the writing-room to deal with neglected correspondence. She was interrupted at noon by the sound of a carriage turning into the yard, and moments later the butler Simmons appeared, bearing a package.

'Sedley is back from Twyford, Miss Kate. He required me to give you the parcel directly, it being very urgent, he said.'

'Thank you, Simmons. Tell him I'll be out to see him shortly.'

Kate was already tearing the wrappings from the parcel. The last layer of tissue cast aside, she drew out a flat box of tooled leather, and opening that, exposed a book, also bound with leather, and fastened with a silver hasp. She did not disturb the book, but closed the box and carried it up to her bedchamber, where she locked it in her bureau.

That done, she went out to the stable yard, where Coachman Sedley was settling a pair of rangy greys in their stalls.

'Changed at Frome,' he informed Kate. 'Didn't wish to strain our 'osses on the 'ills yere abouts. Momsen'll be bringin' 'em along, easy like.'

'You did quite right,' Kate approved, and Sedley shrugged.

'Would have been back sooner, if Mrs 'Orning could have found that there mouldy ol' book. Hid away in a pesky cupboard, it was, 'stead of being where a Christian would expect. Then she must needs dust un off and passell un up warm as a newborn babby. And "niver you drop that, Sam," she tells me. "Niver you let that out of your sight", an' so I didn't.'

'I'm very grateful to you,' Kate said. 'It's a very precious book, you see; very old, and with beautiful writing and pictures in it. I mean to give it to a person of great importance.'

'Oh, ah.' Sam's expression said that though he personally wouldn't say thank you for such a gift, there was no accounting for tastes.

'The lady lives near Midsomer Norton,' continued Kate. 'I shall require you to drive me there tomorrow, when the horses are rested.'

Her casual tone covered a certain trepidation. She did not look forward to telling her uncle and aunt of her latest plan, and knew they would vigorously oppose it. As it turned out, however, that confrontation was averted by a quite unlooked-for event.

On entering the house, she found Simmons engaged in agitated discussion with a thin female clad in a black bombazine gown and a beehive bonnet of lavender straw.

'Cousin Agnes!' exclaimed Kate, hurrying forward to embrace the newcomer. 'What in the world brings you here?'

'Necessity,' said the lady grimly. 'You know my dislike of travel, but needs must when the Devil calls.'

Kate's heart sank. Mrs Agnes Fitt was a widowed cousin of the Beachers who had made her home with Anna and Thomas Durrant. In return for a comfortable living, she rendered what small services she could. She never allowed these to strain either her purse or her person, and to see her so far from the fleshpots of Corsham was in itself alarming. Nor was her next sentence reassuring.

'Where are your uncle and aunt?' she demanded. 'I must speak with them immediately.'

'They are out, making calls,' Kate said. 'I expect them back very soon. Won't you come and sit down? You look exhausted.'

'Yes, I should think I am. I've not slept a wink all night; it was one thing after another, first Anna and then Cousin Thomas . . . the doctor, the midwife, the Rector . . .'

'Rector?' Kate turned pale. 'Good God, what need was there for him?'

'None at all,' said Mrs Fitt tartly, 'and so I told him, more than once, but after Thomas fell down the stairs, he said it was his duty to remain, though all he did was get in the way and add to the confusion.' Mrs Fitt pressed a hand to her chest and closed her eyes. 'Just thinking of it is like to bring on one of my spasms.'

Mrs Fitt's spasms, and the proper treatment of them, were well known to members of her family.

'Come and sit down,' said Kate firmly, 'and Simmons shall bring you a glass of brandy.'

'And plum cake,' said Mrs Fitt, extending a hand towards Kate and opening her eyes. 'Lend me support, child, or I shall faint quite away. I have been in such a fever of worry, and the children so hysterical one could do nothing with them. Where are Charlie and James?'

'Out with Elinor.' Kate succeeded in edging Mrs Fitt into the small salon and settling her in a comfortable chair. Simmons appeared unbidden with brandy and cake on a tray, which he placed at the widow's elbow. She lifted the glass, sipped, sipped again and nodded. 'Very tolerable. There's nothing like a good Armagnac to restore the flagging pulse.'

Kate said impatiently, 'Pray tell me at once, is Anna's baby born?'

'Born,' agreed Mrs Fitt, taking a large bite of plum cake and chewing busily. 'Two weeks before time, but a fine healthy girl, according to Dr Duby.'

'And Anna? Is she well?'

'Well as may be expected, in the circumstances.' Mrs Fitt swallowed the last morsel of cake and dusted crumbs from her fingers. 'I thank my lucky stars Duby was with us, for no sooner had he delivered the baby when Thomas fell downstairs and broke his leg. After that, the doctor was box and cox between the two bedrooms, until daybreak.'

'How did Thomas come to do such a thing?'

'Little Johnny Head-in-air,' declared Mrs Fitt, 'Came to the head of the stairs to tell the Rector the good news, missed his footing and fell heel over crown to the bottom of the flight. Broke his shin bone. Duby set it for him; a clean break, he said, and didn't pierce the skin. Thomas will be confined to his bed for some days, which is why I'm here. With the best will in the world, I can't mind the house, two invalids, and children, one of them newborn. I must take Amyas and Emily back to Corsham . . . and the two boys, of course.'

Before Kate could answer, Mr and Mrs Beacher walked into the room, both of them looking extremely anxious, for they had seen the Durrants' carriage at the door. The news of Anna's early but safe delivery, and Thomas's unfortunate accident, naturally led them to ask a great many questions; and no sooner were these answered than Elinor arrived with the children, and the explanations had to be given all over again.

The Beachers decided that they must set out at once for Corsham. Servants were despatched to pack valises, the boys' nursemaid was told to dress them in clean clothes, and the cook instructed to prepare a picnic nuncheon for the travellers. Mrs Beacher scribbled a list of reminders for Kate.

'I feel very badly, abandoning you like this,' she said, 'but I confess it's a comfort to know that you and Nell are here to hold the fort. I don't doubt we'll be home within the week, but pray explain to Mrs Montagu-Gore and Mrs Wrensley why we are forced to break our engagements with them. Oh, and Mr Spooner was to call tomorrow with patterns for the new paper in the dining-room; Simmons must send word to him not to come. Your uncle is writing a draft on his bank, in case there should be any untoward expenses, and Cook will tell you if she needs supplies. Oh, my head is quite in a whirl! I'm sure I've forgotten half the things I should say to you!'

'Don't fret,' said Kate, giving her aunt a hug, 'We'll go on famously, I promise. Give Anna and Tom my love, and say I'll write very soon.'

At last all the arrangements were completed and the party embarked, the Beachers with Mrs Fitt and the two boys in their travelling-coach, Mrs Beacher's maid and the nanny in the Durrants' carriage. Kate and Elinor stood on the front steps to wave goodbye, then re-entered a house that seemed unnaturally empty and quiet. In the hallway, Elinor picked up a lead soldier, dropped in the scramble of departure.

'They'll be so disappointed,' she murmured.

'Who will?'

'Charlie and James. Mr Walcott promised to take them to Astley's farm tomorrow, to help him choose a puppy. I fear it's too late to warn him not to come.'

'Why should you do so?' Kate asked. 'You may still go with him.'

'Indeed,' answered Elinor, with a slight heightening of her colour. 'It would be a shame to bring him all this way for nought. I'm told the kennels are famous hereabouts. Will you not come with us?'

Kate smiled, but shook her head. 'I've business to attend to that will occupy me for most of the day.' She hesitated, half inclined to make a clean breast of her plans, but she knew how strongly Elinor would oppose them, and resolved to hold her peace.

X

Mr Walcott arrived promptly at ten o' clock on Friday, neat as a pin from his polished boots to his curly-brimmed hat. He listened with grave concern to Elinor's report of the dramas assailing the Durrants, expressed his pleasure at the news that mother and child were doing well, and urged Kate with every appearance of sincerity to join the expedition to Astley's Farm. When she declined the invitation, he bowed gracefully and turned to Elinor.

'I think, ma'am, we should set out at once. I've promised to collect Nick Barr from The White Hart at two this afternoon,' he said.

He handed Elinor into the carriage, climbed in himself, and signed to the coachman to drive on.

Kate lost no time in going to her bedroom, and there exchanged her muslin gown for a more formal one of honey-coloured poplin. She gathered up a cloak with a hood, her reticule, and the box Sedley had fetched from Twyford. Descending to the front hall, she placed a letter addressed to Elinor on the table, propping it against a vase so that it could not be overlooked. She then went quietly through the door that gave access to the stable yard.

Her coach stood ready there, and next to it Sedley was in close conference with the stable-lad. He glanced up at Kate's approach, and touched his forelock.

'Mornin', miss,' he said. 'Beggin' yer pardon, but I doubt we should drive so far as Midsomer today.'

'Kate stared. 'Whyever not?'

'Weather,' explained Sedley.

Kate lifted her gaze to a cloudless blue sky. 'The weather's perfect,' she said. 'What's this all about, Sam?'

Sedley looked sheepish. 'Jem yere says we'm in fer a powerful big storm. Seein' as 'e's a local lad, I thought we should mebbe . . .'

'Mr Walcott is a local man, and he said nothing about a storm.' Kate contemplated Jem, a gangling youth with lank fair hair and an obstinately jutting lip.

'Why do you think it will storm?' she demanded.

'Storm like billy-oh,' he said flatly, and jerked a thumb towards the west. 'She'm out there, and she'm a-movin' in fast.'

Kate sighed. Good sense told her that the unseasonable heat might very well bring thunderstorms. It also told her that today was her last chance to make the journey without wearisome arguments with her family. If she delayed, she must take Elinor into her confidence. Elinor would very likely warn their uncle and aunt of the situation, and altercations would surely result.

'How long will it take us to reach Midsomer Abbey?' she asked.

Jem pondered, examined the sky, eyed the waiting horses, rubbed his snub nose and said, 'Two hours to Midsomer Norton. Maggoty ol' town, that be. Abbey's 'nother five miles. Maggoty ol' road, maggoty ol'—'

'Yes, well, never mind that. We shan't be there long.' Kate nodded briskly to Sedley. 'Take him up on the box with you, he knows the way. We'll leave at once. I shall complete my business by early afternoon, and we'll be home before the storm breaks.' She climbed into the carriage and shut the door with a firm jerk.

Seeing further argument was useless, Sedley climbed to the box and nodded to Jem to join him. The chaise rolled out through the yard gates and took the road that climbed the steeps of Beechen Cliff.

For the first hour they followed the Radstock pike road, which was in fair condition. They made good progress, and in ordinary circumstances Kate would have enjoyed the drive, but today her thoughts were on the meeting that lay ahead of her.

What if Dame Celia proved to be as mad as her uncle claimed? Pictures of a crazed Amazon armed with a crossbow rose unpleasantly in Kate's mind. She resolutely dismissed them and tried to concentrate instead on the good she knew of Dame Celia. Even Dymoke admitted she'd been a scholar once, and her father had considered her a historian worth consulting. Surely Papa would not have encouraged his only child to consort with a dangerous lunatic!

Her musings were interrupted by a sudden lurch of the chaise, and looking out of the window she saw that they had left the pike, and were on a branch road. It was narrow and pot-holed, which forced Sedley to drive at a snail's pace for long stretches. Jem's description of it as maggoty was all too accurate, and worse, Kate saw that the sun had dipped behind banks of rolling cloud, and that puffs of wind tugged at the grassland and stirred the trees along the way.

It was after noon when they reached Midsomer Norton – a pretty place that gave the lie to Jem's denigration – and Kate directed Sedley to stop at the inn so that she could ask the way to Midsomer Abbey. The landlord looked at her askance, but told her that they must take the right-hand fork at St Mary's Cross, and keep on up the hill. About three miles on, they must again turn right, and that would take them to the Abbey.

Following these instructions, they reached the stone cross, which was weatherworn and propped up by a cairn of stones. The right-hand fork led them uphill, past a hamlet that consisted of a forge, a cluster of cottages and a tannery where a cart was offloading a pile of malodorous hides.

Once past the hamlet, the track became steadily worse, winding between low hillocks. They turned right again, and after a series of twists and turns, emerged into a wide basin of land bisected by a sluggish rivulet. The fields on either side of the stream were planted with mangold-wurzels, woodland clothed the western rim of the basin, and far to the north lay pastures dotted with sheep.

It was a landscape unremarkable save for the extraordinary building that dominated it.

If Midsomer Abbey was a ruin, it was a ruin with a difference. At its western end was a tower that must once have been part of a fine church, built of stone in the square Norman style. The belfry at its crest was broken down, the bells long gone, but the ragged stonework had been capped to prevent further decay. From a flagstaff at one corner of the tower dangled what appeared to be a personal standard, idle on the breathless air.

Next to the tower ran a line of cloisters, also of stone, and to the right of these was a magnificent barn of ancient brick, with a slate roof.

Round the whole complex ran a green-slimed moat, spanned by a drawbridge that led to an archway at the base of the tower. The archway was sealed by heavy wooden gates that looked as if they had not been opened in years.

It was like an old tapestry, thought Kate, or a painting in some medieval book of hours. She would not have been surprised to see a band of pilgrims on the track ahead, or a nobleman riding by with hawk on wrist. She could discern no sign of human activity. Not even the cry of a bird disturbed the silence of the hanging woods. She had the eerie feeling that to advance would be to challenge some ancient and puissant spell.

She realized that the carriage had come to a halt, and leaned her head out of the window.

'What is it, Sedley?'

Sedley bent to call down an answer. ' 'Tis Jem, Miss Kate. Powerful scared, 'e be. Says there's a witch lives yonder.'

'Tell Jem,' said Kate, 'that as good Christian folk we need have no fear of witches. Drive on, please.'

The carriage started forward once more, swaying along the winding course of the rivulet to a broad stretch of packed earth directly in the shadow of the tower. Kate opened the carriage door and alighted, clutching her parcel to her.

'Wait here,' she told Sedley.

'Miss, I dunno as you should . . .'

He spoke to thin air, for Kate was already hurrying across the drawbridge.

The planks echoed to her determined tread. The massive oak gates debarred her. Set into elaborately carved stone, they must once have formed the main entrance to the Abbey. Now they guarded a fortress.

She saw that a small sallyport had been let into the right-hand gate, and that beside this was an iron bell-pull. Seizing hold of it, she gave it a sharp tug. Far away a bell jangled, then the oppressive silence rolled back.

She sounded a second peal on the bell, and this time heard footsteps approaching. A face appeared at the iron grille set in the door; a round face, young, framed by butter-yellow curls on which was perched a mobcap of starched muslin. Round blue eyes stared at her unblinkingly, and a voice with an accent like clotted cream said, 'Yeu'm trespassing! Be off wi' yeu!'

Kate met the insolent stare, her own temper rising.

'Tell your mistress, if you please, that Miss Safford of Twyford Lindum is here, and desires to speak with her.'

'Missus aint 'ome.'

'Yes, she is. Her personal flag is flying on the tower.'

'She'll loikely set 'ounds on yeu,' promised the yellowhead with relish, and Kate heard the sound of heavy snuffling along the foot of the gate. Lifting the package, she held it against the bars of the grille. 'Take this to Dame Celia at once. I shall wait here for her answer.'

The girl hesitated, chewing her lip, then pulled the parcel through the bars and retreated, whistling the dogs after her. Kate wondered if she'd seen the last of both servant and gift.

A step sounded on the drawbridge, and she saw Sedley approaching, his jaw set.

'I don't fancy the look o' thikky place, nor that wench, neither.

No more manners than a nalley cat. I'll teach 'er!'

Kate smiled. 'Thank you, Sam, but we have to play this game by *their* rules. You'd best keep an eye on young Jem; he looks ready to bolt for home.'

Sedley scowled at the youth who crouched on the driver's box, clutching the reins in rigid fingers, his eyes wide with terror.

'Bats in the belfry, that one,' Sedley averred. 'But 'e were right about the weather, miss. Look yonder.'

He pointed westward, to where huge flashes of lightning criss-crossed a blackening sky. 'We mun get the 'orses to shelter,' he said. 'If there's naught to be had yere, we mun make a run for Midsomer Norton.'

As he spoke, there came the sound of bolts being drawn back, and the small door behind her opened. This time it was not the yellow-haired girl who stood there, but an old man in a long black robe that was held at the waist by a velvet sash. On his head was a black cap with side-flaps that half hid his cheeks, and in his right hand he held a tall ebony staff tipped with silver. He looked as old and withered as Time, and peered at Kate through clouded eyes.

'Miss Kate Safford?' His voice was cracked, but gentle.

'Yes,' Kate answered.

'I am Robert de Morford,' the old man said. 'Dame Celia's seneschal. She bids me apologize for having kept you waiting. She invites you to come in.'

'I'm grateful to Dame Celia,' Kate said, 'but what of my servants and my horses? There's a storm brewing.'

'Indeed. I hear it.' The old man appeared to meditate for a space, then said, 'I believe we must grant them shelter. My mistress found your gift most acceptable, especially as today is her birthday. Pray direct your coachman to drive round to the rear gate. I will send someone to admit him to the precincts.'

Stepping back from the door, he indicated with a bow that Kate should follow him. She spoke rapidly to Sedley. 'Do as he asks, Sam. See the horses are fed and watered, but be sure to offer compensation for whatever is provided.'

She followed de Morford through the gloom of the archway to a vast yard paved with cobblestones. It was enclosed on the west by a lofty stone wall, against which was a row of stables. On the north side of the square lay a long building of weathered brick, its lower storey devoted to a coach-house, a forge, a bakery, dairy and kitchens. The upper storey seemed to accommodate haylofts, storerooms and servants' lodgings.

While her guide paused to give orders to a groom, Kate studied the scene before her. It was easy to see why the outlying fields had seemed so deserted. Every living soul on the estate must be here in this yard. Men scurried about carrying provisions, tables and barrels of ale. In the kitchens and bakery, women appeared to be preparing a gargantuan meal. Spits revolved, pots seethed, and the aroma of roasting meats and fresh-baked bread was heavy on the air.

A group of children passed, their arms full of cut greenery, and the seneschal waved them towards the barnlike building Kate had seen from the head of the valley. It ran the full length of the east side of the square, a distance of some three hundred feet.

De Morford beckoned her on. 'All our people will be in the Great Hall tonight,' he told her, 'to join in the celebrations and drink to Dame Celia's health. A place of honour shall be reserved for you, Miss Safford.'

'Oh, but I cannot stay so long,' Kate said in alarm, but the old man was already striding away along the cloisters. Kate followed. They reached a second set of oak doors, on which de Morford rapped three times with the head of his staff. The doors swung slowly back, and they moved into the presence of Dame Celia.

She stood before a great fireplace in which massive logs were laid; a tall woman clad in a dark-blue robe that fell in bunched folds from shoulder to ground. A girdle of worked silver encircled her waist, and a silver brooch was pinned to her left shoulder. Hair that had faded from gold to a yellowish-white hung in two braids to frame a long, bony face. One heavily beringed hand rested on the head of a wolfhound at her side. Her eyes, which

115

were large and burning blue, fixed Kate with a stare that seemed to last forever. Then she said preremptorily:

'Come!'

The seneschal signed to Kate to go forward. She advanced to within a yard of her hostess, and dropped a curtsy. Dame Celia nodded approvingly.

'A pretty face, and manners to match,' she said. 'A rare combination in these graceless days.' She caught a flicker of surprise on Kate's face, and smiled. 'You think I've no right to speak of courtesy, when I'm reputed to shoot intruders?'

Kate swallowed. 'No doubt you have your reasons, ma'am.'

'Yes indeed, many.' The jewelled hand described a circle in the air. 'They lie all about me.'

Kate glanced round uncertainly, and was astonished by what met her eyes.

The hall occupied two thirds of the building, a heavily carved rood-screen dividing it from whatever lay beyond. Opposite the screen, at the south end, was a low dais on which stood a table and several chairs as ponderous as thrones. Other tables and benches occupied the floor of the hall, and these Kate thought might accommodate as many as a hundred people.

Rugs of homespun wool were scattered over flagstones polished to a marble smoothness. Light fell from tallow candles set in iron wall-sconces, and in six iron chandeliers.

The primitive austerity of the room was redeemed by two features. One was the great rose window above the dais, which was of a beauty and lustre that put Kate in mind of Chartres. The other was the tapestries that covered every inch of the walls.

Each tapestry depicted a different scene. One showed a young man being dragged towards an open boat by a group of armed ruffians. In another, the same youth appeared as a shepherd; in a third he stood in a Roman palace; and in a fourth he wore the mitre and vestments of a bishop.

'They're wonderful,' Kate said. 'It's easy to understand why you guard them so closely.'

116

Dame Celia's brows rose. 'Lud, child, it's my *people* I seek to protect! While I live, they will not be driven from their rightful territory by bullies and speculators. As for the tapestries, I value them less for their beauty than for what they represent. Do you know what that is?'

'I think, the story of St Patrick of Ireland.'

'St Patrick of the Severn,' retorted Dame Celia. 'Patricius Magonus Sucat was born not far from here.' She moved to a table on which Kate's gift lay. 'You have given me this book that describes his life. I've not had time to examine the text, but the illustrations are very fine. It shall have an honoured place in my collection, and I thank you.' She turned her luminous gaze on Kate. 'What made you choose such a present?'

'My uncle told me you claim descent from St Patrick.'

'Descent? No, how could that be? I'm no more than his distant kinsman. My family has lived on the Severn Estuary for fifteen hundred years. Calpurnius Sucat, Patrick's father, was a deacon of the early church, and a minor local official in the fifth-century Romano-British establishment. My name, Sickert, is a corruption of Sucat. And now, Miss Safford, we will sit together and you will tell me the purpose of your visit.'

The words were spoken with an authority that allowed no argument. Kate took off her bonnet and sat down on one of the long benches. Dame Celia took the place opposite her, leaned her elbows on the table, and said bluntly:

'In your first letter to me, you wrote that you are making a search for the Twyford Gold. Why is that?'

'It was my father's last request.'

'A precious odd one, to be sure. But Clive Safford was a notable scholar, his opinions must always be respected. Did he believe the gold still lies at Twyford?'

Fixed with a penetrating stare, Kate felt she was in some way being tested. This strange old woman sought more than answers to idle questions.

'Papa told me that most historians believe the gold was

removed from Melburn centuries ago,' she said. 'But according to the legends, it's buried there still.'

'Was he in his right mind when he made that statement?' As Kate frowned, Dame Celia smiled. 'If I take no offence at being termed mad, why should anyone else?'

'He was certainly of sound mind when he wrote me a letter, suggesting I look for the gold. Later, when he was ill and in a high fever, his thoughts . . . seemed to ramble.'

'What do you mean, "seemed"?'

'I mean that though what he said sounded irrational, I felt compelled to believe it. He spoke with such urgency – as if even in his delirium he had recognized some truth, and was trying to convey it to me.'

'What precisely did he say?'

'He said I must find the dry river. He said the blackthorn is anathema.'

'Anathema?' The old lady's gaze sharpened. 'A strange word for a dying man to employ. Do you know what it means?'

'Yes, I looked for it in the lexicon. It's a solemn ecclesiastical curse, carrying the threat of excommunication from the Church.'

Dame Celia clicked her tongue impatiently. 'No, no, your lexicon is too modern for our purpose! Look to the Good Book, child. "Cursed be the man who moves his neighbour's boundary". 'Our Anglo-Saxon forbears marked their boundaries with blackthorn fences, and to them, anathema condemned land-thieves to eternal damnation. You must be clear on the meanings of words, you know, or you'll go woefully astray.'

'And the dry river?' enquired Kate. 'What does that mean?'

'I have no idea. It's gibberish, a contradiction in terms.'

'Mr Dymoke says it refers to the Winterborne streams, which dry up in summer.'

Dame Celia shrugged. 'That may be so. Dymoke's a prating fool, but even fools are sometimes right.'

Kate looked crestfallen. 'So you don't think there is treasure at Melburn?'

'Think? What has thinking to say to anything? Thought tells me that if the Danish murderers failed to find the gold, the Godwin scavengers did not. Earl Godwin betrayed his people to the Danes, and Cnut gave him half of Dorset as reward. The Godwin greed would never have allowed gold to lie unclaimed in the earth. Thought, my dear, tells me that you are on a wild goose chase. *Faith*, on the other hand—'

She was interrupted by a clap of thunder so sudden and loud that Kate gave a startled cry. Her hostess chuckled.

'Don't worry, it's still a long way off. It won't reach us till sundown. What was I saying?'

'Faith,' said Kate weakly.

'Ah, yes. Faith is made of sterner stuff than reason, you know. Faith moves mountains; faith walks on the water.' Dame Celia pressed her bony hands to her chest. 'I have faith. I have faith that I will find my cross. I have searched for it all my life, without success; but now, in the twilight of my years, you have been sent to aid me. Your gift is a sign from Heaven. I am to be rewarded at last. You will help me find my cross.'

Kate stared at her hostess in growing alarm. Uncle Amyas was right, not a doubt of it. Dame Celia was afflicted with religious mania. She might become violent, if crossed. She must be humoured.

'I'm afraid,' said Kate, in what she hoped was a matter-of-fact tone, 'that the only cross I know of is the Cross of St Dunstan, which is said to be part of the Danish treasure.'

'I care nothing for Dunstan!' said Dame Celia fiercely. Leaning forward, she caught Kate's wrist in a powerful grip. 'I speak of the Cross of St Patrick, which he let fall on the Severn shore, on the day the Irish pirates carried him off to slavery. That cross was in my family's possession till the Saxons came. Then it was sent to Glastonbury for safekeeping. It was never returned to us, the rightful owners. Surely you know the story?'

'No,' said Kate humbly. 'I fear I'm very ignorant.'

'Then I shall relate it to you tonight at the feast, and tomorrow

I will show you my library, and the replica of the Sucat Cross.'

Kate managed to release her wrist from the old lady's grip, and stood up. 'You are very kind, ma'am, and I thank you for your gracious invitation, but I cannot remain here tonight. If I fail to return to Bath, my family will be very much alarmed.'

Dame Celia put up her brows. 'Did you not inform them that you were coming to visit me?'

'I left a letter for my cousin,' admitted Kate, 'but . . .'

'In that case,' said Dame Celia with hauteur, 'they can have no possible cause for concern.'

Her arrogance infuriated Kate. 'There you mistake,' she said roundly. 'They will very likely think you have shot me with your crossbow, or laid a curse on me!'

Dame Celia broke into laughter. 'Saints above, do they take those old wives' tales for truth? I assure you, I have never shot any living creature, and as for curses, how else should an old hag like me protect herself and her people? If harsh words frighten off predators, then God be thanked.'

Kate set her jaw. 'I intend to leave at once, ma'am. You cannot stop me.'

'Of course I cannot. I would not, if I could. I observe the old rules of hospitality: welcome the coming, speed the parting guest.' She glanced upwards. 'With luck you may be half-way to Bath before the storm strikes.'

As she spoke, lightning flared, turning the rose window to living fire. Thunder rolled from end to end of the sky. Kate was visited by the unnerving thought that the old woman had the power to summon the tempest at will.

'Why *should* I stay?' she demanded. 'You wish me to help you find your cross, but you refuse to help me find mine! I've paid you my tribute, and you give me nothing in return!'

Dame Celia bowed her head, seeming to give this accusation her consideration. At last she said, 'I know nothing about the treasure of Melburn, whether it exists or not. I do know – by faith, not by reason – that we two are meant to help each other. The saints have presented us with an opportunity. If you leave, it will be lost to both of us. The choice is yours, Kate Safford. What will you do? Go, or stay?'

Kate pressed her hands to her temples. She must be mad to listen to such a rigmarole. Every dictate of good sense reminded her of her family's anxiety, of the impropriety of her actions, of the possible dangers of spending a night in this outlandish establishment. Yet meeting Dame Celia's gaze, she found she cared not a jot for good sense.

'I'll stay,' she said.

XI

Mr Walcott and Elinor spent a delightful hour at Astley's Farm, visiting each of the kennels and discussing the rival merits of various litters of puppies. Mr Walcott eventually chose a hound and a bitch that would be ready to leave their dam in two weeks' time, and went to settle his account with the head kennel-man.

On his return, he found Elinor standing by one of the pens, gazing wistfully at the puppies at play in the straw.

'Thinkin' of makin' a purchase yourself, Mrs Crane?' he asked, and Elinor nodded.

'The little one with the black muzzle,' she said. 'Only see how brave he is! He faces up to the others, as if he doesn't give a rap for their growls.'

'Regular giant-killer,' agreed Mr Walcott. 'His size is against him, though, if you want him as a workin' dog.'

'But I don't! I want him for myself, as a friend and companion.'

'Lucky fellow,' murmured Mr Walcott, but Elinor was not paying attention.

'I shall call him Jack,' she decided. 'Jack the Giant-killer. I shall pay for him now, and come to collect him the minute he's old enough.'

'You plan to remain in Bath for another fortnight, then?'

Elinor's face fell. 'Oh, no, I'd forgotten! Kate and I leave for Twyford next Friday.'

Mr Walcott seized his chance. 'That's easily remedied. With your permission, I'll bring the little fellow to you myself when I visit Nick Barr next month.'

This arrangement made, and Jack's price duly paid, Elinor and her companion set off for Bath, very well pleased with themselves and the world in general.

Their complacency was shattered when they arrived at the Beachers' residence, to be met on the doorstep by Simmons and the cook, Mrs Peabody, both of them in a state of high agitation.

'Miss Kate left this for you, ma'am,' said Simmons, handing Elinor a letter and at the same time casting a darkling look at Mrs Peabody. 'Had I been informed earlier of Miss Kate's intention, I would have done my best to dissuade her from such a course, but I learned of it only after I returned from the wine-merchant's shop.'

Mrs Peabody bridled. 'How was I to guess what was in Miss Kate's mind, ma'am? Never a word did she say to me. 'Twas only by chance I 'appened to be standin' by the kitchen window, and I 'eard Miss ask that lobcock Jem how long it'd take to drive to Midsomer Abbey.'

Elinor silenced the wrangling with a lift of the hand, and broke the seal on Kate's letter. She scanned it quickly, shaking her head in disbelief. 'She's taken leave of her senses!' she exclaimed. 'I must go after her at once. The carriage, Simmons. No, that won't answer; Uncle has taken it. Oh, what am I to do?'

She turned instinctively to Mr Walcott, who rose nobly to the occasion. Taking her hand in a firm clasp, he said soothingly, 'Don't distress yourself, I beg. Just tell me what's wrong.'

'Kate has gone to Midsomer Abbey to see Dame Celia Sickert,' said Elinor distractedly. 'What can have possessed her, to take such a risk for a treasure that doesn't exist?'

Unable to make much sense of this plea, Mr Walcott latched on to its salient-point. 'What risk?' he asked.

'The woman's as mad as a hatter! She attacks any stranger who sets foot on her property. Kate may be lying dead or injured at this very moment! I must hire a carriage; please tell me where I may do so.'

'No need to hire anythin',' said George. 'I'll take you to Midsomer myself. You should fetch a warm cloak, I think. The weather is like to break soon.'

124

'But I cannot impose on you . . .'

'Yes, you can.' He gave her hand a comforting pat, and with a sigh of relief she hurried away up the stairs. He turned to confront Simmons and Mrs Peabody.

'Tell me, what time did Miss Safford set out?'

'Soon after you left with Mrs Crane,' offered the cook. ' 'Bout ten o'clock, I'd say, sir.'

'Then she'll have reached Midsomer by now,' said Mr Walcott. Mrs Peabody broke into a quavering wail, and he fixed her with a stern eye. 'That's enough. No harm will come to Miss Safford. I undertake to bring her safely home. In the meantime, no word of this escapade is to be heard, in or out of this house. The last thing we need is foolish gossip. Is that understood?'

Mrs Peabody nodded, stifling her sobs. Simmons ventured to enquire what Mr Walcott would do if the storm broke before he could return to Bath.

'We will find shelter at Radstock or some such place. My groom, Lyte, must ride over to Solsbury and inform my parents that because of the threatening weather, Lord Barr and I have decided to remain in Bath tonight.'

One of Mr Beacher's hacks was saddled, Lyte was given his instructions, and Mr Walcott returned to the carriage. He was joined moments later by Elinor. She had exchanged her bonnet and shawl for a cloak with a hood, and carried a long leather case which she held out to Mr Walcott.

'Uncle Amyas's duelling-pistols,' she explained.

George took the box with an indulgent smile. 'I doubt if we'll be reduced to such straits,' he said, 'but there's no harm in bein' prepared. Shall you mind if we drive by way of The White Hart? I engaged to take up Nick Barr. He'll have to come with us to Midsomer, or make his own way to Solsbury.'

Lord Barr had passed the morning in Mr Shipton's office, making a realistic assessment of his financial position.

'It's a damned Augean stable,' he said, contemplating the piles of bills and documents spread across the solicitor's desk. 'As fast as we clear one load, another comes pouring in.'

'I think we can claim to have dealt with the most pressing of your obligations,' said Mr Shipton carefully.

'Not good enough, though, is it?'

'No, I fear not. Even if we achieve the target set for the sale of the contents of the house, we will still not be able to redeem the mortgage, or set aside money for the proper running of the estate.'

Dominic smiled bleakly. 'In other words, all we've done is turn a rout into a defeat.'

'An honourable defeat,' Mr Shipton replied. Over the past weeks he had revised his opinion of young Lord Barr, discovering beneath the veneer of a man of fashion, an admirable courage and honesty. 'The world must respect your efforts, I believe.'

'My world has no respect for a man without means,' Dominic answered. He sat for a moment twisting the signet ring he wore on his left hand. At last he said, 'Tell me, if you please, what's next to be done.'

Mr Shipton touched a finger to an eyebrow. 'We must meet with Mr Horace Pickford, who holds the mortgage on Melburn. He has been generous in giving us time to settle with other claimants, but if he decides to foreclose then I'm afraid it will mean . . .'

'Melburn will be sold.'

'Yes.'

'How soon?'

'It's hard to say. An estate as large as Melburn can't be disposed of in a week. A proper value must be set on the Hall itself, the lands, the tenant farms and cottages; the work could take a month or two. Mr Pickford will appoint his own assessors, as we will. We must try to ensure that your losing Melburn won't be a mere ritual sacrifice, but will provide you with the means to rebuild your life.'

Since the deaths of his father and brother, Dominic had been prey to many emotions – shock and grief, anger and self-reproach, but he had never despaired of saving his family home. Wealth and social consequence, he found, counted for little compared with his desire to remain Barr of Melburn. Now that that hope was finally crushed, he must face reality. He must conclude his business in Bath and return to Twyford. The members of his staff must be warned of the probable sale of the estate. He must make time to visit London, to inform his mother of the situation.

When he arrived at The White Hart Inn, it still lacked twenty minutes of two o'clock, and he was surprised to see George Walcott's carriage in the yard, and George himself pacing beside it in an agitated manner.

Catching sight of Dominic, Walcott hurried to meet him and said in a rapid undertone, 'Nick, dear boy, 'fraid there's been a change of plan. Find myself obliged to drive Mrs Crane to Midsomer. Delicate matter, d'ye see? Storm brewin', may be forced to stay overnight in Radstock. Unchaperoned female. Beg you'll accompany us, make all *comme il faut*.'

The idea that he was being invited to lend respectability to any undertaking made Dominic smile, but George's next words were sobering.

'Miss Safford's gone to Midsomer Abbey,' said Mr Walcott, taking hold of Dominic's elbow and propelling him towards the carriage. 'Taken it into her noddle that Dame Celia can tell her where to find the Danish gold. Mrs Crane fears the girl will meet with violence. Frettin' herself to flinders, poor little soul.'

At this moment, Elinor leaned from the window of the carriage and exclaimed, 'Oh, Lord Barr, thank God you are here! Now we may set out at once.'

It would have required a heart of stone to ignore the appeal in her eyes. The two gentlemen took their places, George rapped on the roof, and the carriage moved forward at a brisk pace.

In after years, Dominic was to think of the journey that followed as a turning-point in his life, but at the time it seemed at once tedious and bizarre. His own mood was far from sunny, and Elinor Crane's fluctuated between a desire to reach Midsomer

Abbey as quickly as possible, and a conviction that when they arrived there, they would be refused admission.

'Dame Celia only receives people who bring acceptable gifts,' she declared. 'Kate must have hit on something acceptable. Simmons told me that Sedley brought her a parcel from Twyford, and she took it with her this morning. We have no gift. We'll be turned away, or shot.'

Mr Walcott patted his pocket. 'We'll pass,' he said. 'I shall sport my blunt. Never knew anyone who couldn't be sweetened by hard cash.'

'I don't think Dame Celia will take a bribe,' Elinor said.

'No, no,' soothed George. 'Nothin' so crass. Handle the matter with kid gloves. Pledge a neat sum to her favourite cause.'

But despite the best efforts of her two companions, Elinor remained convinced that Kate was in the clutches of a homicidal lunatic. To make matters worse, after they passed Radstock, the road deteriorated and the storm heightened, lightning flashes turning the sky an ominous blue-green. It was past five o'clock when they reached Midsomer Norton, and they were further delayed when they enquired directions of the village simpleton.

At last they found themselves on a rough lane that seemed to lead in the general direction of Midsomer Abbey.

'Be there in no time,' averred Mr Walcott. 'Can't be more than a mile or so to go.'

Neither of his companions made a reply, Elinor because she was sitting with her eyes shut and her hands clapped to her ears, and Dominic because he was straining to catch sounds that challenged the thunder.

Somewhere on the road ahead, men shouted and a horse neighed in terror, and forming a strange descant to this cacophony came the sound of harp music, and a man's voice raised in song.

XII

The carriage slowed to a crawl, rounded a bend in the lane, and came to a dead halt.

Elinor opened her eyes and said in a trembling tone, 'What is it? Why have we stopped?'

For answer, the coachman's face appeared at the glazed trap in the roof.

'Girt ol' wagon a-lyin' in the way, sir,' he announced. 'Gypsies, by the look of it. Proper shambles.'

Mr Walcott sighed and alighted from the carriage, Dominic followed, and the two advanced towards the wagon. It lay on its side against the bank, its left-hand wheels in the ditch, its canvas tilt torn. Baggage and stores had spilled from it, and were strewn across the track. The percheron cart-horse that had drawn it kicked and squealed against a broken shaft, trapped in a tangle of harness. Three men milled about the beast, a fourth lay in the roadway with blood streaming down his face, and a fifth sat perched on the outcrop of rock that crowned the right-hand bank.

It was this man who was providing a vocal obligato to the increasing roar of the storm. He sat with a lap-harp on his knee, plucking the strings and singing at the top of a powerful baritone.

He looked to be about sixty years old, and was extremely fat, with a tangle of black hair under a battered tricorn hat. Linen breeches cross-gartered with strips of leather encased his legs, and a patchwork cloak was thrown about his shoulders. He paid not the slightest heed to the confusion surrounding him.

Mr Walcott moved to attend to the injured man. Dominic joined the group at the ditch. Two of them were making ineffectual attempts to calm the horse, which intensified its struggles with each clap of thunder. The third man, a giant in a frieze overcoat and a rabbit-skin cap, was seeking by main force to lift the wagon from its muddy bed. Dominic tapped him on the shoulder.

'You'll have to cut the traces,' he said. 'Once we have Dobbin out of the way, we'll be able to shift the cart.'

The big man glared at Dominic as if he thought to challenge his advice, but after a moment he shrugged and spoke to his companions in what sounded like the Welsh tongue. One of them drew a knife from his belt and cut the traces. The big man laid hold of the sound shaft and heaved it towards him, allowing the horse to lumber to its feet. Dominic caught its head-leather, ran a hand down its neck, and checked its legs and quivering flank. Finding no serious injury, he bade the man with the knife lead it away.

The giant dropped down into the ditch to inspect the underside of the wagon, and Dominic turned to see how the injured man fared. George and Elinor Crane had carried him to the strip of turf on the far side of the road, and were binding his wound with strips of what had to be her petticoat.

The minstrel on the rock was still singing, and irritated by his lack of concern, Dominic went to stand beneath him.

'We must get your friend to cover,' he said. 'Before the rain comes.'

The fat man spat. 'No friend of mine. Drunk as a fiddler's bitch he was, and has ruined all our chances. What are madrigals without a tenor? Bricks without straw, look you. Let him rot where he lies!'

'He's lost a great deal of blood. Do you want his death on your conscience?'

The fat man snorted. 'Conscience? Don't speak to me of conscience! That one has none. Drinking all night in the taverns, never a thought for his comrades, or for the Lady Celia.'

Dominic moved closer. 'Were you contracted to sing for Dame Celia tonight?'

'What would I need of a contract? Minstrel to the Sickerts, I am, like my forebears back to the first bards. A fine birthday my lady will have, without the gift of music!'

As he spoke, a particularly vivid flash of lightning lit the landscape, thunder crashed, and drops of rain spattered the dust underfoot.

Dominic turned up the collar of his coat. 'It so happens,' he said, 'that my friends and I are bound for the Abbey. 'We'll be happy to convey you and the injured man to shelter.'

The fat man laughed. 'Lying, you are! Dame Celia never invited the likes of you to her banquet.'

'Invited or not, we are going to the Abbey.'

'Then you'll waste your journey. She admits only those she counts as her friends.'

'*And* those who pay suitable tribute.'

'Ah, don't think to buy your way in, my fine cockalorum. It's gifts of the spirit my lady looks for, not your gold that you've stolen from honest working men.'

Dominic ignored the taunt. 'I have a gift,' he said.

'Indeed, and what is that?'

'I sing tenor.'

The effect of these words was startling. The fat man's face swelled, and he stabbed a callused finger at Dominic. 'Sing high, sing low,' he shrilled, 'you'll not ride in on my back. I'll not play donkey to the exploiters of the poor.'

This proved too much for Mr Walcott, who had come to stand at Dominic's side. He raised a monitory hand. 'That's enough, sirrah! I'll have you know that you're addressing Lord Barr of Melburn.'

'Lord Barr of Melburn may go to Hell, and take you with him, my prancing macaroni!'

To Mr Walcott, pink of the ton, the word 'macaroni' was the

ultimate insult, and he danced forward, fists flourishing. Dominic caught his arm.

'Softly, George, softly.'

'Teach the fellow a lesson!' roared Mr Walcott. 'He's a ravin' revolutionary!'

'Possibly, but he may serve our purpose.' Dominic faced the harpist again. 'Do you or do you not require the services of a tenor for your performance tonight?'

The fat man glowered, jaws champing. Then he leaned back against the rock face and waved an imperious hand.

'Sing!' he commanded.

Dominic was now the cynosure of all eyes, save for those of the injured man, who was unconscious. Mrs Crane and George were regarding him with stupefaction, while the harpist and his crew seemed to be taking a deep professional interest in his actions.

He considered. He enjoyed singing. At Oxford he had joined a choral society; in London, one might take part in a duet at a gathering of friends; but for a peer of the realm to throw in his lot with a bunch of roving minstrels would be seen by the ton not merely as eccentric, but as downright improper.

The past few weeks, however, had given him a contempt for the vapourings of polite society. If a song would provide access to the Abbey, then so be it. Clearing his throat, Dominic broke into the opening bars of 'Voi che sapete'. He sang while the storm rolled round the valley, and rain ran down the back of his neck. When he had made an end, the fat man slid down from his perch and faced him.

'Do you sing by ear, or can you read music?'

'I can read music.'

'Well, I suppose you're better than nothing. I'll take you in with me, but you'll have to rehearse, mind, and do as you're bid.'

'I won't come without the other members of my party – Mrs, Crane, Mr Walcott and the coachmen.'

'Can they sing?'

Elinor stepped forward. 'I can hold a tune, and play the lute.'

'Lute, is it?' The harpist's eyebrows soared. 'And how well do you play, my dear?'

'Well enough to be instructed by Signor Gabrielli of London,' retorted Elinor, putting up her chin.

'Heaven preserve me from gifted amateurs!' said the fat man. 'Well, we'll see. And you, Mister Macaroni, what's your talent?'

Mr Walcott refused to dignify the question with an answer, and Dominic spoke for him.

'Mr Walcott is tone-deaf, despite the fact that his grandmother hailed from Caernarfon.'

'There's good basses come out of Caernarfon,' admitted the fat man. George regarded him coldly.

'My grandmother was a contralto.'

'Ah, there's lovely. Nothing to beat a true contralto. But if you've no ear, bach, I've no use for you.'

'He can act as dresser,' suggested Dominic. 'Might give your company a new touch.'

The fat man sniffed. 'It would take the magic of Merlin to do that,' he said, 'but I suppose he can shift furniture. Very well, you can all of you come. You'll get no pay, see? A fine meal, and a bed for the night, that's all I can promise.'

He began to shout at his followers, bidding them tie their bundles to the back of the percheron. That done, horse and men moved down the road, into the rain that veiled the valley.

The injured man was placed in a corner of the carriage, with Elinor and George in attendance. Dominic and the harpist were the last to board.

'You have the advantage of me, friend,' Dominic said. 'You know my name, but I don't know yours.'

The harpist looked at him in astonishment. 'I'm Nairn,' he declared, as a man might have said, 'I'm King of England.'

'Then, Nairn,' said Dominic cheerfully, 'let's make a push to find shelter from this damnable weather.'

Her audience with Dame Celia concluded, Kate was shown to her room. It was in the former cloisters, several cells having been knocked into one to form a long dormitory. The floor was of stone, covered with woven rugs. There were no windows in the outer walls, but three that overlooked the courtyard. White curtains masked them, and white quilts covered the three cot beds.

For the rest, there was an oaken clothes-closet, two straight-backed chairs, a table on which stood a bowl of roses, and a lectern bearing a massive bible. A silver crucifix, finely wrought, hung above the lectern. In one corner of the room an archway led to a small powder-closet.

An elderly maid of forbidding aspect brought hot water and towels, and a tray of refreshments. Kate washed, ate, and stretched out on one of the beds. The linen smelled of herbs and lavender. She closed her eyes and allowed her thoughts to drift.

Strange though the events of the day had been, she felt neither anxiety nor doubt. The tumult of the storm seemed not a threat but a powerful force that was sweeping her on to some appointed goal.

She was roused from her reverie by a commotion in the yard, the sound of heavy gates being thrown open, and men shouting. Going to her door, she saw that an elegant carriage had entered the premises, followed by a percheron cart-horse, laden with bulky packages and surrounded by a raggle-taggle group of men.

As she watched, the old seneschal advanced to meet the carriage, and the next moment, to Kate's astonishment, Dominic Barr and George Walcott sprang down and proceeded to lift out the prone form of a man whose head was swathed in a blood-stained cloth.

Kate started forward, but before she had taken many steps, a figure in a sodden mantle came running towards her, crying, 'Kate, Kate! Thank God you're safe!'

'Of course I'm safe, you goose!' Kate moved to embrace Elinor, but she backed away.

'Don't touch me, my cloak is bloodied.' Elinor pulled off the garment and dropped it to the flags, and Kate saw that her gown also was streaked with blood. Kate put an arm round her shoulders and pulled her into the bedroom.

'Nell, are you hurt? What's happened to put you in such a state?'

'An accident.' Elinor sank down trembling on one of the chairs. 'The poor man bled dreadfully. I fear he may die.'

'What man? What accident? Was Mr Walcott's carriage involved?'

'No, no. It was the musicians' wagon. We came upon it lying in the ditch, and stopped to help. The harpist said we couldn't come here, but Dominic offered to take the tenor part in the madrigals, and Mr Walcott is to be dresser.' Tears began to course down Elinor's face. 'Such humiliation! They are to be paraded with a bunch of wayside mummers!'

'Gammon,' said Kate roundly. 'No one can make them do anything they don't choose.'

'That man can,' wailed Elinor. 'He agreed to bring us past the gates, on condition that Dominic and Mr Walcott take part in his miserable concert.'

'Who, pray, is this tyrant?'

'The chief of the minstrel band. He is the rudest creature I ever encountered. He called Dominic a cockalorum, and Mr Walcott a m-macaroni!'

'No, did he?' said Kate, entranced. 'What happened next?'

'Mr Walcott wished to fell him to the ground,' Elinor said. She fished for a handkerchief and dabbed her eyes. 'But Dominic prevented him, which was a great shame, for I'd dearly have loved to see that man given a sound drubbing.'

Kate laughed. 'Lord, I wish I could have been there.'

Her laughter proved the last straw for Elinor's strained nerves. 'It is no laughing matter, Kate. A man has been grievously injured, to say nothing of the anguish of mind you have caused to me and our friends. They would never have been subjected to it, had they not come to rescue you!'

135

'I don't need rescuing,' said Kate reasonably. 'I am indeed sorry that you have been so worried, but to tell you the truth I am enjoying myself excessively, and unless I mistake, this venture will prove very profitable.'

'How can it profit anyone to be trapped in this ruin with a bunch of lunatics? What is more, if it becomes known that we have passed a night here with two unmarried gentlemen, our reputations will be ruined past recall!'

'Fustian,' said Kate. 'Who could cavil at our spending the night in an Abbey, surrounded by dozens of perfectly respectable folk?'

Luckily, the dispute was cut short by a tap on the door. Opening it, Kate saw that the elderly maid was back with more towels and hot water and accompanied by two other women, one with a tray of food and the other bearing on her outstretched arms what looked like church vestments. These last, when spread out on a cot, proved to be gowns of archaic style; one of white silk trimmed with crystal beads, the other green, embroidered at cuffs and hem with designs of birds and flowers.

These tributes delivered, the women withdrew. Kate moved to inspect the garments on the bed. She lifted the green gown for Nell to see.

'Fit for a queen,' she said. 'You'll take the shine out of us all tonight!'

Elinor shook her head. 'It is not at all modish,' she declared. 'I should feel a figure of fun in something so outlandish.'

However, when she had washed, and eaten a little bread and butter and an apple, she consented to try the green robe, and admitted that it became her well enough. She demanded to hear about Kate's meeting with Dame Celia, and at the end said that while she couldn't approve of that lady's high-handed treatment of strangers, she seemed to show a proper concern for the well-being of her people.

'I hope she will fetch a doctor to the man who was hurt,' she added, 'for one thing is sure, that swagbelly Nairn cares nothing for his welfare.'

136

Kate paused in the act of pinning up her hair.

'What name did you say?'

'Nairn,' answered Elinor. 'The leader of the troupe, who treated us so rudely. He claimed, if you please, to be Hereditary Minstrel to the Sickert family! From the way he spoke, one might have thought it conferred some kind of nobility on him.'

'So it does,' said Kate softly. 'The nobility of the bard, who is welcomed in kings' palaces, and goes into battle armed only with his music and his courage.' Her eyes sparkled. 'Oh, Nell, at long last I've been granted guidance in my search!'

'Guidance? Whatever can you mean? How could such a lout guide you to anything?'

'His name is Nairn,' Kate answered. 'Don't you see? It was the poet Nairn who first set down "The Song of Edina", that described the siege of Melburn and the Danish Gold.'

The rehearsal for the concert was held in the chapel that stood between the tower and the cloisters. Nairn quickly showed himself to be a slave-driver of the worst sort, describing the efforts of the group in general, and Lord Barr in particular, in vitriolic terms.

Mr Walcott, meanwhile, unpacked the contents of two large baskets of clothes, and examined them with a jaundiced eye. Many of the costumes were soiled, and all were sadly crumpled. He visited the Abbey's laundry, and bribed a rabbit-faced wench into putting them in better shape.

He then found a bench in the cloisters, sat down on it, and lit a cigarillo. Its pungent fumes did much to restore his frame of mind. He noted that the storm was veering eastwards, and the rain steadily diminishing. With luck, the roads would be passable by morning.

He was joined in due course by an aged wolfhound, who fixed him with a mournful and contemplative stare. Mr Walcott extended a hand. The hound advanced, sniffed, sighed, and faintly wagged his tail. Mr Walcott reached for the sensitive spot behind a leaning ear, and scratched it. The hound groaned appreciatively, flopped down on the flagstones, and fell asleep.

Some time later the laundry wench, staggering back with an armful of costumes, stared in amazement.

'Masser,' she said in awe, 'you niver tetched owld Festus?'

'He seemed to invite it,' said Mr Walcott, and in affirmation Festus thumped his tail.

'Well,' marvelled the wench, 'if that doan't beat arl. Last 'un as took the liberty nigh lost 'is right 'and! Where will I put the duds?'

Mr Walcott stood up. 'We'll hang them over the backs of the pews,' he said. He pitched the stump of his cigarillo into the mud of the courtyard, relieved the girl of part of her burden, and led the way to the chapel. The wolfhound, sighing gustily, staggered to its feet and followed.

XIII

At six o'clock, the seneschal conducted Kate and Elinor to the banqueting hall which had been splendidly decked with greenery and swags of bunting. The high table was set with plates and goblets of polished silver, the lower tables with pewter vessels. Tapers burned in the side sconces and chandeliers, and in their flickering light the figures in the tapestries seemed to bend and shift as if alive.

Servants were already moving in from the kitchen regions, with platters of roast meats and vegetables, bread and pastries, tarts, jellies and great round cheeses. In one corner of the hall, aproned tapmen presided over promising barrels of ale.

Dame Celia had taken up her place near the main door. She wore a gown similar in design to Kate's and Elinor's, but more splendid. Its scarlet silk was embroidered with threads of gold. A gold torque was fastened about her neck, and ropes of pearls were plaited into her hair. So magnificent was her appearance that Kate stood spellbound, almost forgetting to make her curtsy.

Dame Celia greeted them kindly, saying to Elinor, 'I must thank you, Mrs Crane, for helping poor Hodge.'

'It was nothing, ma'am. How does he do?'

'Well, I thank you. He's demanding brandy, which we'll not give him. He has a deep wound, but there's no damage to his thick skull.' She lifted a hand to summon de Morford.

'Let the revels begin,' she said. 'Come, ladies, it's time to take our places.'

She moved to the dais, motioning Elinor to sit at her right hand and Kate at her left. The seneschal raised his staff and struck the floor three times. In answer came the sound of flutes and drums, and the jingling of silver bells.

The music grew louder, and added to it were the stamp of feet and voices chanting a simple, repetitive tune. A procession swung into sight and advanced up the hall; first a group of young girls, clad all in white and wearing garlands on their heads; next the young men, red-faced and shining in white shirts and breeches, carrying small sticks trimmed with ribbons and bells; and last of all, the elders of the community, dressed in sombre black, as if for church.

The procession passed slowly by the dais in salute, then retreated to fill the benches round the table. When all were seated, the seneschal rapped again with his staff, and six children came two by two through the door, their scrubbed faces solemn, their lips moving as they marked the figures of their dance. They stopped facing the dais, and each laid a posy at its base. Then they too retreated to take their places on the benches.

Scanning the audience, Kate saw that Sedley, Jem and the Walcotts' coachman were present, but of Lord Barr and Mr Walcott there was no sign.

The music ceased abruptly. Dame Celia rose to her feet, and raised both arms high.

'People of the Abbey,' she cried, 'you are welcome! May God bless you, and send you long life and happiness.'

'Amen' went up the chorus of many voices, and without more delay the feast began. Plates were filled, tankards foamed, and in a short while the hall rang with talk and laughter.

Kate indicated the posies at the foot of the dais. 'A charming tribute,' she said.

Dame Celia gave her an enigmatic glance. 'Charming, yes, but it's not meant for me, you know.'

'For whom, then?'

'Dear knows,' returned the old lady. 'The song they sang, the customs they enact tonight, existed long before our Saviour was born. Before the gods of the Romans and Greeks. Our distant ancestors worshipped Cernunnos of the Animals, Condatis of the Waters, Naponus the god of fun and music, and the Three Grim Goddesses, too. When the Romans came, they took those Old Ones into their pantheon. The Christians in turn adopted the ancient sacred days, and made them sacred to our Lord.

'Our faith is old, Miss Safford, but the land is older. Before this tithe-barn was built, an Abbey stood here, and before the Abbey there was a Roman villa with its temple, and before that there were other shrines in which folk put their trust. We islanders are not pure-bred. As our blood is the blood of many nations, so our thoughts and prayers are compounded of many philosophies, many religions. No man can know with certainty who are his ancestors. We are no more than the driftwood of history.'

The servants brought food and wine to the high table, and Kate, who had tasted little since breakfast, ate with a will. Dame Celia conversed on many topics, and was eager for news of the outside world.

When the flow of questions ended, Kate said, 'You promised, ma'am, to tell us the story of your kinsman, St Patrick.'

'So I did, so I did.' Amusement gleamed in Dame Celia's eyes. 'It may surprise you to know that Patricius Magonus Sucat, the patron saint of Ireland, was not Irish at all. He was of Romano-British stock, born on the banks of the Severn.

'When he was sixteen, he was captured by Irish raiders and sold into slavery in Ireland. For six years he toiled as a shepherd, and during that time he turned to the Lord. One night he was warned in a dream that he must make his escape, and that a ship awaited him at Wicklow. He reached the port, and found passage on the boat, in return for which favour he took charge of a leash of wolfhounds.'

Kate eyed the two massive dogs couched near the fireplace. 'Ancestors of those, perhaps.'

'Perhaps. From Britain, Patrick made his way to Arles, and possibly to Rome. He entered a monastery on the Isle of Levins, near Cannes, and studied at Auxerre under St Germanus, returning at last to Ireland as a bishop of the Church.'

Elinor, who had consumed several goblets of wine, said suddenly, 'He drove out the snakes.'

Dame Celia smiled. 'The snakes are legend, my dear, not fact.'

'And the Sucat Cross?' Kate's tone was challenging. 'Is that legend, or fact?'

Dame Celia met her gaze. 'Humphrey Dymoke calls it legend. I believe it to be fact. I hope you will prove me right.' She raised her goblet in a half-mocking salute, and drained it.

A diversion occurred at that moment, in the form of Mr Walcott, who appeared at the main door leading a pantomime horse and accompanied by the wolfhound, Festus. The horse, whose canvas sides were adorned with large red spots, unwisely aimed a kick at Mr Walcott, and Festus, with a ferocious growl, sank his teeth into the horse's leg. It took the united efforts of Mr Walcott and the seneschal, as well as a large beef bone, to persuade the hound to loose his grip, but at last the dog disappeared to the yard with his trophy. The horse, to the accompaniment of cheers and guffaws, began a series of clowning tricks, curtsied to Dame Celia, kissed a pretty girl, and made a determined effort to carry away a barrel of ale.

Dame Celia beckoned Mr Walcott to the high table.

'Welcome to Midsomer Abbey, sir. I see you've found favour with old Festus. No mean compliment, I assure you. He's finicky in his choice of friends.'

Thankful to be back in the world of politesse, Mr Walcott executed a graceful bow and thanked Dame Celia for her hospitality. She greeted the remark with a derisive smile.

'Evidently Nairn has made you earn your keep. His arrogance is insufferable. I tolerate him only for his music.'

'I count myself lucky to have escaped playing the hind half of that horse,' said George with feeling. He took his place next to

Elinor, accepted a stoop of ale from a steward, and raised it with a smile.

'Your very good health, Mrs Crane. How goes it with you?'

She shook her head. 'I can't be easy in these odd circumstances. I'm too strait-laced to enjoy what's strange, and I feel a frump in this gown.'

'No need for that. A trifle out of style, I grant you, but the effect is most becoming.' His face creased in a grin. 'If you feel a frump, do but wait until you see Nick Barr.'

The banquet ended with the concert – lute, flute and fiddle, and finally the madrigals. Though under-rehearsed, these went with enough of a swing to draw warm applause from the diners, and a well-filled purse from Dame Celia.

The main body of the audience then dispersed, leaving only Dame Celia, the Bath party, and the minstrel Nairn in the hall. Dame Celia and Nairn fell into a discussion of plainsong, Elinor and George moved away to examine the tapestries, and Kate and Dominic sat together near the dying fire.

The costume that had so amused George Walcott – a red silk cope embroidered with a sprawling gold dragon – seemed to embarrass him not at all. He lounged with legs outstretched, and dreamily sipped his wine.

Watching him, Kate thought how greatly the past few weeks had changed him. His careless arrogance was gone. He looked older, more vulnerable. Unwilling to break in on his thoughts, she sat quiet, her hands in her lap. Presently he glanced up, and she smiled at him.

'You sang well tonight.'

He gave a grunt of laughter. 'I wish you would convince Nairn of that. "Niffy-naffy warbler" was his kindest comment.'

'Thank you for coming to my rescue.'

He regarded her lazily. 'Did you need rescuing?'

'No, but I appreciate the thought.'

He glanced about him. 'I wouldn't have missed this for worlds. It's not every day one has the chance to travel back in time. I imagine life hasn't altered here for centuries.'

'Dame Celia aims to protect her people from those who would exploit them.'

Dominic shrugged. 'A losing battle, I'm afraid. The age of the beneficent despot is over. When the old lady goes, her little kingdom will go with her. Her people will leave for Bath, or Bristol, or the factories in the North.' He paused, then said abruptly, 'Did you speak to her of the Danish gold?'

'Yes. She said she had little knowledge of it. I think her interest is fixed on earlier times. She told me about the Sucat Cross, which St Patrick, her kinsman, dropped on the Severn shore when he was kidnapped by pirates.'

Dominic stared. 'She claims kinship with a saint?'

'Distant kinship.' Kate told him of her conversation with Dame Celia, saying at the end, 'She told me not to rely on reason, but on faith. I am to expect miracles.'

'A tall order.'

Kate frowned at the glowing logs on the hearth. 'In this place, anything seems possible. If Dame Celia can spend a lifetime seeking her cross, then surely I can spend a few more weeks looking for mine.'

'What will you do next? I don't wish you to run any more risks, Kate.'

'No risks. I plan to visit Father Francis Tuckitt of Wells.'

Before he could query that, they were joined by Elinor and George, and then by Dame Celia. Nairn remained apart, brooding on the chimney bench, and after a while Kate went to sit beside him.

She complimented him on the success of his concert, and was answered by an irritable roll of the shoulders. Abandoning flattery, she said bluntly, 'Your name is Nairn, is it not?'

'It is.'

'Do you know "The Song of Edina"?'

Nairn cackled. 'Know it? My forebears wrote it. Handed it down, generation to generation.' He eyed Kate sideways. 'What's it to you, I'd like to know?'

'I intend to find the Danish gold.'

'Do you now? And what put that crazy notion into your head?'

'It was my father's dying wish.'

Nairn yawned. 'Dead men's wishes, food for fishes.'

'Don't you believe there was a treasure?'

'If there was, the Danskers took it long since.'

'Dame Celia says one must have faith.'

He snorted. 'I've faith in this, and this.' He touched his fingers to his harp and his throat.

'Will you sing "The Song of Edina" for me?'

'No, I will not.'

'I'd pay you a fair fee.'

'Then you'd waste your money, for the song's in Welsh, and not a word would you understand.'

'I see.' Kate thought a moment, then said, 'Tell me, if you will. In your version of the Song . . .'

'My version? *My* version?' Nairn's little black eyes snapped dangerously. 'I told you, it's our Song. *Ours*. All the rest are shoddy imitations.'

'Very well. Does your Song give a description of St Dunstan's Cross?'

'No, it does not.' As Kate's face fell, Nairn smiled with undisguised malice. 'Poor lady, you've been taken in by imitations, have you not?'

'I'd have thought the cross would figure in some detail. Edina was a devout Christian.'

'Oh, the cross figures, sure enough.' Nairn got to his feet, and slung his harp across his back. 'The cross figures, but not St Dunstan's Cross. It was not St Dunstan's Cross that was sent to Twyford Lindum, but St Patrick's Cross, the Sucat Cross.' And with the swagger of a man who recognizes a good exit line, Nairn sketched Kate a mocking bow, and sauntered from the hall.

Kate found it hard to fall asleep that night. Conflicting ideas

145

crowded her mind, and the more she struggled to bring them into order, the more confused she became.

Her father had directed her to trust the old legends. Dymoke said they were not to be taken seriously. Dame Celia first told her that the Danish gold must long since have been removed from its hiding-place, then urged her to search for it at Twyford. The minstrel Nairn scoffed at history, maintaining it was the Cross of St Patrick, not of St Dunstan, that had formed part of the treasure hoard.

Every answer she received seemed to give rise to fresh questions. The more she delved, the deeper the mystery was buried. Logic bade her abandon a wild goose chase, yet she knew she could not. The search she had begun almost light-heartedly had become all-important to her. She would pursue it to its end.

She fell asleep in the small hours, and was awakened what seemed moments later by the sounds of the household going about its tasks. She dressed quietly so as not to disturb Elinor, and strolled along to the tower entrance. To her surprise, the heavy doors stood open, and stepping through them she crossed the drawbridge and surveyed the scene about her.

The whole landscape was dotted with toiling figures. Cowmen and shepherd boys led the beasts to pasture, men with scythes and bill-hooks worked in the fields and along the hedgerows, and on the fringe of the woods a team of foresters was dismembering an elm that had been blown down in the storm.

Moving away along the river road was a wagon with a torn tilt; the one, she supposed, that had capsized the day before. She would have no further chance to talk to Nairn. She turned back towards the building and saw Dominic standing in the gateway. He greeted her cheerfully.

'Good morning, Kate. You're up betimes.'

'Not as early as that wretch Nairn, it seems.'

'Yes, he knocked on my door at first light, demanding that I help him raise his wagon from the ditch. I told him that was no part of our contract.'

'He's an insolent bully,' said Kate. 'I dislike him intensely. He's overset all my theories.'

'Has he? How?'

'He insists it was St Patrick's Cross that went to Twyford, not St Dunstan's. When I dared to question his opinion, he flew into a rage and told me he's descended from the Nairn who wrote Edina's Song, that his version is gospel, and all the others are worthless imitations.'

'Nairn's malicious, you know. Perhaps he lied to tease you.'

'I don't think so. He wouldn't lie about the Song; he regards it as a sacred trust. The rub is, if his version is right, then the legend we know, and accredited history as well, are indeed worthless. I no longer know what to believe.'

Dominic eyed her curiously. When first she had told him of her madcap scheme, he'd given it his consent without much thought, seeing it as the passing whim of a romantic girl. Now he saw his mistake. Kate was neither whimsical nor romantic. She had set about her unpromising task in a practical manner, and pursued it with a good deal of resolution. He owed her the truth.

Offering her his arm, he led her back through the archway.

'Kate, my dear, it's only fair to warn you. By the time your tangled skein is unravelled, Melburn may have a new owner.'

She glanced at him quickly. 'You've decided to sell?'

'The choice is not mine. It rests with Horace Pickford, who holds the mortgage. He's been kind enough to allow me time, but Shipton thinks, and I agree with him, that foreclosure must come soon.'

'How soon?'

'A few weeks.'

'Then we must use those weeks,' Kate said earnestly. 'Don't despair yet, Nick. Even if Melburn changes hands, I believe that treasure-trove belongs to the finder, and not to the owner of the land.' She frowned. 'It's a point I must clear with my lawyer.'

He shook his head, between amusement and impatience. 'If you're determined to waste your time . . .'

147

'It's not wasted; I know it's not. I feel that every day brings me closer to the truth.'

'The end of the rainbow exists only in fairy-tales. We have to live in the real world.'

'At least allow me those weeks,' she pleaded. 'If by the end of them I've found nothing, I'll admit defeat. I'll not trouble you further, I promise.'

Her eagerness warmed him, and he laughed. 'You have your weeks. Dig up the whole estate, if you wish. The new owner can repair the ravages, Devil take him.'

Back in her room, Kate found Elinor up, dressed, and full of praise for their hostess.

'So kind and courteous,' she said. 'No effort spared to make us comfortable. My dress washed and ironed, not a stain on it. Dame Celia sent word that breakfast will be ready for us in the hall at nine o'clock, and that after that, she will be in her library, should you wish to see her.'

They ate lavishly of cold meats, baked eggs and grilled kidneys, and bread hot from the oven. When they were done, George and Elinor went off to speak to their respective coachmen about the return to Bath, and Kate and Dominic went in search of Dame Celia.

The room she chose to call her library was as unusual as its owner. The north wall was of ancient brick, buttressed at each end by a sturdy stone pillar, and pierced by three tall windows. The south and west walls were windowless, every inch of them being lined with shelves of books or scrolls. Half-way along the eastern wall was a wide recess which might once have been a lady chapel. It contained a long table and several chairs, evidently for the use of readers.

What struck Kate most forcibly was the floor of the room. It was a mosaic of many-coloured marble chips, and depicted a young man of barbaric aspect, clad only in a leather kilt, his wild hair tumbling about his naked shoulders, his throat encircled by a torque of twisted gold.

'Naponus,' explained Dame Celia. 'He was the Celtic god of fun and music. Beautiful, is he not?'

'Extremely handsome,' agreed Kate, 'though I find it odd that a pagan god should have been tolerated in a Christian abbey.'

Dame Celia chuckled. 'Perhaps the good monks felt it wiser to humour his followers, rather than offend them by tearing up the floor. More likely, they feared to disturb the hypocaust. Its pipes run under the mosaic, you see. In Roman times they carried warm air from the bath-house to the corn store, which lies just beyond the north wall. When the Saxons came, they destroyed most of the Roman mansion, but those two pillars and the floor survived their attentions.

'The Benedictines covered Naponus with boards for decency's sake, and made this their library. The Danes burned the Abbey, and the Normans rebuilt it. The Plantagenets added the rose window in the hall, which escaped the havoc wrought by Henry VIII's vandals.'

'And your kinsmen? The Sickerts?' asked Dominic.

'We held to our land. Ludovic Sickert built the tithe barn in the seventeenth century. My grandfather restored all the buildings in 1701, and during that process unearthed the Naponus mosaic.'

'It's masterly work,' Dominic said. 'A pity no more of the Roman house remains.'

'But it does,' corrected Dame Celia, and beckoned them to follow her into the recess.

'These walls are Romano-British,' she said, 'and there is the mark of my ancestors.' Carved in the worn stone was a cross of Celtic design. Its arms were decorated with formal patterns, and at the foot of the cross, so eroded by time that it was barely discernible, was the likeness of a small bird.

'The Sucat Cross,' Kate breathed, and Dame Celia nodded.

'When St Patrick's Cross was sent to Glastonbury for safekeeping, the Sickert of the day ordered his mason to carve its likeness on this wall. Soon after, raiders came and destroyed the house, but this wall, like Naponus, survived the fire, as it has survived all other attempts to destroy it.'

'And the bird? Is it the dove of peace?'

'Nothing so uplifting, my dear. It's a wren. In the Celtic tongue, the word meant 'chief'. Apparently the mason considered himself without equal in his field, and signed his efforts with that emblem.'

Kate stretched out a hand to touch the carving. 'So many centuries. It's a miracle!'

'It has the protection of the saint,' Dame Celia said.

Kate sighed. 'It will take St Jude to work my miracle! There is so little time.'

Dame Celia's sharp gaze switched to Dominic. 'So you are to sell Melburn?'

Dominic frowned. 'Of necessity, madam, not by choice.'

'Cynric Cerdinga fought to the death for it,' Dame Celia said. 'Earl Godwin betrayed his nation to gain possession of it, and you will let it go to the highest bidder?'

'Yes, rather than see it fall to rack and ruin.'

Dame Celia waved a derisive hand. 'Fine words, my lord, but they cut no ice with me. You must find a way to hold what's yours.' She beckoned Kate to her side. 'Yesterday, girl, I told you there was little chance of finding the Danish gold, but I'll give you this piece of advice. Study the names. Wherever you go in this land of ours, you'll find history enshrined in the names of the towns, the rivers, the people.

'Twyford is the place of two fords; Lindum means a marsh. Melburn is the mill stream. There must have been a mill in Cynric's day, since the name existed then. You are a Safford, which derives from Sallowford, the ford beside the willow trees. As for Barr . . . a barr is a gateway, in the Saxon tongue.'

She gave Dominic a challenging look. 'At the moment the gateway is closed, through wrong thinking or vain pride or lack of faith, but it can be opened again, if the will exists.' She placed a hand on Kate's shoulder. 'Where do you go from here, child?'

150

'Back to Bath, ma'am, and then to Wells to meet with Father Francis Tuckitt.'

'A fine scholar. I hope he may help you. And then?'

'To Twyford Lindum, to begin digging.'

'You have men qualified to do such work?'

'Oh, yes. My father trained them.'

'Then it only remains to wish you success. May the saints bless your endeavour.'

She walked with them to the courtyard, where their carriages stood waiting. She received the thanks of her guests with a smile, shook hands with Elinor and Mr Walcott, and enveloped Kate in a warm embrace. Her last words were for Dominic.

'Remember what I say, Barr of Melburn. Hold to what is yours, by every means in your power.'

XIV

It was comfortable to exchange the archaic splendours of Midsomer Abbey for the homely routine of Queen's Square. It was also, Kate found, somewhat dull, though the dullness was relieved on Monday when a groom rode over from Corsham with a letter from Mrs Beacher.

Anna is recuperating fast, and I thank God suffers no complications after the delivery. The baby thrives, and a wet-nurse has been found. Tom's leg is mending, tho' he's impatient of being confined to his room, and summons the factor a dozen times a day to instruct him in matters with which he is perfectly conversant.

Cousin Agnes remains a sore trial. Her disposition is not sanguine, and I have had to forbid her to visit Anna, as she persists in recounting mournful tales of the plight of babies born before term. She is addicted to strong spirits, and I have warned Badger to guard the keys of the liquor-store; but she is extremely sly, and procures stores which she conceals in out-of-the-way places about the house. Yesterday I discovered a quartern of gin hidden in the linen cupboard. So bad for the morale of the servants!

I cannot abandon the Durrants to her care, but I fancy I've found the solution. Old Nanny Adkin has agreed to return. She will see that things run smoothly, and that the children behave. They are a trifle above themselves, due to all the disruptions of late.

All things considered, your uncle and I should be free to come home at the end of the week. I look forward to seeing you very soon, my dears.

PS The baby is to be named Beatrice, which means 'she who brings joy'.

'Poor Aunt and Uncle,' said Elinor. 'They must be at their wits' end, having to cope with so many problems.'

Kate laughed. 'I think they must be in their element: Aunt is never happier than when she's in the bosom of her family, setting them all to rights. As for Uncle, by now he will have introduced a new system of accounting in Tom's estate office, and dragooned the gardener into using his improved method of preparing compost. I daresay they'll return very well satisfied with themselves.'

Later that day they received a visit from Mr Walcott, who brought them an invitation to dine the following night with his parents at Solsbury Hill.

'Mama bade me apologize for the shortness of the notice,' he said, 'but when she learned you were off to Twyford next week, nothin' would do but she must arrange an impromptu gatherin' in your honour. Nothin' elaborate, you know. Just ourselves and Nick Barr, and our neighbours, Lucy and Jack Wyndham. Jack was at school with Hugh Crane and me, so we can talk of old times.' He looked anxiously at Elinor. 'Mama sincerely hopes you will find it possible to accept.'

'*George* sincerely hopes you will accept,' Kate said, when Mr Walcott had taken his leave. 'And his mama is resolved to see for herself what sort of female has taken her son in tow!'

'Nothing of the sort,' exclaimed Elinor, much shocked. 'Why, I have only been acquainted with Mr Walcott for three weeks!'

'What has that to say to anything? The man's head over ears in love with you – and I fancy you're not entirely indifferent to him, are you?'

'He is all that's kind and amiable,' replied Elinor, putting on a prim face, 'but it's far too early to be talking of love.'

Despite this, it became apparent to everyone that she set great store by the projected visit. She summoned Mrs Beacher's *coif-*

feuse to cut her hair in the new, shorter style; treated her face with applications of cucumber and crushed strawberries; and spent hours trying on first one gown and then another. One was rejected as being too sombre, another as being cut too low on the bosom, and a third as giving her the appearance of a cottage loaf. At last Kate felt compelled to protest.

'Dearest Nell, don't take on so! Mr Walcott will think you delightful, even in a gunny sack!'

'It's not him I must please,' cried Elinor, abandoning all pretence, 'it's his mama! I'm sure she has already taken me in dislike! At Lady Lynam's she stared at me as if I was something out of a freak-show, and at Mr Dymoke's lecture she barely addressed one word to me. She has such high aspirations for George; she will never countenance his marrying a female who's past her first youth, and a widow to boot!'

'Fiddle!' said Kate. 'At twenty-nine you are hardly one foot in the grave, and as for your being a widow, Mrs Walcott may dislike it, but the Colonel won't forget that your husband died fighting for his country. If she tries to spike your wheels, she'll find herself at odds with both husband and son, for neither of them is the sort to submit to petticoat government.'

'What if she hears of our excursion to Midsomer? She'll take me for a harpy, scheming to entrap George.'

This image of her decorous cousin as a scarlet woman came close to reducing Kate to giggles, but she said bracingly:

'She won't hear of it, Nell. Our own servants value their positions too much to gossip, and the folk at Midsomer are too far from the beaten track to spread tales about us.'

On Tuesday evening, they set out for Solsbury Hill at five, as the Walcotts kept country hours and dined at 6.30.

Elinor wore a gown of dove-coloured gauze over rose satin, which admirably set off her fine complexion. Her hair fell in soft curls at each side of her face; she wore no jewels but a string of pearls, and insisted on retaining her fine lace cap. She carried a shawl of silver tissue, and a beaded purse.

155

Kate's gown was of amethyst silk, the hem quilted to give it the new wide line, the bodice delicately ruched at the shoulders. Diamond earrings and a fine Madeira shawl completed an ensemble she felt to be modish, yet modest enough to satisfy Mrs Walcott's critical eye.

The evening passed surprisingly well. The Colonel and George welcomed Kate and Elinor with the utmost affability, and if Mrs Walcott's manner was less cordial, the presence of the Wyndhams obliged her to present a smiling face.

True, when dinner was over she contrived to separate Elinor from the other guests, and questioned her closely on her antecedents, her first marriage, and her opinions on every subject from popery to parenthood; but Elinor endured the catechism with patience until she was rescued by George, who bore her off to talk to Lucy Wyndham.

Kate joined her host and Lord Barr in a stroll along the terrace. The old man begged her permission to light up a pipe.

'Caught the habit in my army days,' he explained. 'M' wife can't abide the smell of tobacco, so I resort to blowin' a cloud out of doors.'

Kate prompted him to talk about the Peninsular War, on which subject he held unorthodox views. 'Boney could have been rolled up in half the time,' he declared, 'if only the High Command had seen fit to abandon their Gothic notions.

'A modern army needs more than gunpowder and guts, saving your presence, Miss Safford. It must have machines that are superior to those of the enemy, and men who know how to use 'em. It must be able to bring its battalions across flooded rivers and waterless deserts, and over mountain passes in the depths of winter. Wellington and his staff looked down their noses at officers from our Indian regiments, but I say we can learn a lot from those fellows. They've developed skills and tactics that aren't taught at any military academy.'

Kate regarded him with interest. 'Was Cnut the Dane a good tactician, sir?'

The Colonel chuckled. ' 'Fraid I can't say, m'dear. Bit before my time, he was. Why d'ye ask?'

'I was thinking of the siege of Melburn,' she answered. 'I wonder if the Danes found a way to divert the waters of the Rem, to beat Cynric's defenders by thirst?'

The Colonel pursed his lips. 'It's possible, of course, though much would depend on the force of the river's flow. It's easy to dam a sluggish stream, but a spate the size of the Rem is another matter. Very effective trick, if they could bring it off. It takes months to starve a garrison into submission, but cut off their water supply and you'll see the white flag hoisted within days. Men can't fight without water – especially wounded men.'

When they returned to the drawing-room, Dominic led Kate to a sofa near the window, and taking his place beside her, said, 'You think that's the explanation of the "dry river" in the legend?'

'It came to me when the Colonel spoke of crossing waterless deserts,' she said. 'I suppose it's far-fetched.'

'It seems logical to me. The Danes dammed the river, it ran dry, and Edina was able to cross it without using the bridge. The Colonel's right, though, about the force of the Rem. It runs swiftly, and its bed is deep. To block it would be difficult.'

'Could there have been two rivers at that time? Perhaps that's how Twyford came by its name. Two fords across two rivers. The main stream of the Rem ran by Sallowford, the ford of the willows, and a lesser stream ran past Cynric's stronghold. If we can show that to have been the case, we'll know where to search for the site of old Melburn.'

'There are a dozen rivulets that cross the Twyford valley,' Dominic replied. 'We've no way of knowing which one served Melburn.'

Kate sighed. 'It might not even exist today. Papa spoke sometimes of the Roman River, as if it were a thing of the past and not the Rem we know.' She pressed her hands to her temples. 'Once, when I was a child, I dropped a coin on Saunton Beach. I dug and dug for it, and turned up buttons, and shells, and an old bottle, but not my penny. It's the same with this search. The more I dig, the more I turn up, and none of it is what I seek. Perhaps Father Tuckitt will help me to put my thoughts in order.'

'When do you mean to visit him?'

'On Thursday.'

Dominic hesitated, then said abruptly, 'Would you permit me to accompany you?'

She looked at him in surprise. 'Why, yes, I should like it of all things.'

'Good, then. What time will you set out?'

'Early. As soon after nine as may be possible.'

'I'll join you at nine. I promise to be prompt.' He took her hand and raised it briefly to his lips, as if to seal a bargain. ' 'Till Thursday,' he said.

A short while later, the tea tray was brought in, and at eleven o'clock the carriages were brought round, and the guests took their leave. The Colonel and George went out to bid them good-night, and Dominic was left alone with Mrs Walcott. She beckoned him to sit beside her.

'You are George's friend and confidant,' she said bluntly. 'Tell me, does he mean to marry Mrs Crane?'

'I have no idea, ma'am.'

'It's plain he's in love with her.' As Dominic made no answer, she said, 'You think I should not speak so? I have had experience of hasty marriages. My mother died when I was five, and my father took a second wife. It was a bad decision, for him and for his children. We suffered. It has made me determined to do what I might to keep my children from making bad matches. Can you blame me for that?'

'No, but it is something you should discuss with George, not me.'

'Tell me, at least, do you like Mrs Crane?'

'I'm not well acquainted with her, but I find her pleasant and kind. I believe she's well liked in Twyford. Kate Safford is very fond of her.'

'And her opinion commands respect. Miss Safford is a young

woman of sense. Pretty, too, and with her share of the world's goods. I understand Mrs Beacher means to take her to London next year. No doubt she will enjoy great success there.'

'No doubt,' said Dominic stiffly.

Mrs Walcott fixed him with a bright stare. 'George hoped that *you* might marry Miss Safford. It would be a commendable match, from every point of view.'

'It would be said that I married her for her money, to save Melburn.'

'Even if that were true, which I know it is not, no one would think the worse of you. We live in a hard world, and must make hard decisions.'

Dominic remained silent. He could not explain that it was not the world's opinion he cared for, but Kate's.

In childhood he had looked on her as part companion, part nuisance; a devoted slave who could be relied upon not to blab a secret, and who made no complaint when she was excluded from purely male excursions with gun or rod.

When his mother absconded with Lord Savernake, and the hideous scandal of the divorce burst about his fourteen-year-old ears, he resolved to spend as much time as he could away from Melburn, and found plenty of school and university friends who were happy to include him in their holiday plans. At the age of twenty-one he removed to London, where his sporting prowess, his easy manner and his apparently ample purse quickly made him a favourite, both with the bucks of the Town and with society hostesses.

If he remembered Kate at all, it was as a thin little snip of a child with a tangle of beech-brown hair. Later people began to speak of her as the girl his brother John was like to marry. He imagined Miss Safford must have grown up meek-mannered, malleable, and dull.

Over the past few weeks, he had found this image to be very wide of the mark. Kate was possessed of a strong will, independent views, and a lively imagination. She was brave, honest, and loyal to her friends. She was pursuing this cursed Danish treasure not for her own gain, but to save Melburn, and on that score alone he stood in her debt.

But that was not all. He was discovering in Kate a delightful companion, with a sense of humour that matched his own. More than once, when something particularly amused him, he had found himself seeking her eye, to share the joke. Tonight, when she had come into the room in her elegant gown, her face alight with friendliness and interest, he had felt a pleasure he hadn't thought possible at this point in his life.

The cynical survivor of many desperate flirtations and not a few passionate liaisons, he had believed himself immune to love. Kate had proved him wrong. When she turned and smiled at him across the room, it had taken a conscious effort of will to prevent him from going at once to her side. Just watching her filled him with a dizzying happiness.

Oddly enough, it was Mrs Walcott's well-meant words that had brought him back to earth.

Kate Safford was the girl he desired above all others, the one girl he wished to marry, and the one girl he could not pursue. He could not ask her to share his penury, and he could not – *would* not – agree to live on her income. There could be no surer way to sour a relationship – he had seen it happen all too often – than when a man married for money.

Given time, he might re-establish himself and be in a position to offer her the home and the social position she deserved; but that would take years, not weeks or months. Meanwhile, she would make her come-out in London, where her pretty face, her charm and her great fortune would not be missed by the pack of hopefuls on the hunt for a wife. If she did not return to Twyford betrothed, it would be nothing short of a miracle.

'I must put her out of my mind,' thought Dominic miserably. 'I should never have offered to go with her to Wells.' The memory of how pleased she had seemed with the offer did nothing to ease his conscience.

160

'On Friday,' he decided, 'I shall go back to Twyford, and from there I'll go to London to consult with Pickford. Once Melburn is handed over, I'll go abroad, to Russia or the Antipodes or some other godforsaken place. Kate will marry, and forget all about me, and the Danish gold, and that will be the end of it.'

It was a commendable decision, but one that took no account of the meddlesome ways of family, friends, foes and Fate.

XV

Arriving at the Beacher residence a little before nine on Thursday morning, Dominic found the Safford carriage already waiting at the flagway, with Sedley mounted on the box and Flite the groom loading cushions and a hamper into the interior.

He left his borrowed hack in the charge of Jem the stable-lad, and approached the front door, but before he could knock, it opened and Kate appeared. She was in high spirits.

'Good morning,' she said. 'How lucky we are in the weather! There were clouds on the hills when I woke, but they've all rolled away.'

She looked delightful, he thought, in a gown af jonquil-yellow muslin and a straw hat trimmed with matching ribbons. She carried a short jacket, a parasol, her reticule, and a large folder of papers.

'I've been making notes,' she explained, tossing all her possessions onto the seat of the carriage. 'I've so many questions to put to Father Francis, I scarcely know where to begin.'

'I hope he may be able to answer them,' Dominic said, and she nodded gravely.

'Yes. I know I mustn't raise my hopes too high, but Papa held Father Francis in the highest regard, said he was not merely scholarly, but wise, which is more than one can say of Mr Dymoke.'

'Poor Dymoke,' said Dominic, holding out his hand to assist her to climb into the coach. 'I see he'll be for ever in your black books.'

163

'I will forgive him,' answered Kate, settling herself and making way for him to take his place beside her, 'but only if we find the treasure. Then I shall be able to point out to him that he was wrong all along in his Winterborne theory.'

'Nothing like rubbing salt in a man's wounds,' agreed Dominic.

The carriage set out at a brisk pace. On reaching Radstock they were warned that the roads across the Mendip hills were in a poor state, so they held to the route through Frome and Shepton Mallet, and there turned west for Wells.

For the first part of the journey, Kate tried to explain to Dominic the contents of her dossier; but as this involved a great deal of cross-reference from one document to another, as well as scribbled notes, and random ideas, he soon threw up his hands in protest.

'Stop, Kate! My head's spinning!'

She smiled ruefully. 'I know. It sounds like gibberish, but I'm sure the truth is in there, somewhere. Perhaps Father Francis will find it for me.'

Dominic thought that unlikely, but he kept his doubts to himself.

They reachad Wells at noon, and were set down at Francis Tuckitt's door, Sedley and Flite taking the carriage on to The Bellwether Inn, where they would see to the horses and find their own refreshment.

The house was small, and stood so much in the shadow of the cathedral that Kate felt the air about it must always be aquiver with the clamour of bells.

A housekeeper in a neat black uniform opened the door to them and led them to a parlour that overlooked a lawn starred with crocuses, and a walnut tree in early leaf.

The old man who rose to greet them was tall and spare. His features were not handsome, seeming in some way to be larger than life, the forehead very high and bumpy, the nose long with a bulbous tip, the eyes huge under beetling brows. His thick silver-white hair was combed straight back to fall almost to his shoulders. He wore a cassock green with age, and the cord at his waist might have been filched from one of the sash windows.

His voice, though, was beautiful, rich and soft as fine old burgundy, and he possessed what Kate's father would have termed 'presence'; a magnetic quality that radiated from him like light from a lantern.

In her imaginings of this meeting, Kate had seen herself behaving in a brisk, no-nonsense manner. She would put her questions to Father Francis without roundaboutation, receive his answers, offer her thanks, and depart.

She found this was not Father Francis's way. He seemed to have all the time in the world at his disposal. He ushered his guests to comfortable seats, served them with sherry and sweet biscuits, settled himself in his wing chair, and entered benignly into what Kate thought was an irrelevant conversation with Dominic.

'I was never acquainted with your father,' he said, 'but I knew your grandfather. Before you were born, that was. He called me in to give my opinion about the Twyford Tump. The landowners on your eastern boundary wished to demolish it, and plough the land. Your grandfather quite rightly held that that would be sacrilege. It was not, of course, a Christian burial-ground, but graves of *any* kind are sacrosanct, don't you agree?'

'I remember Grandfather saying something about ancient graves that shouldn't be disturbed,' Dominic answered.

'Very ancient indeed,' nodded Father Francis. 'Those burial-mounds were there before the Celts came, or any of the more recent invaders.'

Kate seized on what she felt to be the salient point. 'In your view, then, sir, the Tump was never the site of Cynric's Melburn?'

'Never. Cynric may himself have been a convert to Christianity, but his forebears were pagans who worshipped Wotan and Thor. Even if he had wished to build on the Tump, the feelings of many of his followers would have forbidden it. Cynric built his fortress elsewhere – close at hand, perhaps, but not on the mound.'

'Can we find the site?' asked Kate, and the old man smiled at her gently.

'Not by wishful thinking, child. Accident may find it for you, or archaeology, which entails a good deal more than going out with a spade and digging holes at random. Our earth is like an onion – layer upon layer, civilization upon civilization, each over-laying the other. Before our cathedral was built, there was a Saxon chapel on the site, and I've no doubt that beneath that lie Roman remains of one kind or another. At Sherborne Abbey they have found tesserae from a Roman mosaic.'

'At Midsomer Abbey there's a whole Roman floor,' Kate said. 'Dame Celia showed it to us.'

'Ah, yes. The mosaic of Naponus. Very fine work, albeit an unlikely godling to grace a monastery. It proves my point, however. The very ancient may lie buried beneath the merely old. When primitive folk sought to build a house, they looked for three things; suitable ground, a supply of fresh water, and build-ing materials within easy reach. Once such a site was located, it was like to be used over and over again.'

'If that's the case,' said Dominic, 'why was the new Melburn not built on the site of the old?'

'Probably because one or other of the requirements I've mentioned ceased to exist,' replied the old man.

'The water,' said Kate excitedly. 'When the Danes besieged Cynric's Melburn, they diverted the water supply and it never returned. Mr Dymoke wrote to me only last week, advising me to explore the Roman canal cut—'

'Dymoke said that?' Father Francis shook his head in disbelief. 'He has always held that Melburn was in the Winterborne coun-try.'

'He said so, when I spoke to him at Weymouth, but in his letter he said as a historian he must consider every possibility.'

'A leopard may change its spots . . .' murmured Father Francis. He leaned back in his chair. 'Miss Safford, when your father urged you to make this search, he did so as a historian. He would have to find proof that Cynric's Melburn existed, to expose the site and find a few artefacts that would establish his theory as fact. He sought historic truth, but you want rather more, do you not?'

Kate blushed, but she held the old man's gaze. 'Yes. I want to find the gold so that Dominic – so that Lord Barr can claim the reward from the State, and not have to lose Melburn.'

'And if the treasure is found, my lord, is that the use you will make of it?'

'Yes,' said Dominic at once, but he added more slowly, 'I realize it won't be as simple as it sounds.'

'It won't be simple at all,' said Father Francis grimly. 'Any hint of buried treasure engenders enormous public excitement, not to say greed. All sorts of people will enter the fray – government officials, ministers of the Crown, antiquaries and private collectors, idle busybodies, and above all, the Church.'

'The Church?' Dominic looked puzzled, and Father Francis sighed.

'Surely you've not forgotten the source of the treasure? The histories of the time, and the legend you seek to authenticate, state that when Cnut the Dane began to ravage Britain, the custodians of the King's Treasury decreed that "much store of gold and holy vessels, including the Cross of Dunstan" be sent north for safekeeping. If that treasure *is* found, at Twyford or anywhere else, the Crown will lay claim to coinage and gold bullion, and the Church to the holy vessels and Dunstan's Cross.'

'Which church?' said Dominic, with a half-smile. 'The Church of Rome? Our Protestant establishment? The Benedictine Order?'

'You begin to see the nature of the problem,' said Father Francis. 'The treasure may prove to be a Pandora's box that will bring a host of gadflies to buzz about your ears. In my experience, the wheels of State turn even more slowly than the mills of God. Your share of the haul will come too late to save Melburn.'

Kate, who had been silent for a space, said suddenly, 'According to the minstrel Nairn, it was not the Cross of Dunstan but the Sucat Cross that was sent to Melburn.'

Father Francis blinked. 'I think you mistake, Miss Safford. Nairn's Song of Edina exists in several versions, and they all of them refer to Dunstan's Cross.'

'I don't mean the dead Nairn,' Kate said. 'I mean the Nairn who's alive and is minstrel now to Dame Celia. He claims descent from the Nairn who wrote Edina's Song, and swears it tells how the Sucat Cross was sent to Twyford. When I argued with him, he grew very angry and insisted his version was the true one.'

'Did he sing the Song to you?'

'No, because it's in the Welsh tongue, and I don't have Welsh, alas.'

'*I* do!' Father Francis's eyes were bright with interest. 'I would dearly love to hear this man's version of the tale. Sucat, eh? That is remarkable. Fascinating!'

'I wonder—' began Kate, and then paused, shy of venturing an opinion to so notable a scholar. Father Francis nodded encouragement, and she continued:

'I wonder if the Sucat Cross, which was St Patrick's, and the Cross of St Dunstan, which figures in most versions of the legend, could be one and the same? I know it would take a miracle to prove it . . .'

'I am in a profession that believes in miracles,' said Father Francis. He stretched out a hand to the small silver bell on the table at his side, and rang it briskly.

'We will discuss this further,' he said, 'over a light luncheon and a glass or two of wine.'

The dining-room overlooked an inner court, and its windows stood wide to admit not only the warm spring air, but also the importunings of a small bird that hopped from sill to sill and eyed the bread-board with eagerness. Father Francis scattered a handful of crumbs for it, and returned to the head of the table.

'An omen perhaps, Miss Safford?'

She caught his meaning at once. 'The wren? There's a wren on the replica of the Sucat Cross at Midsomer. You've seen it, sir?'

'Many years ago.' He waited while his guests' plates were filled, then said, 'To return to your suggestion that we are seeking not two crosses, but one . . . we must go back to the fifth century AD. St Patrick had been kidnapped by Irish pirates. The Romans were withdrawing from Britain, to defend Rome. Here in Wessex, King Vortigern sought to guard his territory against new invaders, the Saxons. He made the mistake of forming a pact with the Saxon mercenaries, Hengist and Horsa, who held the southeastern shores. They betrayed his trust, and helped the Saxon raiders to seize control of the Severn Estuary. The Sucat family sent the Cross to Glastonbury. It was never returned to them.'

'Stolen, Dame Celia implied,' said Kate. 'Though one can't credit that a religious order would steal such a precious relic.'

Father Francis rubbed his nose. 'It's been known to occur,' he said. 'At any event, centuries passed and the Saxon Cerdinga clan became the rulers of Britain. They produced many notable men and women, one of whom was Dunstan.

'He was born in 909 and died in 988 AD. He was a West Country man, and studied at Glastonbury. He was appointed Abbot of Glastonbury by King Edmund, and was entrusted with the keeping of part of the royal treasury.

'After Edmund was stabbed to death at Pucklechurch, Dunstan fell foul of his successor and was exiled to the Low Countries, but he returned in 959 when Edgar took the throne, and in 960 he was made Archbishop of Canterbury. A man of huge prestige and power.'

Kate clasped her hands before her. 'Glastonbury is the link! Dear sir, you believe that at Glastonbury the Sucat Cross passed into the possession of Dunstan, and so was identified with his name?'

It was on the tip of Father Francis's tongue to say that the link between Patrick and Dunstan was not an icon, but their service to God and the Church; but looking at Kate's eager face, he hadn't the heart to snub her. He sighed.

'The Cross could not have been owned by Dunstan, but if it

was in his care, it might indeed have become identified with him.'

'A cross associated with two saints,' said Kate, in a hushed voice, 'would be very precious, would it not?'

'Unimaginably precious. But, my dear Miss Safford, even if the Cross was sent to Twyford, there is not a jot of proof that it remained there.'

'The legend says it did,' said Kate obstinately.

'History says it did *not*. The Danes were hot on the heels of the treasure wagons. Cynric and Edina can have had little time to devise a safe hiding-place for so much gold.'

Dominic, who had listened to the conversation in brooding silence, now spoke:

'What if both history and legend are right? Cynric and Edina were devout Christians. To them, the Cross and the other sacred vessels must have seemed far more important than gold coins or bars. What if they hid the church treasures in a safe place, but left the rest where the Danes could easily find it? Like tossing the gold apple to Atlanta.'

Kate beamed at him. 'Nick, how clever of you! I'm sure that's what occurred! If only we can discover where old Melburn stood, we shall be able to find at least part of the treasure.'

Neither of her hearers made an immediate reply. Dominic was thinking that the task was impossible, and the kindest thing would be to tell Kate so.

Father Francis, on the other hand, was experiencing an emotion he had not felt since the day he was ordained – an uplifting of the heart, a conviction that something momentous was about to begin.

Rising from his chair, he went to the next room and returned carrying a heavy volume, which he handed to Kate.

'This may help you,' he said. 'It's Radcliffe's book on Roman architecture. It describes the construction of a typical Roman villa – living-quarters, atrium, kitchen and bath-house, possibly a temple.' He waved aside Kate's thanks. 'A word to the wise, my dear. If you dig, do so with the utmost care, or you may destroy more than you discover.'

Half an hour later, as Kate and Dominic were about to take their leave, a thought occurred to her.

'One last question,' she said. 'When Papa was dying, he said, "The blackthorn is anathema". Dame Celia told me anathema was a curse laid on a person who infringed his neighbour's boundary rights. But how will that help us to find the gold?'

The old man shook his head. 'I can only guess at your father's meaning. The blackthorn is a very ancient plant. Even in prehistoric times, it was used to mark the limit of a man's property. So where one finds a dense thicket of blackthorn, one may in fact be looking at an old-established boundary line.'

He came to the door to wish his guests godspeed, and remained on the front steps until their carriage was out of sight.

I must have been mad to encourage such flights of fancy, he thought. I should have told the child not to waste her time.

Yet, looking up at the soaring face of the cathedral, he knew that far from being repentant, he was hoping against all reason that Miss Safford would be successful.

'After all,' he murmured, as he turned back into the house, 'miracles do happen, and if it's miracles we need, why, then two saints must be better than one!'

XVI

The journey to Bath passed quickly. Kate was elated by their meeting with Father Francis.

'He's given me fresh heart,' she said. 'He didn't patronize me as Dymoke did, he didn't laugh at my theories. Somehow, talking to him has given me a far better idea of where we may find Cynric's Melburn. We know he very likely built over an old Roman site, close to a river that existed in Roman times but ran dry at the time of the siege. When I return to Twyford, I shall try to discover where the Romans settled. Perhaps the Vicar will be able to advise me, and I have Father Francis's book to guide me as well.'

Dominic forbore to put a damper on her spirits. The Romans might have settled in any of a dozen vales in Twyford. To search them all would take years, and they had only weeks.

He held his peace, content to watch Kate's glowing face and listen to her plans. How different she was from the languid beauties of Town, with their parroted opinions and shallow social rounds.

A man could never be bored in Kate's company. She would lend interest to the most commonplace event, she would be the most delightful of companions, the best of wives . . .

He checked his pipe dream.

Tomorrow he would start for Twyford, and from there go on to London, to arrange for the final disposal of Melburn.

*

They reached Queen's Square when the shadows were lengthening and the sun lending a roseate hue to the columned face of the buildings. As the carriage drew up outside the Beachers' home, Elinor appeared at an upper window, and Simmons at the front door, for all the world like figures on a weather-clock. Something in their demeanour warned of ill tidings, and Kate sprang down from the carriage and hurried up the front steps. After a moment's hesitation, Dominic followed her.

'Simmons?' said Kate, as she stepped into the hallway. 'Is anything amiss? My aunt and uncle . . . ?'

'They are home, miss.' Simmons spoke in the hushed accents of an undertaker. 'They have been waiting all afternoon to speak with you.'

Elinor came running down the stairs, dismissed Simmons with a nod, and embraced Kate.

'Thank Heavens you're home!' she said. 'Such a brouhaha as we've had here. Aunt is distraught.'

Dominic, realizing he had intruded on some family drama, made as if to retreat, but Elinor surprised him by grasping his arm.

'Pray don't go, Nick. Uncle is anxious to see you. They're in the morning-room.'

Mystified, they followed her to the small parlour at the rear of the house. The scene that met them as they crossed the threshold was hardly reassuring. Mr Beacher stood with his back to the fireplace, stiffly erect and wearing the expression of a man braced for unpleasantness. His wife reclined on the *chaise-longue*, a sodden handkerchief clutched in one hand, a bottle of smelling-salts in the other. Kate hurried to her.

'Aunt? Tell me, quickly. It's not Anna or the baby?'

'No, no, they're quite well. Quite well.' Mrs Beacher seized Kate in a convulsive hug and kissed her on both cheeks, then said in a trembling voice, 'You mustn't take it to heart, my love. It's a mistake, a dreadful mistake. Your uncle will set it all to rights, never fear.'

174

'Set *what* to rights?' demanded Kate, but as Mrs Beacher pressed her fingers to her mouth and shook her head distractedly, she sought her uncle's eyes. 'Tell me what's happened,' she begged.

Amyas cleared his throat. 'As your aunt has said, my dear, there's been a misunderstanding. God knows how it can have come about, but we'll rub through it somehow.' He nodded at Dominic, who was standing near the door, intent upon making his escape at the earliest opportunity.

'Come in, if you please, my lord. This concerns you as much as it does us, and I'm anxious to clear up the matter at once. I lay no blame at your door, as I trust you will lay none at mine. We will find the perpetrator, and deal with him as he deserves.'

'What perpetrator?' cried Kate. 'What are you talking about? Oh, if someone doesn't explain I shall run mad!'

For answer, Mr Beacher reached into his coat pocket and drew out a page torn from a newspaper. He offered it to Kate, who studied it with widening eyes, then passed it wordlessly to Dominic.

In the centre of the torn sheet, prominent among the court notices, was a paragraph that read:

The betrothal is announced of Lord Dominic Barr, son of the late Lord Justin Barr of Twyford Lindum and Letitia, Countess of Savernake, to Miss Kate Safford, daughter of the late Sir Clive and Lady Safford, also of Twyford Lindum.

Mrs Beacher held out a tremulous hand. 'I do assure you, Lord Barr, this is no work of ours. No member of this household would stoop to such an outrageous trick.'

'Of course not.' Dominic achieved a smile. 'Pray don't distress yourself, ma'am. We've been friends for far too long to doubt one another.' He handed the paper back to Mr Beacher. 'Whoever sent that notice to *The Times* committed forgery,' he said bluntly.

Mr Beacher nodded. 'I agree. The main part of the text could have been penned by anyone, but the signature must have resembled yours.'

'My signature is easily imitated,' Dominic said. 'The one word "Barr" would suffice.' He was silent for a moment, then went on with some difficulty: 'I fancy I know who is responsible for this piece of malice. Rest assured, I'll discover if my suspicion is correct, and I'll take suitable action. I shall, of course, write to the newspaper at once, demanding they publish a correction of the blunder.' His gaze shifted to Kate, who stood white-faced at his side. 'I need not tell you how sorry I am that you should have been embarrassed in this way. I'll leave you now. There's a good deal to be done, and I must post up to London tomorrow, to warn my mother that the announcement is mere fabrication.'

Mrs Beacher began to weep again. 'Such a shock for poor Lady Savernake. Such a shock for us all.'

Elinor moved quickly to offer her aunt a draught of hartshorn. Mr Beacher and Dominic started for the door, but before they reached it, Kate said, 'Wait! Please wait!'

As the two gentlemen halted in surprise, she clasped her hands nervously and said, 'I don't think the announcement should be denied. At least, not immediately. You see, whoever was unkind enough to send it to *The Times*, did so for a reason . . . expecting certain consequences . . . and I don't think we should fall so easily into the trap.'

'What consequences?' said Mr Beacher, bewildered.

'Well, firstly, the person concerned might have believed we would accuse Dominic of inserting the notice without our permission, and that he in turn would accuse us.'

'Poppycock,' said Mr Beacher. 'We've been friends for too long to do any such thing.'

'Yes, but the person might not understand that. The person might expect that there would be a dreadful quarrel between us, and . . . and a rift that couldn't be healed.'

Kate saw that Dominic was watching her closely, and addressed her next remarks to him.

'If the betrothal is cancelled so soon after its announcement, there'll be a great deal of gossip, will there not?'

Dominic nodded. 'Yes, the long tongues will wag, but the ton has a short memory. In a week or two they'll find some new bone to chew on.'

'I'm not thinking of the ton,' Kate said, 'but of your creditors. If the betrothal is cancelled, they'll know that I'm no longer in a position to help you financially.'

'That may be so,' answered Dominic grimly, 'but you must not let it concern you, Kate.'

'It does and *must* concern me!' Tears sparkled in Kate's eyes, 'Someone has tried to strike at you through me, and I won't stand for it! I won't be a pawn in such a dirty game!'

Mrs Beacher made a sound of distress. 'Dearest, you must see that we can't allow the misunderstanding to persist. You and Lord Barr are not betrothed, and the sooner people understand that, the better.'

'We're not betrothed, but now isn't the time to say so.' Kate pressed a palm to her flushed cheek. 'Oh, this is so difficult!'

Mr Beacher, who had been listening with chin sunk on chest, looked up and said heavily, 'Difficult, and mighty unpleasant for you, puss, but your aunt's right. Neither you nor his lordship would wish to be party to a lie.'

'The lie isn't of our making,' said Kate. 'If we leave things as they are for a few weeks – allow Nick's creditors to think we are betrothed, they'll hold off.' She directed a challenging look at Dominic. 'That's true, isn't it?'

'It may be, but it's not a course I choose to take.'

'Oh, don't be so precious! We needn't be engaged for long, only until I've had time to find the treasure. Then you may announce we've decided to cry off.'

'A fine figure I'd cut!' said Dominic indignantly, and Mr Beacher nodded vehemently.

'Quite right. A gentleman can't jilt a female. Not done.'

'Then I'll jilt him, or we can say we're parting by mutual

177

consent. That's not so uncommon, is it? I do think you're making a fuss over nothing.'

At this point, Elinor, who had remained silent throughout the discussion, suddenly spoke her mind.

'Kate's right,' she said. 'To deny the betrothal would be to do just what the wretch who sent the notice desires. The scandal will be horrible, Lord Barr's creditors will move in like wolves for the kill, and all of us who have his and Kate's welfare at heart will suffer. I say, let the engagement stand.'

She came to put an arm round Kate's shoulders. 'It won't be easy for any of us to keep up the deception, but we must at least try. Dominic will need to take his mama and Savernake into his confidence, and perhaps Mr Walcott as well. No doubt they'll be shocked, but they're sure to offer their support. After all, to deceive society is not yet considered a hanging matter.'

The debate continued for nearly an hour, but at the end of that time everyone agreed to maintain the pretence of a betrothal. It was also agreed that Dominic would travel to London at once to acquaint his mother with the true state of affairs, and that Kate, the Beachers and Elinor would follow in a few days, to lend credence to the subterfuge.

It was after seven o'clock when Dominic mounted his horse and rode away to Solsbury Hill. He left behind him an exhausted little group.

Elinor assisted her aunt upstairs and helped her into bed, where she lay sobbing, unable to stem the flow of her tears. 'I thought,' she said brokenly, 'that to read such a notice in *The Times* would be the happiest moment of my life. Imagine if it were true, Nell, and we might expect to see dear Kate a bride and mistress of Melburn! But it is all come to nought. My dreams lie in the dust!'

'We mustn't despond,' said Elinor bracingly. 'We must live each day as it comes, and not refine too much on the past.'

Mrs Beacher sank back on her pillows and closed her eyes. 'I have not your stoical nature. I don't know how I shall contrive to face people – to lie to my friends. It is all so very dreadful!'

'You will manage, for Kate's sake. Now try to sleep. You'll feel more the thing in the morning.'

Downstairs, Mr Beacher poured a large measure of brandy for himself, and a glass of wine for Kate.

'A bad business,' he said, 'very bad, but we'll come through it. Barr behaved with generosity, I think. I feared he might cut up rough. Suspect *me* of sending the notice to the newspaper.'

'I'm sure it never crossed his mind.'

Mr Beacher looked sheepish. 'I'll admit I've been known to meddle, in the past, and to be plain with you, I did give Barr a hint that he might be well advised to marry you.'

'I know,' Kate replied. 'Nell told me.'

'I meant no harm, puss. Only did it because I thought it was for the best.' Amyas sighed heavily. 'I'd dearly love to lay hands on the knave who brought us to this pass.'

Kate drank some of her Marsala. 'You could hardly lay hands on a woman, Uncle.'

'*Woman?*' said Mr Beacher in a startled tone, and Kate nodded. 'Unless I mistake, it was Madeline Cheveley who sent the notice. Nick has thrown her over, you know, and this is her way of paying him out, and of dealing me a backhander as well.'

'Are you saying she forged Barr's signature?'

'Yes,' said Kate coolly. 'They're well acquainted.' A sparkle lit her eyes. 'The one thing I hope for, in this whole sorry mess, is that I'll be privileged to see the creature's face when Dominic presents me to the ton as his affianced bride!'

On Saturday, Kate and Elinor left for Twyford, with the alacrity of refugees fleeing from an advancing army.

The news of the 'betrothal' had spread round Bath like wildfire, and it seemed that everyone of their acquaintance felt bound to pay a courtesy call in Queen's Square and offer felicitations.

In any circumstances the engagement of Barr of Melburn must have created something of a stir, but the news that he was to marry Miss Kate Safford, the owner of an extremely prosperous estate and handsome fortune, added much spice to the gossip.

Mr and Mrs Beacher met the flood of well-wishers with fortitude, and after a while Mrs Beacher began to believe her own
utterances, to preen at the encomiums of her friends and to
murmur in suitably lowered tones that of course there could be no
large-scale celebration of the announcement as dear Lord Barr
was so recently bereaved.

'We take our girls to London next week,' she told Lady Ingram,
'to present them to Lady Savernake. Our stay in Town will be very
short, but we look forward to meeting Barr's close circle, and to
visiting the London shops.'

'Bride-clothes,' agreed Lady Ingram sagely. 'One cannot begin
to buy too early, my dear Emily. When our Margaret married, I
thought I would never reach the end of the shopping-list. I advise
you to take comfortable shoes and a well-filled purse.' She
paused, then took the plunge. 'You won't take offence if I say that
Ingram and I are delighted at this turn of events. It's a splendid
match for Kate, and Melburn will be saved, which is something to
gladden all our hearts.'

Kate and Elinor reached Safford Manor late on Friday, and
early next day the Vicar appeared on their doorstep, all smiles.

'My dear Miss Safford, I rejoice to hear your news! That two
of our best-loved families are to be united in the sacred bonds of
matrimony . . .'

Kate said hastily, 'We've not had time to set a wedding-date, Mr
Pruitt.'

'So his lordship told me. He was kind enough to call on me on
his way through to London. He explained that in view of the
recent deaths in his family, the engagement might be a long one.
But what matter? The happy day will dawn, in God's good time.'

The country came in their carriages to offer good wishes, and
the villagers sent a deputation of elders, led by old Tom Kendall.
They presented Kate with a quilt sewn by Doll Kendall's grandmama, a famous needlewoman.

'Lucky quilt, that be,' Tom announced. 'Five sons it brung me,

180

an' two darters. Reckon it'll fill 'is lordship's quiver for 'im.'

Kate smiled, but protested that the quilt was an heirloom, and should stay in the Kendall family. Tom shook his head.

'Ain't no way any of us'll survive 'thout Melburn, Miss Kate. So 'tis the time for sacrificial gifts, an' prayer an' the lightin' o' candles, so 'tis.'

This widespread support and approval was a two-edged sword; it brought Kate comfort, but with the certainty that it couldn't last. She tried not to think of the day of reckoning to come, and concentrated her mind on the task she had set herself.

She summoned her factor, Arne, and explained that she must make a short visit to London, but that on her return she intended to conduct some archaeological research in the Twyford Valley.

'It was my father's wish,' she said. 'I want you, while I'm away, to make all the preparations you were used to make for his digs. Assemble the men he trained, Crawford and Pooke and the rest. See that all the tools are in good order, set out the trowels and sieves and sorting-tables in the barn, clean and fill the water tanks.'

'And the pay, Miss Kate? Will that be the same as usual?'

'No. Raise the rate. We'll have to work fast, and the hours will be long.'

'May I ask what it is they'll be looking for?'

Kate answered with a half-truth. 'Roman artefacts,' she said. 'Coins, pottery shards, mosaic chips and the like. I'll call the workers together when I get back from Town, and tell them what I plan.'

In the middle of the week the Beachers arrived, and on Thursday Kate and Elinor set out with them for London.

XVII

As Dominic had, feared, his interview with his mother was not easy. He arrived at Savernake House in the middle of the afternoon, and found Lady Letitia in her writing-room, a stack of correspondence at her elbow. He stooped to kiss her, saying:

'I came as fast as I could, Mama. Stopped only at Twyford, to speak to Pruitt. I take it you've seen the notice in *The Times*?'

She touched the pile of letters and cards. 'I, and half of London.'

'I'm truly sorry. I know what distress it must have caused you.'

'*Anguish* is a better word! Could not you have warned me, Dominic? To learn of your betrothal in the public press, without one word from you! I've tried to tell myself that you must have had reason for such unkindness, but I cannot imagine what it might be!'

He caught her hands and held them tightly.

'That announcement was a hoax, Mama. I did not send it to *The Times*, and nor did the Beachers, or Kate. None of us knew of it until we saw it in cold print.'

She shook her head in bewilderment. 'But who in the world can have played you such a cruel trick?'

He met her eyes. 'I suspect Madeline Cheveley. She and I have been . . . close.'

'Yes, yes, I knew of the affair,' said Lady Letitia impatiently, 'but why would the woman do such a thing?'

'To strike at me,' Dominic said. 'To cause trouble between my

183

family and Kate's. I made a foolish mistake. I told Madeline that Amyas Beacher had suggested I offer for Kate's hand. Madeline took the idea seriously. We quarrelled, and I made it clear to her that our relationship was at an end. This, I suppose, was her notion of revenge. She imagined I'd accuse the Beachers of trying to trick me into a betrothal. Nonsensical, but logic has never been Madeline's strong point.'

'I see.' Lady Letitia was watching her son's face carefully. 'Tell me, when Mr Beacher made his somewhat brash approach, what was your response?'

'Oh, I made a high-sounding speech. Told him I wouldn't sink to being a fortune-hunter, even to save Melburn. Said I couldn't offer Kate such an insult as to invite her to marry a bankrupt.' Dominic sank his head in his hands. 'God, what insult I've exposed her to now!'

'Is she very distressed? Angry?'

'No.' He looked up, his face haggard. 'She's been generosity itself. She wishes to let the betrothal stand for the time being. We're to cry off once I'm free of debt. She says my being engaged to her will keep my creditors quiet, and the devil of it is, she's right. When I called at Barr House an hour ago, I found a load of congratulatory notes, half of them from the very jackals who've been snapping at my heels for weeks.'

'It seems to me,' said Lady Savernake, 'that Miss Safford is both practical and kind. I'm inclined to agree that at this juncture, silence may well be golden.'

'I find it past bearing!' Dominic jerked to his feet and went to stare out of the window. 'I would do anything to free Kate from this imbroglio.'

Lady Letitia gazed thoughtfully at his rigid back. Though he had always shown her love and tenderness, she was aware that he had the reputation of being cold-hearted and arrogant. The careless indifference he displayed to those outside his own intimate circle had caused her many a sleepless night.

Today she saw him in a different light, his hurt made plain, his self-blame and regret beyond doubt. She did not have to look far for the cause of this change. Her rakehellion son had at last fallen in love.

Aloud, she said calmly, 'What do you intend to do?'

He came back to her side. 'I've agreed, very much against my will, to let the engagement stand. The question is, can *you* bring yourself to support such a pretence, introduce Kate to our closest friends, act as if you welcomed the news? It goes against the grain to ask you to lie for me, but I see no alternative.'

'I shall be happy to do whatever I can,' she answered. 'Does Miss Safford mean to come up to Town?'

'Yes. The Beachers will bring her, and her cousin Elinor Crane, in a few days' time. Kate has a house in Curzon Street – they will stay there. They won't remain in London above a week.'

'Understand, Dominic, I must take Ivor into my confidence over this. I won't lie to him.'

'I do understand. I regret putting him in this awkward situation.'

Lady Letitia smiled. 'Do you know, I believe he'll derive a certain entertainment from deceiving the ton. His sense of humour was always quixotic. Now I suggest you leave me to draw up a list of the people I shall invite to a select gathering in honour of your Kate.' She saw the haunted look that crossed Dominic's face, and reached out to pat his hand. 'Don't fret. We'll rub through this well enough, I dare say.'

Later that evening, she regaled her husband with the whole history of Dominic's break with Lady Cheveley, his stay in Bath, the false notice sent to *The Times*, and the decision to let the betrothal stand.

Lord Savernake listened in bland silence, and only at the conclusion said gently, 'Do you trust this girl? You don't think this is a ruse to ensnare Dominic?'

'No. She's the soul of honesty, and she's spent the past two months attempting to learn the whereabouts of the Danish gold, to save Melburn.'

'A novel approach, certainly.'

'Dominic is so unhappy, Ivor. I believe he's in love with the girl; I wish with all my heart he could marry her, but I see no hope of it. His pride forbids it.'

'I offered to lend him the blunt. He refused the offer.'

'That, too, is his pride.'

Savernake lifted a languid shoulder. 'Perhaps Miss Safford will find the treasure, and everyone will live happy ever after.'

'Don't jest, Ivor.'

'I beg pardon, my love. Tell you what, I'll take a stroll down Bond Street tomorrow, and pick out some pretty trinket for the chit.'

'That will rub salt in Nick's wounds.'

'Salt,' retorted his lordship, 'if judiciously applied, has healing qualities. A pair of earrings, I think, don't you? What is Miss Safford's colouring?'

'She has brown hair, hazel eyes, a fine complexion with colour on the cheekbones. In stature she's petite, but she wears her clothes with distinction. Her manner is direct. She has a charming voice. I'm not well acquainted with her, you know. We met only once or twice, last year.'

Savernake nodded affably. 'Leave it to me. I'll drop in at Asprey's, and see what they have to show me.'

In after years, Kate was to remember that brief sojourn in London as having a dreamlike quality. She moved through her daily round like a character in a child's cardboard theatre. The people she met were no more than an audience, blurred beyond the footlights.

The day after the family arrived in Curzon Street, Dominic paid them a morning visit, bringing with him his mother's invitation to a soirée at Savernake House.

Seeing the anxious look on Kate's face, he said quietly, 'Don't worry, Mama's aware of the facts, and so is Savernake. I've also confided in George Walcott, who came to Town yesterday. He says we've done just as we ought, and will support us all along the line. He believes the whole thing will resolve itself if we don't make too much of a splash, or . . . or behave like April and May.'

'Quite so,' approved Mr Beacher. 'We'll puff it off as an agreement between two young people who've known each other since they were in leading-strings. After all, people expected Kate to marry your brother, so this arrangement won't exactly come as a surprise.'

This view proved to be over-sanguine. While the match was seen by society as entirely suitable, the circumstances of the double death in the Barr family, and the fact that the heir to Melburn was in dire financial straits, figured largely in the talk in clubs and drawing-rooms. On one occasion, Kate heard the loquacious Lady Jersey say to Princess Lieven that it was a mercy Nick Barr had found a way out of his difficulties; and it was certain that many members of the ton accepted that on his part at least this was a marriage of convenience.

One terrifying old beldame went so far as to congratulate the young couple on their good sense. 'People of quality cannot resort to vulgar love-matches,' she declared. 'If we don't hold to our rank and our property, we shall have our heads chopped off like the French, and serve us right!'

The mercenary attitude of such people was assuaged by the kindness shown to Kate and her family by Lord and Lady Savernake. At the soirée, Kate knew herself to be among friends who were genuinely eager to wish Dominic and his fiancée well. Lord Savernake proposed a toast to them, and presented Kate with a small box containing a very beautiful pair of pearl eardrops. Overcome, she gazed up at him and murmured:

'Oh, no, I cannot. It would not be proper!'

'More proper,' he returned, 'than to spurn the gift of your prospective father-in-law. Come, put them on. They will go very well with your gown, I think.'

She did as he asked, privately resolving to return the gift at some future date. Dominic came to her side, and took her hand.

'Charming, Kate.' He turned to Lord Savernake. 'You are very kind, sir. We appreciate it, both of us.'

His lordship smiled, nodded, and sauntered away to join his wife.

'I like Miss Safford very well,' he announced.

'Yes, so do I.' She heaved a sigh. 'If only things had happened differently – if Amyas Beacher hadn't set Dominic on his high horse with his meddling suggestion. Truly, I could strangle the man!'

'Not here, I beg. Too many witnesses.'

His wife fixed him with a kindling eye. 'Do you take nothing seriously?'

'Why, certainly, my love. You, my pictures, and my fishing-rods are sacred in my eyes.' He slipped a hand through her arm. 'Angus Quinn has found the brandy bottle, I see. He's already sunk to the Plimsoll line. Let us go and tow him to safer waters.'

A number of invitations arrived addressed to Kate, her family, and Dominic.

'The Devonshires we must accept,' he said. 'Also the Kirks and Stanfords, and of course we'll dine with George, but the rest we may decline.'

Kate was grateful for the let-off. All too often, on outings with Dominic, they encountered people who were eager to congratulate them, and she found it hard to respond with warmth, feeling herself to be wearing false colours. Her diffidence did her no harm in the eyes of the high sticklers.

'A modesty that must please,' commented the haughty Mrs Cavendish. 'Barr is fortunate in his choice.'

One of Kate's first actions on reaching London was to arrange a meeting with the publisher, Mr Lombard. Arriving at his place of business, she found him wreathed in smiles, firstly because he had read of her betrothal, and secondly because he was able to present to her Mr Henry Godbold, who was to write her father's History of Dorset.

Mr Godbold was sixty years old, bow-legged and barrel-chested with a face tanned by warm southern suns. He had merry blue eyes that almost vanished when he laughed. He wrung Kate's hand and said that he looked forward keenly to their joint venture.

'I've studied Sir Clive's notes. Wonderful stuff. Wonderful. I've already drafted a chapter or two, and when I've fleshed 'em out a little, I shall beg a further meeting with you, Miss Safford, so that you may give me your opinion. I desire to keep as close as may be to your papa's intentions and style. This is to be his gift to posterity, not mine.'

The generous statement set the tone for a happy discussion, at the end of which Kate was so delighted with Mr Godbold, and so impressed by his learning, that she urged him to come and stay at Safford Manor as soon as her family returned there.

To this he readily agreed, and Kate left him and Mr Lombard to thrash out the details of the project.

Back in Curzon Street, she found Dominic kicking his heels in the library, and at once launched into an account of her morning.

'It's such a relief to know that Papa's documents are in good hands,' she said. 'Mr Godbold's knowledge is not only wide, but precise. Apart from being an expert on the Middle Ages, he knows a great deal about Roman ruins. He told me he's worked on many sites over the past twenty years, and he gave me such useful pointers. He said we must watch out particularly for mosaic chips in the surface soil. They are thrown up by the plough, he says, and even in molehills. Imagine, Nick, we may be led to the treasure by a Gentleman in Velvet!'

Dominic was becoming her chief confidant. They had many opportunities for conversation, for they drove or rode in the mark each morning, and met every evening at dinner with friends, or their respective families.

The growing rapport between them was not missed by those close to them.

'I fear Kate is becoming too fond,' said Mrs Beacher to Elinor.

'One has only to see how she runs down the stairs when Barr's curricle stops at our door. How can we warn her that to him this is just an interlude? What hope is there that he will offer for her in earnest?'

'None, I fear,' said Elinor sadly. 'Mr Walcott says Dominic will never do so, as long as he's a pauper. He has told George that a marriage where the husband is the wife's pensioner, is doomed to failure.'

'I think him as stubborn as a mule,' said Mrs Beacher unreasonably. 'Heaven knows how we shall ever be free of this tangle. My only wish is to be back in Bath, away from this horrid, tattling, money-grubbing Town!'

XVIII

Dominic had decided that the best way to deal with Madeline Cheveley's conniving was to ignore it. A direct challenge would provoke outraged denials and provide fresh fodder for the scandalmongers. By the same token, if society welcomed the betrothal, Madeline would not dare denounce it as as sham.

He did his best to avoid taking Kate to any place where Madeline might put in an appearance, and his luck held until the day before the Beachers were due to leave London. He had taken Kate to call on his great-uncle, who had rooms in Albany. The visit over, they strolled slowly back towards Piccadilly, Dominic pointing out the apartments that had been home to such famous figures as Lord Byron, Macauley, and 'Monk' Lewis.

As they approached the mouth of the cul-de-sac, Dominic saw with a shock that a carriage was drawn up there, and that leaning from its window was Lady Cheveley. She was watching him intently, a cat-smile curving her lips.

His reaction was immediate and instinctive. He put a protective arm round Kate's shoulders, and drew her close to him. Kate, who had been gazing about in the hopes of catching sight of some famous personage, looked up at him and smiled radiantly. The smile swept away all Dominic's good resolutions. He bent his head and kissed her mouth.

As unthinkingly, she put her arms round his neck and returned the embrace. He broke her grip and said roughly:

'No, Kate. I'm sorry. I should not have done that. Forgive me.'

She stared at him in confusion. Then the sound of the carriage moving away made her turn her head, and she saw Lady Cheveley glaring at her in fury.

Colour rushed into Kate's face. She said disjointedly, 'I beg pardon . . . I didn't realize . . . I never saw . . .'

Dominic shook his head. He ached to tell her that he loved and desired her with every fibre of his being, that Madeline Cheveley meant nothing to him, but from that kind of admission there could be no going back. He forced himself to say in a matter-of-fact-tone, 'She won't trouble us again, I fancy. Now we must be getting back to Curzon Street. You'll wish to make ready for the journey tomorrow. At what hour do you leave?'

'Early.' Kate made a play of straightening her bonnet. Her face felt stiff and tears stung her eyes. After a moment, she summoned up a smile, and said brightly, 'We plan to set out at nine, so pray don't plan on seeing us off. We'll meet soon enough in Twyford.'

'Yes. I'll be home in a few days' time.' He offered her his arm, and they made their way through the bustling crowds of Piccadilly, neither of them able to think of anything to say. At Kate's front door, Dominic held out his hand.

'*Au revoir*, Kate. I want you to know that this has been a very happy time for me. I'm eternally grateful to you for all you've done.' It seemed he might say more, but he checked himself, and murmured, 'Thank you, my dear Miss Safford.' He walkly quickly away towards Barr House.

Kate did not stay to watch him go, but rang a sharp peal on the doorbell, and fled past an astonished footman to the sanctuary of her bedroom. Locking the door, she cast off her bonnet and shawl, and sank down on the chair that faced her looking-glass. Her reflection stared back at her, white and trembling.

She was appalled at the emotions that gripped her; hurt and embarrassment, and a fierce self-disgust.

How could she have been so mistaken in herself? She had thought herself level-headed, perfectly well able to play her part in the betrothal charade, immune to romantic freaks. She saw now that the only person she had fooled was Kate Safford. Why had she not seen that she was falling in love with Dominic? Why had it taken a kiss to wake her, as if she were the sleeping beauty of a fairy-tale? Worst of all, how could she have forgotten that he did not love her? He had kissed her only to convince the Cheveley woman that the engagement was fact, not fiction.

She had made an idiot of herself.

She sat numb, her chagrin too great for healing tears. Someone tapped on her door and softly called her name, but she made no sound. The person moved away.

After a while, she picked up her hairbrush and tidied her hair, went to the wash-stand and splashed cold water on her face, found her phial of rosewater and dabbed some of the liquid on her neck and wrists.

The prosaic actions helped to calm her. She sat by the window for some time, thinking what she must do.

It was not the end of the world. She mustn't allow a trifling mistake, a mere kiss, to deflect her from her course. She had set out to find the Danish gold, and she would not give up now. She would go back to Twyford Lindum and put all her energy into finding the site of old Melburn.

Rising, she went to pull the bell-rope that would summon a maid to help her pack her belongings.

Lady Cheveley stormed into her elegant house in a towering rage. She snapped an order to the butler to deny all callers, and was about to mount the stairs when a voice spoke behind her.

'A word with you, Madeline, if you please.'

She spun round to see her husband standing in the doorway of his study.

'What is it?' she said coldly. 'I'm tired. I need to rest.'

Lord Cheveley made no answer, merely indicating with an outstretched hand she join him. With a flounce of her skirts she complied. He set a chair for her and regarded her with a faint smile.

'You're a handsome termagant, my dear, but have a care. Temper begets wrinkles, and *that* is to be deplored.'

She said between her teeth, 'Come to the point!'

'Very well. You must stop your childish efforts to engage Barr's attention. I won't say affection. He has never felt any for you, as you will admit, if you are honest with yourself.'

She turned her face away, and Cheveley sighed. 'Come now, Madeline, you are far too well versed in these matters to believe Barr has ever loved you. Accept that fact, and desist from your efforts to drive a wedge between him and Miss Safford.'

'I don't know what you mean.'

He settled in a wing chair and held up a warning hand. 'Don't waste my time, my dear. You know I keep a careful eye on what's mine. I'm aware that in Bath, you waylaid Miss Safford in the Sydney Gardens, and tried to put her in disgust of Barr. When that failed, you sent a notice to *The Times*, announcing their betrothal. An imbecile notion if ever there was one. What has it done, but force them into a closer alliance? Left to themselves, they might even make a match of it. Is that what you want?'

Madeline's shoulders sagged. 'I don't know. I saw them, not an hour since, kissing in the street, like common . . . common . . .'

'Lovers?'

She shook her head dumbly. Cheveley said softly, 'So, no more tricks, Madeline. Do you understand?'

She rounded on him. 'How can I understand? Why does he prefer that chit of a girl above me? It's only because she promises to pay his debts!'

'She will not be permitted to do that.'

'If that lunatic search of hers succeeds . . .'

'It won't. Kate Safford has been set on a false trail.'

'And if she declines to follow it?'

'Then I shall take other steps.'

'What steps? What's in that twisted mind of yours? I won't be associated with foul play!'

Cheveley laughed. 'There'll be no violence, nothing so crude. I shall supply pressure where it will produce the effect I desire.'

She stared at him, her face pallid. 'And what is that? What do you desire?'

He took his time answering. At last, he said simply, 'I desire to strip Barr of everything he has. His great possessions, his standing in society, his friends, his future. Everything.'

'Why? *Why?*'

'You know the answer to that question.'

'No, I do not. There have been other men who dangled after me; you never sought to destroy them.'

'Because I knew you cared nothing for them.' Cheveley leaned towards her, his face suddenly dark with blood. 'None of your backdoor bucks has ever touched what you're pleased to call your heart. Only Barr has achieved that distinction. I envy him. I envy him his great name, yes! I owe my title to a grandfather who bought the right people; what is that compared to the Barr legend? I envy him his easy friendships, a popularity I have never known. I envy him his sporting skills, his sense of humour, his solid worth. Above all, I envy him the feeling you cherish for him. Shallow and transient as it no doubt is, it's more than you ever gave to me!'

Cheveley checked himself abruptly, raising both hands in a placatory gesture. 'But it serves no purpose for us to trade insults. Do as I ask, Madeline. Leave all to me.'

She stared at him in silence for a moment, then rose to her feet and sauntered from the room. Her footsteps faded on the marble tiles of the hall.

Cheveley closed the door, crossed to his desk and settled in the chair. Unlocking a drawer, he drew out a heavy ledger. This he studied for some time, pausing occasionally to make a note on a sheet of paper. Presently the butler came to announce dinner, but his lordship waved him away.

'I shall dine at the Club,' he said. 'Have the carriage brought round at ten o'clock.'

*

The Club in question was not White's, nor Watier's, nor even Byron's Dandy Club, but an institution much less widely known, and in a sense much more select. Its members were without exception men whose interest lay in the world's staple food – money.

Some were bankers, or financiers, some merchants; some had knowledge of far countries, of gold or gems or great works of art. They came to this discreet house on the fringes of St James's to enjoy an excellent dinner and talk, or listen to others talk. From that talk, decisions sprang. A war could be won or lost in the coffee-room of the Club, an expedition launched to Peru or the Spice Islands, a new invention promoted or pooh-poohed.

That night, Lord Cheveley found the place thin of company. He dined alone, then passed an hour in the reading-room, and at a few minutes to midnight was informed that his guest had arrived and awaited him in the blue salon, a room where a member could conduct an undisturbed interview with a client or a friend.

The man who rose from his chair to greet his host was tall and thin and on the wrong side of sixty. His appearance suggested the dandy of an earlier epoch, his greying hair being tied back in an unfashionable queue, and his face delicately painted, with a patch at the corner of the mouth. He looked less than pleased about his situation, his bow being little more than a ducking of the head.

Cheveley waved him to a chair. 'Evening, Pickford. What will you take? Brandy? Wine? Coffee?'

Horace Pickford held up a white hand. 'Nothing. Pray tell me, my lord, to what do I owe the invitation?'

Lord Cheveley smiled. 'There is a matter of business I wish to discuss with you, sir.'

'I cannot think what it might be.'

'No? Then let me explain. It concerns the mortgage you hold on Melburn Hall, the house and acreage willed to Dominic Barr by his father, Justin Barr.'

Mr Pickford frowned. 'I cannot conceive how that should concern *you*.'

196

'But it does, Mr Pickford; it concerns me very closely. You hold the mortgage. When you foreclose . . .'

'I do not intend to foreclose. Justin Barr was a good friend of mine. I have promised his son that I will give him time to arrange to pay me what he owes. I do not break my promises.'

'I fear you must break this one.'

Mr Pickford got to his feet. 'I don't know what lunacy prompted you to arrange this meeting,' he said. 'I will be charitable and conclude you have drunk too much wine. I take my leave of you.'

He started for the door, but Lord Cheveley said sharply, 'Before you go, I think you had better read this.' He held up a folded document.

Mr Pickford stopped. 'What is it?'

'A statement of your own financial position.'

Mr Pickford hesitated, then came slowly to take the papers. He glanced through them, and his face paled under the paint. He sat down in the chair he had vacated.

'Who wrote this?' he demanded.

'I did,' Cheveley replied. 'The facts set down were gathered by various of my staff. I employ skilled investigators. Your gambling debts, for instance . . .'

'I am a gentleman, my lord. I pay my debts of honour,' said Mr Pickford hotly.

'Of course, but I really would advise you to avoid faro and the horses. Your losses far exceed your gains in that area. Then, your household expenses – it's a costly business keeping pace with our noble king, and one is conscious of his preference for friends who are plump in the pocket. Then there are your gifts and allowances to the ladies of the night. As we grow older, it's harder to satisfy their greed, is it not? And, of course, there is the mortgage on your own house; an encumbrance you cannot easily be rid of.'

'The mortgage is held by Giles Mortimer. He is a particular friend of mine; he has never pressed me for payment.'

'But he will, Pickford, he will; as will Cumberledge and Grimshaw and the rest of your spendthrift friends. I own them, you see. I have acquired information about them. I have taken over their debts. When I pull their strings, they will dance to my tune.'

'That's a lie! They are men of honour.'

Lord Cheveley laughed. 'There is no such thing, sir. Believe me when I say that if you do not do as I bid you, I will pull those strings. I will ruin you. There will be no more grand houses in London or Hertfordshire; no more visits to White's or Almack's; no more delightful liaisons with the ladies of the night; no more sojourns at Carlton House or Brighton.'

Pickford shook his head, stammering, 'Why are you doing this? Why do you wish to ruin me?'

'Not *you*,' said Lord Cheveley. 'You are merely the means to an end. My target is Dominic Barr.'

Understanding dawned in Pickford's eyes. He said, 'I see what it is. He made you a cuckold, and you seek revenge.'

'Precisely.' Lord Cheveley rose from his chair. 'I will give you thirty-six hours to inform Barr that you intend to foreclose on the mortgage. If you fail to comply, I shall know of it, I assure you.'

Mr Pickford pulled himself upright and pointed a trembling finger at Lord Cheveley. 'You are a rogue. A blackmailer. A poisonous toad. I shall tell Lord Barr of your scheming tricks.'

'Tell him what you please, but do as I bid you. If you fail, I advise you to pack and leave for Paris. Like Brummell, you may find oblivion there. The choice is yours.' Lord Cheveley stretched out a hand to the bell-rope.

'The porter will summon a hansom cab for you,' he said. 'I shall be at home for the next thirty-six hours, to await your decision. Goodnight, Mr Pickford.'

XIX

Dominic returned to Twyford four days after Kate, arriving too late in the evening to make any calls. The following morning was taken up by discussions with various members of his staff, but in the afternoon he rode over to Safford Manor. He had hoped to be able to talk to Kate alone, but found not only the Beachers in residence, but also Mr Godbold.

Their presence put a constraint on the conversation. Dominic confined himself to polite commonplaces. Kate chose to sit in the chair farthest from his, and said little. It was only the determined cheerfulness of the Beachers and Elinor that gave things the appearance of normality.

Elinor at least seemed pleased at the news that George Walcott would be coming in a day or two to spend some time at Melburn.

'He asked me to warn you, Mrs Crane,' said Dominic, 'that he will bring your puppy with him. He advises you to hide all your slippers in a safe place.'

At the end of an hour he took his leave. Kate accompanied him as far as the front steps, and asked the question that had been in all their minds.

'What is the news about Melburn?'

'Not good, I'm afraid. Horace Pickford came to see me in London. He has decided to foreclose.'

'Oh, no! How can that be? He promised to give you time.'

'He is himself heavily in debt. He sees no way out of it, but to foreclose.'

Kate scanned Dominic's face. 'Something has happened, has it not, to make him change his mind?'

He met her gaze. 'Yes. Cheveley has bought out the men who've lent Pickford money. He's now in possession of Pickford's own mortgages, and various other large debts. Pickford is ashamed, humiliated, but he must dance to Cheveley's tune.'

'But . . . does this mean that Cheveley could gain ownership of Melburn?'

'Yes. He's one of the richest men in England. If Melburn comes on the market, he will be able to outbid most buyers.'

'It's infamous! Unbearable!'

Dominic made no answer. In her shock, Kate was on the brink of begging him to go to Ivor Savernake for help, but she realized in time that he must already have considered that option and rejected it. To argue the point would only cause him more distress.

She said quietly, 'How long do we have?'

'Two weeks, possibly three. Shipton posted up to London, and we took advice from Mama's lawyers. It seems there are certain formalities to be completed, but Cheveley is likely to set the wheels turning as fast as he can.' He looked away from her, to the distant façade of his home. 'Frankly, it will be a relief to have it over and done with.'

'We must make it our business to find the gold,' Kate said. 'Mr Godbold joined us yesterday. We talked until late last night. I have every confidence in him, he is so clever and so . . . resolute. He agrees with Father Francis Tuckitt that old Melburn was probably built over the site of the Roman settlement. If we can discover the course of what Papa called the Roman River – the water-course the Danes diverted – we'll be on the way to finding Roman building-sites. If we find those, we've a good chance of discovering where Cynric built his fortress.'

'So many "ifs", Kate.'

'If Godbold thinks it worth the effort, how should we despair?'

'He certainly seems to have inspired you.'

'He has. He says, with so little time, we must form a theory and pursue it to the limit. I'm putting my money on the Roman River.'

Dominic grinned suddenly. 'Well, I was always a gambler. I'll back your fancy. What do you want me to do?'

'Ride with me and Mr Godbold to the top of the Tor, tomorrow morning. He wants to study the valley of the Rem, and we need you to point out the precise boundaries of your estate.'

'I'll be here by nine o'clock. Is that satisfactory?'

'Perfectly.'

'Tomorrow, then.' He mounted his horse, which a stable-lad had brought round, clapped his hat on his head, lifted a hand in salute and cantered away down the drive.

The party set out punctually the next day. Mr Godbold, mounted on a broad-chested grey, rode at Kate's side so that she might point out various landmarks to him. Dominic brought up the rear, content to listen to their conversation and enjoy the sunshine.

Since the floods of late winter, the weather had been uncommonly dry. The waters of the marsh had receded, leaving stretches of malodorous mud that glistened in the sun. Dragonflies hung and darted above the reeds along the causeway, and at the foot of the hills a cowman moved his herd along the road to the village.

They took the track that led up the Tor and reached the summit soon after ten. In the hot clear light they could see the whole expanse of the valley, and the ribbon of the Rem as it wound to its far-off junction with the Frome. Dismounting, they walked to the edge of the plateau, and Kate stretched out an arm.

'You see that the land west of the Rem – Safford land, for the most part – is hilly and broken, with few streams. It's better suited to sheep than to agriculture, and building materials are hard to find. I believe the Romans would have chosen the flatter, well-watered country, east of the Rem – Barr land. Such vestiges of Roman settlements as are known to us are all on this eastern side – the watch-tower up here, the bridge in the village, and the road that runs from the bridge to the pike road to Sturminster Newton.'

She glanced at Mr Godbold, who nodded. 'I agree. Settlers in any generation choose an easy place to live.'

'Shortly before my father died,' continued Kate, 'he rode to the top of this hill. I believe he came here to try to determine the probable site of old Melburn. He was caught in a storm and drenched to the skin. He contracted a fatal inflammation of the lungs. In the grip of that fever, he spoke of the Roman River, the dry river, and he said, "The blackthorn is anathema".

'I believe he was trying to tell me where I must look for old Melburn; close to a Roman settlement, near a river that was once sizeable but no longer exists, and near an ancient boundary marked by a blackthorn thicket.'

She pointed again. 'You can see that there's a blackthorn hedge that runs from the southern edge of the village to the Tump. It's a trifle moth-eaten in places, but the line's quite clear.'

It was true. The straggling line of dark bushes showed up plainly against the tilled land and pasturage.

'If that was the eastern boundary of old Melburn,' Kate said, 'it narrows down our search area quite considerably.'

Dominic frowned at the wide prospect that lay before them. 'There's still the devil of a lot of ground to cover,' he said.

Mr Godbold, who had been staring pensively at the valley, now spoke.

'I don't think we need to look more than a mile or so to the south,' he said. 'The Roman settlers would have clung close to the Tor, and the protection of the watch-tower. In those days, if one came under attack, one took to the hills.'

'Still,' demurred Dominic, 'even if they built their villas within a mile of the Tor, that mile includes a vast part of the valley – and we have no precise idea where we should begin our search.'

'There is perhaps one small clue for us,' Godbold answered. 'Do you see the line of darker green that runs from the marsh south-eastwards, towards the Tump? In a dry summer such as this, old paths and water-courses show up as dark green. One cannot discern it at ground level, but from a height it becomes evident.'

He swung his arm. 'The line down there is ruler-straight, d'ye see? The Romans favoured straight lines. Their roads, their viaducts, run straight as a die for miles on end.'

'You think that marks the course of the Roman River?'

'The Roman canal cut, made to drain the marsh,' Godbold said.

Dominic looked at Kate. She was watching him anxiously. Her face was pale, dark shadows under the eyes. She was wearing herself out in his cause. Her fight was probably hopeless, but it was so gallant that he couldn't find it in his heart to disappoint her. He turned back to Godbold.

'What do you suggest we do?'

'We should start the dig there,' Godbold answered. 'Sink a number of test holes along the dark-green line. Artefacts are often found in old river-beds. If we turn up pottery shards, or coins, or the like, we'll be able to tell if they're of Roman origin. We'll know we're on a sound track.'

'Very well. I can lend you some of my labour.'

'And there are my workmen,' Kate said. 'And men from the village perhaps. We can start tomorrow.'

On the way home, she chatted eagerly to Mr Godbold, full of plans for the dig. Dominic thought she resembled a sparrow flying in the teeth of a tempest, and loved her the more for it.

The search began early next day, teams of labourers from the Manor and Melburn congregating at the edge of the marsh. Mr Godbold outlined the work they were to do, what they should look for, and what to avoid. When he was done, one of the men laughed.

'Hopeful to find thikky ould Danish gold, be ye, sir?'

Dominic stepped forward. 'Yes, Jonas, we are, and if we find it there'll be a substantial reward for all of you, over and above the pay agreed on.'

Jonas lifted heavy shoulders. 'Reckon we'm wastin' our toime, my lord. There's bin dunamany looked for such a' ready, an' niver found so much as a brass button.'

There was a rumble of assent from his fellows, but Ben Kendall, grandson to old Thomas, spoke up from the rear of the crowd.

'What's to lose, Jonas Hubble? If the big 'ouse goes, so do us all.' He thrust forward to face Mr Godbold. 'You tell us where to dig, sir, an' dig us will.'

They began to sink test holes at regular intervals along a line marked out by Mr Godbold, each hole being some twenty yards from the next. All through the long, hot morning they toiled. Sometimes they struck rock a few inches down and were forced to try again. Women from the village were called in to sift through the earth and rubble taken from the holes, and to set aside anything that might interest Mr Godbold. By the end of the morning, he had examined a pile of broken bottles, a rusty ploughshare, and the bones of several animals, but he had seen nothing that remotely suggested a Roman origin.

At noon they broke to eat a meal of bread, cheese and ale, brought from the Manor. Mr Godbold wiped his face with a bandanna handkerchief, leaned his back against a tree, and discoursed on the art of archaeological digging.

'Look for a midden,' he urged. 'Look for bricks blackened by smoke, for layers of ash. Look for stones that might have marked the foundation of a wall.' He pulled a handful of marble chips from his pocket and handed them round. 'These are part of a mosaic,' he explained. 'A pattern made up of small pieces of stone or glass. Anyone who finds such a fragment must tell me of it at once.'

Dominic joined them during the afternoon, helping to heave buckets of dirt to the examination points. At five o'clock Mr Godbold called a halt and sent the workers home.

'Enough's enough,' he said. 'Tired workers make mistakes. Break things.' He strolled away to take a final look at the excavated areas, leaving Dominic with Kate.

Although she had worn a shady hat, and a gown with sleeves

that protected her shoulders and arms, her fair skin was sadly sunburned. The hem of her skirt was torn and muddied, her shoes scored by scratches. Dominic took her hands and turned them palm upward. One was blistered.

'You must take care, Kate,' he warned, 'or we'll be ordering you to the sick bay. Stay home tomorrow. Godbold and I can manage here.'

'You have other business to attend to,' she said wearily, but he shook his head.

'Devil take that! I'll be here, but I won't have you toiling like a ditch-digger.'

'It's what I want to do. It's *my* search, after all.'

He smiled. 'So it is, but at least leave the heavy work to those who are used to it. And wear thick gloves.'

He lifted a hand as if to clasp her shoulder, thought better of it and departed, but Kate went home much comforted by his concern for her.

The digging continued for eight days, the line of test holes moving steadily across the valley towards the Tump. It seemed to the trench-workers that they had shifted a thousand tons of sand and stones, and there were murmurs that it was all a waste of time.

On the fourth day, their spirits were sent soaring when, half-way between the marsh and the village, a broken millstone was unearthed. Kate ran to fetch Mr Godbold.

'Melburn means mill stream, doesn't it?' she said breathlessly. 'And if there's a millstone, there must have been a mill, and a stream to turn the wheel. Surely this must be old Melburn?'

Her hopes were dashed by the arrival of Mr Pruitt, who, drawn by the shouts from the field had come hurrying from St Dunstan's Church. He gazed at their find, pursed his lips and shook his head.

'I fear, Miss Safford, you have hit on the site of the old mill which existed in the fourteenth century, long after Melburn took its name. The find is of course interesting for its medieval connotations, but it sheds no light on the hiding-place of the Danish gold.'

The excavations had by this time attracted the fervid curiosity of the entire population of Twyford. The villagers had thrown themselves into the search with such vigour that Dominic was compelled to limit the number of onlookers, and to set guards at night to prevent incursions by self-appointed treasure hunters.

The Twyford gentry were divided in their views. Some found the hunt mildly amusing; others complained that it disrupted the work on their estates, and criticized Kate for initiating it. It was unseemly, they declared, for a lady of quality to behave in such a hoydenish way, toiling among common labourers.

Mr Beacher, who in private felt some sympathy for the critics, nevertheless said loyally that Kate was free to do as she pleased, and that if she did find the gold, certain people would be laughing on the wrong side of their faces.

Mr Walcott arrived in Twyford at the height of the brouhaha, and did what he could to still the wagging tongues. Miss Safford, he held, could not be faulted for attempting to help her fiancé out of his financial difficulties.

He had brought Elinor's puppy with him – an engaging animal whose innocent gaze concealed an inventive and determined nature. Elinor named him Jack, a title he answered to as and when he chose. Mr Walcott found it incumbent on him to visit the Manor frequently to enquire how Jack did, and Elinor encouraged this touching solicitude.

It was on the evening of the eighth day that Mr Godbold, returning with Kate to the Manor, delivered news that greatly distressed her.

'I'm afraid, ma'am, that we've been on a false trail. There was certainly a stream or canal from the marsh to the Tump, but there is nothing to prove it dates from Roman times. I'm of the opinion it was a medieval drain. The artefacts we've found date from that period. The water-course fed the old mill. It was not the Roman

River your father spoke of, not the river that flowed past Cynric's Melburn.'

Kate gazed at him with a face of tragedy.

'Then all our work is wasted.'

'Not wasted,' he said gently. 'We've tested one theory and found it empty. We know now where we should *not* search.'

'But where shall we turn?' she said miserably. 'We have so little time!'

'I think,' he said slowly, 'that we must concentrate on the streams that presently run south-east from the marsh. One of them may well have been widened by the Roman settlers to become a small river. When the Danes blocked its course, the waters returned to their old course, to the Rem, and that situation has obtained ever since.'

'But there are a dozen such streams!' wailed Kate. 'We can't hope to explore them all. Melburn will be sold.'

Mr Godbold's kind heart went out to her.

'Never fear,' he said. 'I'll burn the midnight oil, and come to you tomorrow with a new plan.'

He was as good as his word. The territory he proposed to cover lay closer to the village, in a basin of land between the Tump and the Melburn hay fields. Mr Godbold had chosen it, he said, because it was likely the Danish invaders would have encamped on flat ground when they laid siege to Cynric's fortress.

Once more the workers sank test-holes. Their task was made heavier by hot weather. Day after day the sun shone, baking the dry earth and drawing a humid haze from the marsh. Day after day the soil was carried to the sorting tables and sifted by George Walcott's helpers. At last, on the thirtieth of May, they made a find that confirmed Mr Godbold's theory. It was a small piece of metal which, when carefully cleaned, proved to be gold.

'Fine workmanship,' said Mr Godbold, pointing to the symbols inscribed on the fragment. 'Must have belonged to someone in a leadership position. The commander himself, perhaps.'

'What is it?' asked Dominic.

'Part of a decoration,' the archaeologist answered. 'Most likely from the shaft of a weapon. These marks are runes. It's evidence the Danes were here. We'll cover the area where it was found, look for signs of an army encampment.' He clapped Dominic on the shoulder. 'We're close, my lord. Close to the site of the siege. Tomorrow, we'll intensify our efforts.'

'I'm afraid you can't count on finding a work-force tomorrow,' Dominic said. 'It's May Day. The villagers will all be taking part in the celebrations.'

'Ah, yes,' said Mr Godbold. 'Maypoles and Morris dancers, eh? I'm glad the old traditions still hold. They're neglected in so many parts of the country, these days.'

'Not in Twyford Lindum, not while old Granny Kendall is alive. She's held to be a white witch, and doesn't allow anyone to trample on the old beliefs.'

Mr Godbold looked at Kate. 'Will you share in the festivities?' he asked.

'Oh, yes, it's expected.' She looked at her blistered hands. 'At least it will give us all a chance to sit in the shade and watch *others* exert themselves.'

That evening, the young men and girls of the village went out to collect may tree boughs, despite mutterings from Mr Pruitt that such gallivantings led to behaviour unseemly in Christian folk. In an effort to give events a more decorous tone, he held a May evensong in St Dunstan's Church, at which prayers were raised for the health and prosperity of all in Twyford.

Kate, seated with her family behind the Barr pew, found herself praying only for Dominic. This might be the last time he would worship in St Dunstan's, she thought, and she asked the saint for a miracle that would let Dominic remain master of Melburn. There was a solemnity in the congregation that made her think she was not the only one to harbour such hopes.

May Day dawned hot and still, with no breeze to cool the air. Kate put on her coolest muslin, and a wide-brimmed bonnet that protected her face and neck from the sun. It would be a long day.

Pretty Susan Jenks, black-eyed and apple-cheeked, was to be the May Queen, with young Ted Liddicombe as her consort. There would be a maypole on the village green, with games and shies for the children, and dancing for the older folk. A feast of roast meats, pastries, cakes and ale would be served at four in the afternoon. But the high point of the festivities was a custom peculiar to Twyford Lindum – the procession of villagers from St Dunstan's Church to Pony's Field, where the crowning of the May Queen would take place.

The field lay on the south side of the village, a few hundred yards east of the Tump. In law it was Barr land, but it had for centuries been used by the local folk as common pasture for cows, goats, and the rough-haired ponies that hauled carts and acted as pack-animals. It was bounded on the north by the yard of the New Mill, on the west by a brook, and on the south by the wheat fields of Melburn. The eastern limit was marked by a stand of massive oaks, under which benches had been set for the spectators.

At eleven o'clock the parties from Melburn and Safford Manor found places together, and they were soon joined by Squire Marchant and his lady, and Mrs Pruitt and her five daughters. Not far from them sat old Granny Kendall, in her ninetieth obstreperous year, gnarled as a willow root, her shrunken form clothed in a white gown with a goffered collar, her head dwarfed by an immense mobcap of starched muslin, secured under the chin by broad green ribbons. She paid no attention to the ranks of the gentry, but focused her gaze on the path that led from the village to the field.

Presently there reached their ears the sound of pipes and drums, and the procession came into sight, the elders leading, the young folk following with arches of may. All wore spotless white, and some of the men had tied round their calves bunches of small bells, which jingled at every step.

Reaching the field, the procession halted and formed up in a broad arc facing the village. Old Tom Kendall stepped forward and delivered a speech intelligible only to those who had spent a lifetime in Dorset. The elders then retired to their seats, and the musicians and young folk began a slow circuit of the field, the May Queen hidden in their midst. Round and round they marched, the circle growing ever smaller until it reached the very centre of the ground. There it halted, and raised a shout that rolled echoing along the base of the Tor.

As if in answer to their summons, there appeared on the path a figure in a long blue mantle, whose head was covered by the carved mask of a horse, with a mane and forelock of yellow hemp. This figure strode slowly across the turf, pausing some-times as if to survey the audience, stepping with majestic authority towards the centre group.

The group parted. The May Queen and her consort came forward and saluted the horse-headed figure, who bowed in gracious acknowledgement.

The musicians struck up a tune and the three began a stately dance, advancing and retreating to the music's beat. The watch-ing crowd made no sound. This was no pantomime to them, but a rite to ensure the fertility of the earth, the people of the valley, and their flocks.

At last the music ceased. The May Queen lifted the wreath from about her neck and slipped it over the horse's head. A cheer went up from performers and audience.

Kate had watched this performance many times, but today it held a special meaning for her. This would be the last time she would watch it with Dominic at her side. Turning her head, she saw him watching her, and without thinking she put out her hand. He dropped a kiss on her fingers.

'I must go and play my part on the green,' he said. 'Will you come with me?'

'I'll join you soon,' she answered. 'I want to thank Granny Kendall for the quilt she sent me.'

He walked away with Mr Pruitt. Kate went to where the old woman sat, and bent to address her.

'Granny Kendall, your Thomas brought me a very beautiful present. I appreciate it very much.'

'Aye, it's 'andsome enough. Lucky, too.' A pair of hooded eyes studied Kate. 'You'll be needin' a bit o' luck, simly, lookin' fer thikky old treasure.'

'We've found little to cheer us, so far.'

'Nor will ye, 'less the Old Uns wish it.'

'Which Old Ones, Granny?'

'Nay, I won't speak of 'em. Devil-talk, Parson says, silly ol' jobernowl.' She leaned forward and beckoned Kate closer.

'You ask Pony's 'elp, my pretty. Allus one fer lovers, 'e was. You ask 'im.'

'Pony? You mean the man in the dance?' But there was no answer. The old woman had lapsed into a doze, her head with its great cap nodding. Kate left her and went to join the revellers on the green.

Whether because she was bone-weary, or feverish from too much sun, Kate slept badly that night. She tossed and turned, and at midnight was roused by a storm that lit the hills with blue fire, and seemed to shake the very earth.

When at last she fell asleep, she dreamed she was filling an endless succession of sacks with flour from a ruined mill, and as she toiled, Mr Pruitt's voice said reprovingly, 'That's Devil's flour, you know, not Christian.' Running in terror from the mill, she found herself in the May Day procession, a wreath on her head, her arm about the neck of a horse. She was whirled into a dance, and found her partner was not a horse after all, but a young man with a naked torso and tangled hair, who smiled at her with Dominic's smile.

She woke with a cry, and saw that the dawn was red outside her windows. Rising, she bathed her hands and face with cool water, then perched on the window-seat and let the fresh morning air blow over her.

Lethargy gripped her. She knew she must fight it, must think, must remember the name of the young man of her dream. It was not Dominic, but someone she had seen before somewhere. If she could but put a name to him, he would help her to find the gold.

She closed her eyes and tried to recall his image. The mass of tangled hair, the smiling eyes, the lips stretched in laughter, and round the neck a torque of gold.

She opened her eyes and sat bolt upright.

It was in Dame Celia's library that she had seen him, a mosaic on the Roman floor.

Naponus, the god of the Old People, the god of fun and music, in whose honour the people of Twyford Lindum had for centuries performed their May Day rite.

Ager Naponi. The field of Naponus. Pony's Field.

XX

'Pony's Field,' said Dominic slowly. 'I'm not sure we can dig that up.'

'It's your land, Nick,' Kate answered.

'In law, yes, but the villagers regard it as theirs. It has a super-stitious significance for them, as well as providing pasturage for their livestock. I can't ride roughshod over their feelings. After all, we've no proof that Pony is a corruption of Naponi, or that there was ever a Roman villa on the site.'

'Mr Godbold thinks it is worth a try,' Kate insisted. 'What else can we do, but clutch at straws? In a few days' time Melburn could have a new owner.'

Dominic agreed to speak to the elders. As he had foreseen, he met with some resistance, but the balance was swung by the Kendalls, who said flatly that beggars couldn't be choosers, and beggars they'd all become if the big house was sold.

That settled, Mr Godbold took command.

'If there's a Roman villa under that pasture,' he said, 'we must search for it in a disciplined manner. I'll use only the most skilled of the workmen. We must quarter the ground, dig with caution, and sift every basket of soil we lift. I'll go down to the field at once, and decide where we should begin.'

No exhortations could hurry him in this task, and Kate and Dominic had to possess their souls in patience through what seemed an interminable day. At sundown, Mr Godbold gave his ruling.

213

'We'll start at first light tomorrow,' he said. 'Over here, by the brook. If it was once the Roman River, then any villa in the area would have been built close enough to ensure an easy supply of water, but far enough away to preclude flooding in winter.' He took a few slow strides. 'We'll make the first cut . . . here. Yes, I think so. With luck, we'll find the bath-house.'

'Bath-house?' said George Walcott. 'Are you saying the gold was hidden in a bath-house?'

'Not in, but under,' returned Mr Godbold, with a smile. 'The Romans were Sybarites, d'ye see? Very set on bathing. A gentleman's villa was equipped with a cold plunge, a tepidarium, a steamroom and a massage-room. The water was heated by a furnace, and pipes from the furnace carried hot air to the hypocaust that lay beneath the floor of the house. That kept the living-quarters at a cosy temperature, and also kept the corn store dry. Being underground, the hypocaust tended to survive, even if the upper structure of the villa was burned, or fell into decay.'

'So there might have been a Roman hypocaust under Cynric's Melburn?' Dominic stared at the turf under his feet.

'Precisely. On Miss Safford's theory, Cynric divided the treasure into two portions. He hid the King's coinage where it was easily found, but the Church treasures, which he considered infinitely more precious, he placed in the hypocaust.'

Dominic was silent for a moment, then he nodded. 'I'll be here with my best workers at daybreak tomorrow,' he said.

They worked without cease throughout that week. The weather broke and they toiled in pouring rain to bring the excavated earth to makeshift shelter. Mud washed into areas they had already cleared, and the walls of the cuts had to be shored up to prevent collapse.

Still they found nothing to give them hope.

On the morning of 8 May Kate stumbled on a mound of rubble and painfully twisted her ankle. Dominic carried her to the gig and sent her home to the Manor.

'No arguments, Kate,' he said. 'Rest, and cold compresses. If the swelling goes down, you can come back tomorrow.'

She spent the afternoon fretting on a *chaise-longue*, while Mrs Beacher held ice-packs to her ankle, and Elinor read aloud from an extremely tedious novel.

But at 4.30 the gig returned, dashing up the drive in a spirt of gravel, to deposit a dirt-encrusted Mr Godbold at the front door. He rushed without ceremony into the drawing-room, and reaching Kate's side, thrust out a palm on which lay several marble chips.

'Tessera!' he declared in triumph.

Dominic and George Walcott dined at the Manor that night. The talk was of nothing but the excavations, even Mr and Mrs Beacher being fired by the enthusiasm of the younger members of the company.

'Remember,' cautioned Mr Godbold, 'we have yet to confirm that there was an Anglo-Saxon establishment above the Roman. We must hope to find artefacts that can be attributed to Cynric's period.

'Bones?' suggested George. 'If there was a siege, there were bodies.'

Mr Godbold shook his head. 'Dust long since,' he said. Mr Beacher struck a more cheerful note. Rising to his feet, he raised his glass.

'Success to the search!' he cried, and drained the wine to its dregs.

When dinner was over, Kate returned to her couch, and Dominic came to sit beside her.

'Are you in much pain?' he asked.

'None. I'm too happy. I feel so sure we'll find the treasure. The tessera are a good omen. Can you not ask Pickford to delay foreclosure for a little?'

'I wrote to him last night. If, as we think, Cheveley's putting pressure on him, he may have no choice in the matter, but perhaps we may gain a few days' respite.'

The week that followed was to test all their nerves to the full. The excavations proceeded at what seemed a snail's pace. Mr Godbold would not be hurried. On the fourth day, when a workman brought him shards of pottery, he was delighted, pronouncing them ninth- or tenth-century work. Other Saxon artefacts were uncovered, cleaned, and stored in the muniments room of Melburn Hall, but of the Danish hoard there was no trace.

Then, on the sixth day, Mr Godbold discovered the furnace and the vents leading to the hypocaust of the villa. The news raced through the village, and Dominic with difficulty prevented its entire population from attacking the site with pick and shovel. Under Godbold's steely eye, a sector of land some seven yards square was stripped of turf and top-soil, and a trench was dug across its centre.

Late on Saturday evening there came into view at the east end of the trench, a small section of mosaic – nothing so splendid as the image of a god, to be sure, but a formal design in red and black marble which Mr Godbold declared to be work of a very high standard.

He would not permit the workmen to dig further. 'We must shore up the walls of the trench,' he insisted. 'An earth-slide could destroy valuable material.'

With obvious reluctance, the villagers went home. There remained at the site only Mr Godbold, Kate, Dominic, Elinor and George – and the puppy Jack, who in the belief that this splendid hole had been devised solely for his benefit, made strenuous efforts to explore it.

Mr Godbold was in a state of high elation. 'We are on the brink of a major find,' he said happily. 'As great, perhaps, as that at Littlecote. It will make a fitting close to your father's *History*, my dear Miss Safford.'

He began to outline the course the excavations must now take. Kate listened with half an ear. Much as she admired his skill, grateful as she was for his generous help, she knew he viewed their discovery with an antiquarian's eye. He worked to advance the cause of history, not to save Melburn from the auctioneer's hammer. He did not love Melburn as Dominic did, as she did.

Her tired gaze roved across the valley, tranquil under a trail of bursting stars. A three-quarter moon rode above the Tor and cast a spectral light on the village, touching the squat tower of the church with fire. A shiver ran down her spine. She had the feeling that she was being watched, that the shades of fifty generations watched her from the quiet fields and hedgerows. She fixed her eyes on the cross atop the church, and sent up a prayer.

'St Dunstan, help us now. You've worked miracles, so they say. Work one for us. Help us find your cross.'

She felt something brush her skirts, and cried out, but it was only the puppy, Jack. He lolloped past her and headed for the trench.

'Jack!' she called sharply. 'Come here!'

He ignored her, and reaching the lip of the trench, began to bounce up and down, barking imprecations at imaginary rats. Kate stepped forward to pick him up, but as she stooped, she felt a tremor beneath her feet, and with a soft slithering thump the earth collapsed, pitching her headlong into the trench. Sand poured in after her, engulfing her body, rising to her neck. She threshed wildly and something gave way under her. She sank deeper and a fresh rush of soil covered her nose and mouth. With a last, desperate effort she forced her arms upwards and felt them grasped, felt herself hauled up into blessed air. Dominic's arms were about her, his face pressed close to hers. For a moment he stood still, then he hefted her up to the outstretched hands of George and Mr Godbold. They carried her to firm ground and Elinor ran to embrace her.

'Kate, dearest! Are you all right?'

Kate spat out a mouthful of sand. 'Jack,' she whispered.

'He's safe, the wicked animal.' Elinor was lovingly wiping dirt from Kate's face. 'You might have suffocated in that dreadful hole. I shall never forgive myself.'

'Not your fault.' Sitting up, Kate saw that the three men had ranged themselves along the brink of the earth-slide and were gazing intently at its depths. She moved cautiously to join them.

'The floor gave way,' she said. 'I felt it go.'

Dominic nodded, pointing downward. Some of the sand at the far end of the trench had fallen away, leaving a wide cavity into which trickles of earth still ran. In the centre of the cavity, wedged between two upright stones, was a dark object, encrusted with baked clay.

'I'm going in,' Dominic said.

'No, my lord!' cried Mr Godbold. 'Wait until we've shored up the sides!'

Dominic paid him no heed, but lowered himself to the bottom of the fall. Planting a foot on each side of the cavity, he leaned down and seized hold of the object. He lifted it to Mr Godbold's waiting hands, and scrambled back to the surface.

Mr Godbold held the trophy in a shaft of moonlight, and gently brushed away the flakes of clay that clung to it. It was a small casket, less than a foot in length, with a flat lid and a hasp secured by a metal pin. The pin would not budge, sealed tight by age and dirt.

'Silver or pewter, most like,' Godbold said.

'Is it the treasure?' whispered Elinor.

He shrugged. 'Impossible to tell what it is, in this light. We must take it back to Melburn.' He turned to Dominic. 'Double your guards, my lord, and instruct them that no one is to come near this field. If we've indeed hit upon part of the Danish hoard, we may expect a lively interest in this area by sunrise tomorrow.'

In the library at Melburn, they spread a white cloth on the map table and set a ring of oil lamps round it. Seated at the end of the table, Mr Godbold painstakingly cleaned the little casket. His companions urged him to make haste, but he ignored them, his whole attention on his task.

At three in the morning, the cleaning done, he leaned back in his chair.

'Solid silver,' he confirmed. 'Roman work, by the designs on the upper surface.' He seemed ready to elaborate, but Kate cut him short.

'Open it,' she said imperiously. 'Open it now!'

He shook his head, but did as she asked, pressing gently on the pin, using a fine brush to ease away the crust that sealed the lid, until quite suddenly it lifted a fraction. Still he worked, his thick fingers infinitely gentle, and at last, at long last, the casket was open. As the watchers leaned forward, they saw a pile of dust that might once have been wrappings. Mr Godbold reached down and brushed it aside, lifted out a small blackened cross and laid it reverently on the cloth.

Despite the black patina of centuries, they could see the Celtic design along the edges of the cross, and at its foot, the engraving of a small bird, its head lifted as if in song.

It was the same symbol they had seen on the wall of the library at Midsomer Abbey; the signature of a master stonemason.

They had found the Sucat Cross.

They rejoiced together, laughing, embracing one another in happiness and relief. Mr and Mrs Beacher, summoned from their bed at the Manor, joined in the general celebration. Even Mr Godbold was seen to pull a kerchief from his pocket, and dab at his eyes.

'You will be the toast of academia, Miss Safford,' he told Kate. 'Your persistence, your devotion, has given us a treasure beyond price. Now that we have found the Cross, we may pursue our search for the gold. It may lie close, in the inner reaches of the hypocaust.'

Kate shook her head. 'I don't think so. I think it was sacrificed to the Danes, to keep the Cross safe.'

Mr Godbold regarded her kindly. 'We can't know that, my dear.' But meeting her gaze, he fell silent, and turned away. Kate saw that Dominic was watching her, and went to him, holding out her hands.

'I'm so happy for you, Nick. So very happy.'

He raised her hands and kissed each in turn. He seemed to be searching for words, and she said anxiously:

'The reward will be enough to redeem Melburn, will it not?'

'Many times over, I imagine.' He smiled as if he had come to a decision. 'I think the occasion calls for wine,' he said cheerfully, and rang for it to be brought.

Many toasts were raised, many praises sung. It was dawn when the Beachers' household returned to the manor, and Kate fell exhausted into bed.

Mr Godbold was back in Pony's Field within two hours, anxious to ensure that the site of the dig was secure against trespassers. Evidently no news of their find had leaked to the village, for which he was thankful.

'Any talk of treasure,' he said to Mr Beacher, who joined him later, 'and we shall have idlers charging in like a brigade of cavalry. All hopes of orderly excavation will be at an end.'

Kate did not visit the site that morning, but went with her family to church. She expected to find Dominic there, but the Barr pew was empty. She told herself that he was engaged in business at the Hall, but when she returned home she found a letter from him awaiting her. It was brief.

My dear Kate,

I scribble this note at daybreak. I would have preferred to talk to you, but there is no time. I am leaving at once for London, where I have business that cannot wait. I ask this great favour of you – that you won't speak of last night's discovery to anyone, nor allow any of our friends to speak of it. Silence is imperative at this time. I will explain all to you when I return, which I trust will be not later than Thursday. I need not tell you how grateful I am to you for all you have done for me, nor how much I regret having to leave you to cope with things alone.

He had begun another sentence, but the words had been heavily scored out. The letter was signed, 'your devoted servant, Dominic Barr.'

Mrs Beacher was incensed when Kate told her the contents of the letter.

'I consider Barr has behaved in a very cavalier manner,' she said. 'There's a great deal to be discussed, and the Lord knows how we shall be able to keep the discovery from the village, not to mention our friends. He is, after all, to receive the reward of your labours. He should at least have been here when he's needed.'

Elinor, seeing the distress in Kate's eyes, was more tactful. 'I expect he's gone to London to consult with Mr Shipton,' she said.

'Mr Shipton's in Bath,' said Kate bleakly.

'Well then, perhaps he will meet with Mr Pickford. Arrange to postpone the foreclosure, or . . . or some such thing.'

Kate nodded dumbly. She could present a brave front to others, but she could no longer deceive herself. Over the past weeks, she had come to believe that she and Dominic shared a common goal, that he was not indifferent to her, that in time he might come to love her and turn their fake betrothal to reality. Nothing of the sort had happened. With the Sucat Cross found, and the promise of riches a certainty, he had elected to withdraw from her, as if he wished for no closer bond than friendship.

Some frail hope still told her not to despair, but reason spoke louder. He did not love her. In giving him financial freedom, she had cut the last bond between them. He had no further need of her.

She could not bear to discuss these feelings with anyone, and throughout that long Monday kept very much to herself. She visited the site, where a preoccupied Mr Godbold had begun new excavations along the hypocaust. She did not offer to assist in them, knowing that her apparent lack of interest would quell the ardour of the villagers.

The night passed, and still no message came from Melburn. It was only on Tuesday afternoon, as she was cutting roses to dry for pot pourri, that she saw Dominic's curricle swing through the gates and sweep up to the front door of the house. He alighted, handed the reins to his groom, and came striding across the terrace towards the rose garden. She set down her basket and waited for him to reach her.

'Kate, my dear. I am sorry I was gone so long. How are you?'

'Well, thank you.' She gave him her hand, but withdrew it before he could kiss it.

'I have been thinking,' she said abruptly, 'that we should not pretend any longer.'

'I agree.' He smiled at her warmly. 'I've a great deal to tell you. Shall we walk a little?'

He tucked her hand through his arm, and led her along a path lined with lavender bushes. 'First,' he said, 'there is something I must say about the Cross.'

'I know.' She looked up at him. 'I was slow to grasp what you understood at once. The Sucat Cross is not ours to bargain with. It belongs to Dame Celia.'

'Yes.'

Kate swallowed. 'What do you wish to do about it?'

'I would like to bring Dame Celia here to see the Cross. I would wish to send a carriage to bring her, as soon as possible, but I want your permission to do so.'

'And if she identifies it, you'll give it to her?'

'I imagine there'll be a great deal of legal argument about that, but I think we're bound to support her claim to ownership.'

Kate saw the last vestige of her dream evaporate. She nodded, unable to speak. Dominic laid his hand over hers.

'I knew you would feel as I do. That's one of the things I particularly enjoy about our betrothal. Our thoughts chime exactly.'

As she glanced up at him in surprise, he turned to face her. 'Kate, my dearest Kate, when I saw you tumble into that damned ditch, I knew that you're more precious to me than any treasure,

222

than Melburn, than anything on earth. That's why I left for London in such haste.'

She said haltingly, 'I don't understand. I thought you went to confer with Mr Pickford.'

'No. I did what I should have done months ago, save that I was prevented by my stupid pride. I went to see Savernake. We talked for hours, and the upshot is, he has bought off Pickford. Taken over his debts, lock stock and barrel. Savernake even holds the mortgage on Melburn. We are free of Pickford and Cheveley and the rest. I'll repay Ivor in time.'

'With the reward. When the Crown pays you the reward . . .'

'No. The reward is yours. I don't intend to speak of that now. Kate, my darling, don't argue, listen to me. Will you forgive me the mistakes of the past, give me a second chance? Will you indeed consent to marry me?'

For answer, she threw herself into his arms and returned his embrace with gratifying enthuaiasm.

Mrs Beacher, observing them from the window of the morning-room, summoned her husband to her side.

'A happy outcome to all our tribulations,' she declared. 'I always knew those two were meant for each other.'

'One kiss doesn't make a marriage,' said Mr Beacher, but she dismissed this cynicism with contempt.

'Nonsense! They are head over ears in love. Oh, how delighted I am! We must hold a reception for them here, and another in London when we go to buy Kate's brideclothes. Only fancy! Lady Kate! What a triumph! And Melburn saved, as well! Where is Elinor? I must give her the good news this instant.'

Mr Beacher smiled slyly. 'Nell's gone out drivin' with George Walcott, to buy that imp of a puppy a collar. I think, my dear, that with a little luck we may expect to celebrate a double wedding in the near future.'

'Luck,' said his wife, 'has nothing to do with it. Marriages are not made in Heaven, but here on earth, by people who know how to arrange matters. I consider we have done very well for our girls. Very well indeed.'

Her husband placed an arm about her waist, and they exchanged complacent looks, comfortable in the knowledge that they were without equal in their chosen field, and that they could expect to enjoy many more years of successful meddling in the affairs of their nearest and dearest.